RIDGE VIEW COMMONS
5200 Case Avenue
Pleasanton, California 94566

# BLOOD LAKE

## Frank McConnell

# BLOOD LAKE

## Frank McConnell

**Walker and Company**
**New York**

*To Celeste*

Published in the United States of America by the Walker Publishing Company, Inc.

Published simultaneously in Canada by John Wiley & Sons Canada, Limited, Rexdale, Ontario.

Printed in the United States of America

# 1

"HARRY, HOW WOULD you like to spend a week in the country?"

I'll tell you, I can't count the times I've dreamed of, say, Audrey Hepburn asking me that. Hell, I'd even settle for Sophia Loren. But it was my boss, Bridget O'Toole, who was asking, and she meant a week in the country on my own. Not that, given Bridget, I would have wanted it any other way.

Bridget, the manager of O'Toole Investigations, Inc., is a sixty-odd-year-old ex-nun. The odd part I'm sure of, by the way. Sometimes I wonder about the ex part. Her face would not only stop a clock, it could probably bust a sundial. She shouldn't be running a private detective agency, but she does; and I work for her, and I should be running a private detective agency.

"How would I *like?*" I replied. "Well, Bridget, I really would not like. I mean, I even get hives watching *Bambi.* I hate the country. But then, you're not really asking, are you?"

Bridget sighed. Ever sit down on one of those big bean-bag things they sell for chairs? That's the way Bridget sighs. I was a great disappointment.

"Oh, dear," she breathed at sigh's end. "You see, Harry, we've been retained by a Mr."—checking the notes on her desk—"a Mr. Howard. Mr. Thomas Howard, from Wilmette. He wants us to—well, to follow his wife for a while. He suspects her of being unfaithful"—I wondered how many people on the planet besides Bridget still called it "being unfaithful"—"and she is about to spend a week, presumably alone, at a Wisconsin resort. Mr. Howard has agreed to prepay expenses there for an investigator. It's at Lake Manitonaqua. Do you know it? Just a few miles north of Rhinelander, and it's supposed to be lovely there this time of the year. In fact, I do believe that I know some people nearby."

This time of year, by the way, was late summer: August, to be exact, on Chicago's North Shore. You can always tell that season in Chicago. The last spring's new crop of potholes in the street have been about half filled, the tar is melting, the air conditioners are humming like a throng of bees on PCP, and the sewers back up from the summer rainstorms; *gurgle, slurp,* we've got your ass *now,* they say. I've lived in Chicago—well, Evanston—all my life, so I can read the signs of the season the way an old sailor reads the sunsets. God knew how you found the late summer in the North Woods of Wisconsin, but it looked like I was going to find out.

"Okay, Bridget," I sighed back at my boss. "So I'll spend a week in the woods. I just hope they get decent TV reception up there, in case Mrs. Howard is only going to check out the ferns and the bunny rabbits. You want the regular tape log, photos, the whole treatment?"

"No, dear. Please. Mr. Howard is very concerned about his wife, but he stressed he didn't want to embarrass her—or divorce her— whatever we may find out. He simply wants to *know,* you know. Poor man, I believe he sincerely thinks knowledge can save his marriage. He was even too shy to come in to the office for an interview. He just spoke to me on the phone, and sent us a certified check as a deposit. Of course," she went on hastily as I cocked an eyebrow at her, "I checked his credentials, banking account, and so forth."

Bridget got that funny look, a faraway look I'd seen come into her eyes a few times before. "I thought of telling him that in fact he'd do best not to consult us in that case. This modern delusion disturbs me, you know; this idea that knowing everything somehow means understanding, controlling everything. . . ." She shook herself back to the moment. "Ah, well. We are, after all, in business."

We were in business. That's what it said, anyhow, on the IRS forms. But we were in business the way an aging hooker with one eye and buck teeth is in business: not so you'd notice, that is. In the old days, when Martin O'Toole—Bridget's father—had run things, the agency had been a comfortable little North Chicago concern, pulling in just enough adulteries and small-change embezzlements to guarantee a Christmas bonus for me and the late Fred Healey, my co-worker. And then Fred had left for another, bigger agency, leaving me to expect to inherit the business after Martin retired. And then Martin had had a stroke—two goddamn years before he would have (I'm sure) handed me the whole enchilada. And then his only child, Bridget, had come out of the nunnery—convent, whatever—to "see to things" for a while.

Now to me, "a while" means a short—dig it, a *short*— period of time. To Bridget, I think it must mean something different. Like until the Second Coming, or until the Cubs win their division *and* go on to sweep the World Series in four. She had been "seeing to things" since right after Nixon's resignation, and these days you can go to any grammar school playground, throw a rock in the air, and it'll hit the head of a kid who doesn't even know who Nixon was. Or is it, what Nixon was? Anyway, she had populated her office (it should have been my office) with enough tropical plants to make Johnny Weissmuller weep for sheer nostalgia. She had assumed, at a high price, her old man's private license. And she had had the reception room (about as big as a beer truck cabin) repainted in aquamarine. It was that last bit that bothered me most. I mean, this lady was *settling*.

And business had gotten bad. Maybe fewer people were cheating on their spouses or pilfering from petty cash. Maybe fewer people cared if other people were. Or maybe, if they did care, they were taking their worries elsewhere. I don't know, though I had my ideas. But slim times had hit O'Toole Investigations. And every time I tried to talk to Bridget about it, what did I get? Meditations on the economy, on the morality of private detective work, reflections that go on for *months* it feels like, for Christ's sake, on the *idea* of crime. That's what I got.

But no more Christmas bonuses.

So, I hear you asking, why don't I quit? So, go ahead and ask—*wer weiss?* A year or so ago, Bridget did me some good favors when I got into a mess involving the murder of my old partner, Fred Healey. That's one. She's really not that bad a boss, just a little flaky. She even brings in doughnuts for the whole O'Toole staff on Fridays. That's two. (I hate doughnuts.) She's got to leave *sometime,* and then it becomes the Harold Garnish Detective Agency: a leaky boat with no rudder, okay, but mine all the same, and a hell of a lot more than I've got now. That's three, and in my book, that's also enough.

So when somebody like Thomas Howard offers to pay us our consulting fee (I love calling it that) and also to rent a cabin in the Wisconsin woods, I rejoice—even if I do hate the great outdoors. I mean, if we're lucky, maybe we *will* find his wife schlepping about with some forest ranger or CPA, right? And then maybe he'll have some friends whose wives or husbands are also playing afternoon donkey, and he'll pass the word on to them what a crackerjack by gum job we do at good old O'Toole Investigations, and . . . Don't laugh. How do you think McDonald's got started?

"Right, Bridget," I said, lighting a cigarette and exchanging a wink with Phil. Phil, who dates from Martin O'Toole's days in the agency, is a philodendron of many years who, I think, has gone plant-senile. He just droops over Bridget's sofa and leaks on the carpet when you water him. Doesn't give a healthy goddamn about being a self-respecting philodendron anymore, you know? Just wants to be left the hell alone. Phil I like.

"Right, Bridget. We're in business. So have you got, maybe, a nice businesslike photo of Mrs. Howard? And her arrival time at—what was it? Lake Maniwakwak?"

"Lake Manitonaqua," Bridget corrected me.

"Yeah. Sure. Whatever. But, what the hell, since Thomas Howard doesn't want pictures or hard evidence, why don't we all just stay home and tell the poor schmuck his wife is clean? It would save him a lot of grief, his wife maybe a lot of embarrassment, and me a lot of poison ivy."

She would have looked less offended, I suppose, if I'd just farted. "Oh, Harry, Harry." She shook her head. "I know you're only joking. Or at least, I hope you're only joking. But I'm afraid I don't think it's very funny, dear. You see, as—as tawdry as this business may appear, it is nevertheless a business and that means we have certain obligations to our clients. We cannot afford to become as tawdry as the people we are employed to investigate."

I should have known. I had just let myself in for another one of those lectures she got such a kick out of giving.

"Look, Bridget, I'm sorry. I was just kidding. But you know, I really can't take this business as seriously as—" It was no good.

"Harry," she interrupted, and I swear, she held up a hand to silence me—just like in fifth grade, right? "Harry, a wealthy merchant once asked Saint Thomas Aquinas to arbitrate his quarrel with a prostitute. The merchant had—ah, retained the prostitute's services, and then refused to pay her on the grounds that prostitution is a mortal sin. And do you know what Saint Thomas said?"

"I'll bet I'm going to find out," I mumbled. Even Phil looked bored.

"Saint Thomas said that though the act itself may have been wrong, the merchant still owed the lady in question her fair pay for a fairly contracted job. Now, do you know what that implies?"

It implied, among other things, that Italian hookers in the Middle Ages must have had it better than Chicago hookers in the 1980s. It implied that if you've got a choice between being hassled by the vice squad or by the Dominicans, pick the Dominicans. It implied that medieval merchants and American Legion conventioneers had a lot in common. But I didn't think any of these was Bridget's point.

"It implies I'm going to spend a week in the Wisconsin woods," I said.

"Yes, Harry," she said. You leave Sunday. And I would appreciate it if you could call me once a day, collect of course, just to check in. Here is a photograph of Mrs. Howard, and here is a brochure about the Manitonaqua Lake Resort. If you need any, ah, *outdoors* clothes, I'm sure Mr. Howard will be willing to pay for them as part of the expenses of the investigation."

Swell. The one thing I could really imagine myself needing was a pair of hip-high fishing boots. What was I going to do, wear them to the seafood counter at the Jewel Grocery?

"Thanks anyhow, Bridget," I said. "I should be okay."

And with that I left the office. Well, maybe *left* isn't exactly the right word. Escaped is more like it. I fantasize, sometimes, about her tropical plants—all but Phil—clutching at me as I exit, trying to bind me down to the floor and whisper lectures in my ear about the private eye business in the Middle Ages.

Anyway, I found my way out, clutching the photograph of my prey for the week and my (I hoped) efficient map of the way to Manitonaqua Resort. I strolled down the hall to my office, where I took a can of Ballantine Ale out of the refrigerator I've got there. (O'Toole Investigations has a reception room and three, count them, three offices. Big-time, you know?)

After I'd sunk into my chair, lit cigarette number five for the day— I was trying to stop—and snapped the top of the Ballantine, I spread out the brochure for Manitonaqua. It didn't look promising: thirty cottages scattered around the shore of a tiny lake, a restaurant that served lunch and dinner, and trained supervisors for waterskiing, scuba diving, and as far as I cared, shark wrestling. The hell with it. I could just drive there, relax, try to keep the lions and tigers and bears out of my bedroom, track Mrs. Howard, and not get hurt. That last part especially is one of my favorite activities.

I mean, I never was a Boy Scout; my mother thought they were all

Protestants, and that the whole movement was some kind of Lutheran plot. So why should I try for my first merit badge at this late date?

I finished the ale and decided to take the rest of the day off. It was Friday afternoon already, and since I was going to spend the next week in the bosom of nature, I figured I could use a day or so of real rest before the excursion. Then I noticed, on my desk next to my eyeglasses, my bottle of pills.

I have hypertension: blood pressure at a dangerous level. Two hundred over one forty are the numbers my doctor keeps telling me, if they mean anything to you. They don't mean much to me, except that my doctor, a young twerp with dandruff, no smile, and more education than me, manages to scare the hell out of me with them. "Stroke city" is one of the knee-slapping lines he's dropped to me about the condition I'm in.

So anyhow, I take two tablets of something called Inderal a day, which is supposed to put my heart on slow motion or something, and I'm supposed not to smoke or take in too much salt. But I always forget to take the damn tablets unless I keep the bottle on my desk, where I can't help but notice it. Thinking about high blood pressure, middle age, and that blood vessel with my name on it made me so nervous that I lit another cigarette. Then I decided to do something, as my doctor says, to "help myself." I took two Inderal tablets at once and washed them down with another can of ale.

I know, I know. Ale is heavy with salt. But Garnish is the anglicized version of a Czechoslovakian name you couldn't even pronounce; and we Central European types have always thought doctors' advice was bullshit if you didn't change it around a little.

On my way out of the office I stopped by the front desk. Brenda, our receptionist, is almost as fat and almost as ugly as Bridget O'Toole. But there the resemblance stops. Brenda's permanent address is the Twilight Zone. She drinks on the job—hell, I don't even know if she knows it *is* a job. And she always looks at you like you've just awakened her from a Hindu trance. She also, though, has the kind of memory they call "eidetic." That is, if somebody came to see you at 1:00 P.M. on December 22, 1975, and if that somebody was later discovered to be a Russian agent bent on blowing up Gary, Indiana, Brenda would remember the time of your appointment, the suit the agent was wearing, the color of his hair, and probably the condition of his fingernails and the state of his breath. Let's hope Gary, Indiana would be gone by then, of course. But good old Brenda could spot the saboteur in a lineup of a hundred guys, and then you'd have to decide whether to shoot the bastard or give him a medal. As I approached her desk she put down her coffee mug. If there was coffee in her coffee mug, eggs were laying chickens. *"Harry,"* she dazed at me. "What can I do for you?"

Actually, what she said was, *"RRRy,* whacn I drfya?" But I'm translating, in case you don't speak fluent snockered.

"Brenda, my love," I said. "I just thought I ought to tell you, in case Bridget forgets. For the next week I won't be taking any calls or taking any appointments. I'll be in Wisconsin. In the woods." Not that I had any red-hot appointments or investigations under way at the moment, but it felt like a professional thing to do. And if you can't be successful, act successful, as John DeLorean used to say.

Brenda's face, anyhow, lit up even more than it had been, and that's lit up like a Christmas tree during a power surge. "Oh, Harry, the Wisconsin *woods?"* she crooned. "They're so beautiful this time of year. Sermons in stones and books in the running brooks."

"Wha?"

"Oh, *Harry.* You know, the Duke in *As You Like It."*

Oh, yeah. Brenda reads.

"Oh, yeah," I said. "Well, I don't like it. Anyway, darling, hold all the calls, okay? And have a real good week."

She beamed benevolence at me and turned her attention back to her coffee mug. And I turned toward the stairwell—we're on the second floor of our building—and met the one person I didn't care to say good-bye to.

Knobby is his name. Well, Peter Conn is his name, but Knobby is his *name,* if you know what I mean. He's short, he's got red hair, he struts instead of walks. He always wears a bow tie and a blue suit, and so with his shock of uncombed red hair it's impossible to look at him and not think about Woody Woodpecker. Except that if he felt like it, Knobby would take you off at the knees and not work up a sweat and not give a damn. He's the other investigator at O'Toole. Bridget hired him a year or so ago, and we don't like one another. He was leaning against the door to the stairs, grinning.

"Boopsie!" he exclaimed. Knobby always calls me Boopsie. "Goin' to the fuckin' woods, yeah? Well, listen, man, you just watch out for them goddamn snipes. You dig? I mean, them snipes'll chew your goddamn balls off, you give 'em the chance. Har, har, har."

Har, har, har. When, one day, I come into some money and can afford to have Knobby killed, no jury in the world will convict me. But today I just smiled. Knobby and I smile at each other a lot.

"Knobby!" I said. "Hell, man, I figured you'd be hard at work this time of day. What's the matter, no action in the men's rooms? Or did the film fall out of your camera again?"

The woodpecker just shoved a stick of gum in his mouth. "Ah, *shee*-it, Harry," he said. Ever notice how some people can make it into a four-syllable word? "*Shee*-it," he repeated, drawing it out even longer. "I'm not looking for trouble, old buddy. I just came to wish you bon voyage, is all. And"—and here the Knobby grin got, as it always does, wider—"don't let no woodchucks crawl up your ass, you dig?"

I was sure that if he could have, he would have bribed a woodchuck to do just that. But so would I, for him. If friendship is perfect understanding, then Knobby and I are a living model of it. We didn't shake hands, just grimaced. And I shoved past him down the stairs.

On my way to the parking lot I passed the window of Ben Gross Dry Cleaners, on the first floor of our building. Ben Gross is one of my pals, a lousy dry cleaner (I bring him all my clothes) and a good advisor (I bring him most of my problems). I decided to pop in and say hello, since I wouldn't be seeing him for a week.

As usual, he was in the back of the shop, drinking tea and reading. Ben was a professor, or a young man about to become a professor, before the Germans did some rotten things to him and his family because he also happens to be a Jew. He's still a lousy dry cleaner.

"Harry!" he exclaimed when he saw me, "sit, my friend, and have a nice cup of tea, right?" I noticed as he folded down the page and put it aside that the book he was reading was something called *The Name of the Rose*. Ben is always trying to lend me his books (the professor training dies hard), and I'm always thinking of reasons not to borrow them (the dummy strain dies hard, too).

"No tea, Ben," I said. "I just came by to say so long for a while, and to see how you're going to make it through next week without me. I'm going to Wisconsin, man, to the woods."

Ben grinned a twisty, sour little grin. "You, Harry, in the woods?

*Nu?* For this, for my Harry to—to rusticate, there has to be a reason, huh? So tell."

So I told. I don't know if Bridget O'Toole knows that most of her business is filtered through Ben's back room. I suspect that she does, but I don't really care. Anyway, I told Ben the whole tale, and as I did the twisty little grin left his face.

"Harry," he said when I was finished. "Harry, Harry, Harry. It's your business, it's how you make your living, *sei gesund.* But such sorrows you wind up fooling around in. I don't think I could bear it, myself. And you're going to be a happy-go-lucky visitor at this . . . this . . ."

"Manitonaqua," I put in.

"Whatever," he replied, waving his hand. "So, what're you taking to play with?"

"Wha?"

"Harry, *Harry.* You're supposed to be a nice, harmless boy from Chicago up for a romp in the woods. You don't have anything to play with? I mean, like a fishing pole, a tennis racket—something so you shouldn't look so much like a private eye on a case?" Ben looked as disappointed in me as Bridget often did.

"Well, Ben," I murmured, "you know, I just heard about this thing an hour ago. I mean—"

"You mean." He smiled. "You mean. You mean, my dear boy, you couldn't find your own *tuchis* with both hands if you didn't have help. But wait."

He got up and went even farther back into the shop, rummaging and mumbling around in a closet I hadn't known was there. I sat, getting even bored enough to think about pouring myself a glass of tea from the samovar, when Ben strolled back, humming happily. In one hand he held a tennis racket that looked like it might have been used in the 1936 Wimbledon finals, and in the other he held two bamboo sticks, fouled as hell with line, that I guessed had once been a fishing pole. Ben was grinning his ass off.

"So here," he said. "I should be in your business. At least I know what camouflage means. With these momentoes of my sportsman's past, you look at least a little like somebody who *wants* to go to lake whatever. Take."

I took, and I thanked him. What the hell, it couldn't do any harm. "And *come back,*" he shouted as I left the shop. *"Safe."*

So I strolled to my car clutching a fifty-year-old tennis racket and a useless fishing pole and a map to a place I didn't want to go and a picture of a could-be adulteress. After all these years of happy city life, here I was, commissioned by an ex-nun and outfitted by a failed rabbi, at long last, going camping.

# 2

MANITONAQUA IS A dopey name, right? Wrong. It's an Indian name, Dakota to be specific, and it means "rusty water," or, if you've got a melodramatic turn of mind, Blood Lake.

I know that because when I finally got out of bed Saturday morning, tuned in to Bugs Bunny on TV, made coffee, and poached my three eggs with Tabasco sauce, I bothered to reread the brochure Bridget had given me. This was around noon. I mean, what good is a private cop who doesn't devote a little time to basic research?

The brochure was stiff blue cardboard, with a clear and misleadingly simple map on the cover and a big drawing of an Indian arrowhead on the back.

Lake Manitonaqua [it said] nestles at the heart of the "Land of a Thousand Lakes" in northern Wisconsin. "Manitonaqua," a name formed from dialects of the Dakota and Winnebago languages, means "Blood-Stained Water." This curious name may refer to the beautiful effect of sunset over the lake. Or it may allude to an ancient Dakota legend that the shore of Manitonaqua was the site of a heroic duel to the death between two brothers for the hand of a beautiful but faithless Indian maiden.

Right, I grumbled to myself, pouring another cup of coffee. That particular Dakota legend was probably as ancient as the resort itself, founded in 1952. I mean, if somebody wants to jazz up things for the tourist trade that's no skin off any particular part of my anatomy. But God. If all the lovely Indian maidens supposed to have been fought over or sacrificed were brought back to life, there would be enough of them to take over Iowa.

Not that it would be missed.

Whatever the origin of the name [my brochure went on] today the lake is the scene only of water sports and fun and relaxation among some of the most beautiful scenery in the world. Fishing off the pier or in one of our boats is fun and challenging. Instruction in waterskiing and scuba diving is available, free of charge, from our talented instructors.

I figured I'd take up scuba diving when World War III broke out. What about eating and drinking? And there it was, on the next page.

Manitonaqua Lodge is a warm, friendly, family place. For cocktails and dinner (5:30–9:00, except on Sundays) informal attire is suggested: jackets for men are optional, and slacks or dresses for ladies.

In other words, dress about as formally as a Californian at a funeral. The hell with it. I wasn't getting paid to make fun of the place. The brochure was signed by one Ross Connors, manager and owner. And the bar opened at 5:30.

And what about Mrs. Thomas Howard, my mark?

Bridget hadn't given me a file on the lady—height, vital stats, like that—and I hadn't bothered to ask for one. Since Mr. Howard didn't want a messy scene, just a word-of-mouth report, and since he was paying anyhow, I didn't care about being too damn professional. I studied the two photos Bridget had given me. Mrs. Thomas Howard, or Cheryl McLean Howard (both names were penciled on the backs of the photos) was a thin-faced, smart-looking blonde. In one photo she was posed in a tweedy suit, smiling a big tourist's smile before one of the stone lions that I recognized as guarding the entrance to San Francisco's Chinatown. It wasn't much of a photo, since the photographer (Mr. Howard, I assumed—had it been a honeymoon trip?) was as interested in getting the lion into the frame as he was in getting the lady's face in the right light. The other was more of a candid shot: Cheryl Howard, in a flannel shirt and with her hair pulled back in a ponytail, was sitting at a picnic bench. She must have just looked over her shoulder and noticed the camera, and the shutter just caught her surprised and, this time, really happy grin. It was a nice grin, and even on Polaroid you got a sense of a kind of—what? Intelligence, good nature, a kind of honesty behind those smiling eyes. Very pale blue eyes, by the way. Photos aren't much to go on, but I was beginning to imagine why Mr. Howard might care so much about her, and why he might not want to know the worst even if there was a worst. By that time it was one o'clock. I get up late on Saturdays. The coffee was cold and the remains of my poached eggs were fossilizing in the dish. Do you know something more depressing than sitting in your pajamas on a Saturday afternoon in a three-room apartment watching your yolks harden? I sure as hell don't, and if you do, Jack, then I'm sorry for you.

Maybe it was the effect of the sexy-looking Mrs. Howard. Who knows? Anyhow, I decided to call a lady I knew and suggest an afternoon at the zoo, the movies, whatever. The way I felt, I was even ready for an afternoon with somebody in the Marshall Fields appliance department.

Her name was Marianne Healey, and she's the widow of Fred Healey, my old partner at O'Toole Agency. She's funny, she's great in bed, and I think I may be the father of her kid, Fred Healey, Jr.

So did I say I was a nice person?

I hadn't been seeing a lot of Marianne lately, though I always sent her a little something once a month for Fred Jr. The kid was eight now, and Marianne wasn't too bad off with her husband's life insurance and with her own job—she was a real estate agent, not a bad gig at all in North Shore Chicago. But I still felt responsible. And, I suppose, I felt more and more responsible the less and less I felt like spending time with Marianne.

My old man, in one of our rare heart to heart talks, once told me something. "Boy," said Anton Garnish, cocking an eyebrow at adolescent me and twitching his nose hairs, "boy, don't never, *never* give up nothin' to get into nobody's pants. You'll be surprised how them grand damn passions fizzle after six months or one good bang." And I guess Pop was a better philosopher than he was a mechanic. At least, my afternoons with Marianne had been becoming more and more exercises in embarrassed silence and less and less fun. I hadn't called her in about a week.

She was home, but from the way she said "Oh. Hello, Harry" I didn't think hearing from me was exactly the sunshine in her Saturday.

"Hi, kid," I chirped in my best Cary Grant, which never works. "Listen, uh, I thought maybe you and Fred Jr. would like to go to

Lincoln Park. You know, feed a few alligators and maybe have dinner downtown. What do you say?"

There was that three-beat pause on the other end that, when you've been chilled out as often as I have, tells you right away they're going to do it to you again.

"Oh, Harry." Marianne sighed. "I could tell you that I already have plans for today. But I don't. Freddy and I are making cookies right now, and tonight we're going to watch *Chiller Theater* on TV. I just— if you don't mind, Harry, I don't feel like seeing you today. Okay?"

Did I say I'd been getting tired of Marianne? All of a sudden cookies and milk and *Chiller Theater* with her sounded like a free trip to Disneyland.

"Well, see," I faltered, "I'm going to be out of town all next week. And you know, I've been so damn busy lately, we haven't gotten to see a lot of each other. So I just thought—"

"Harry," she said, cutting me off. "No. Maybe . . . maybe it's a good thing you're going to be gone next week. I mean—look, we can't talk about things on the phone, and I'm just not up to seeing you today, or tomorrow. Why don't you call me when you get back. Can you do that?"

When I was a kid, I had a real Buck Rogers ray gun. Remember those tin beauties with a clicking trigger and superfuturistic cooling disks all down the barrel? Anyhow, I loved that gun for a month. And then I got bored with it. And then Van Hartledge, the fat kid two doors down, conned me into trading my gun for his Hopalong Cassidy knife. And that night I cried my eyes out in bed because I suddenly realized how great, how *really great* my Buck Rogers ray gun was. Son-of-a-bitch if I didn't feel like I'd *betrayed* something or somebody—maybe myself.

So go ahead: tell me people change.

"Uh. Sure, Marianne," I said. "Look, kid, I'm really sorry. I mean . . . Oh, hell. Okay, I'll call you when I get back. Kiss Fred Jr. for me, will you?

"Right. Right, Harry. Good-bye." And she hung up.

She hadn't even asked me where I was going.

Terrific, Garnish, I thought to myself. You blew it again, it's two o'clock on a Saturday afternoon, and you've got nothing to do but watch the golf tournament—on a black and white TV, for Christ's sake. Or listen to music. I peeked into my cassette player to see what

I'd left there the night before. It was Paul Desmond, that sweet and smart man who died so early and who never got quite the fame, quite the celebrity, his melancholy talent deserved. Nope, I decided: this kind of Saturday wasn't the right time for Desmond, no matter how beautifully he played.

So what to do? Well, you know, you can always have a drink.

I had just flip-topped my first can of Ballantine Ale and lit a cigarette when the phone rang. Of course I knew it was Marianne calling back to apologize and ask me over. Of course I jumped to the phone before its first ring was over. Of course I was wrong.

"Mr.—ah, Garnist?" said a reedy voice on the other end.

"Garnish," I corrected. "Harry Garnish. Can I help you?"

"Yes. Sorry. Garnish. Well"—*cough, cough*—"is this the Garnish who works for Bridget O'Toole?"

"That's a way of putting it," I said.

"Beg pardon?"

"Nothing, and I beg *your* pardon. Yes, this is that Garnish."

"Oh. Well. This is Thomas Howard. I spoke yesterday to your—employer, Miss O'Toole, about a job I want you people to do for me. She mentioned you were the person she would probably assign to it."

I got a kick out of the way he said "you people." You know, the way you say "you people" to the guys who are supposed to have oiled your car and checked the universal bearing, and then tell you that your transmission is shot, it'll cost you five hundred bucks. Mr. Howard wasn't thrilled, I gathered, to be forced to use us people.

What I didn't get a kick out of was the fact that he was calling me at all. One of the rules I've learned—and learned well—is that office business is *office* business. When your clients start calling you at home, your private life is as shot as that transmission I was talking about, especially in my line of work.

But then, I thought, what the hell. What private life? Marianne was making cookies and I was drinking beer staring at an empty apartment.

"Yes, Mr. Howard," I sighed. "Bridget—Miss O'Toole—asked me to, uh, check on the safety of Mrs. Howard while she's at Lake Monitonaqua this week."

*Cough, cough* on the other end. This guy was nervous.

"Look, Mr. Garnish," he blurted out, "you don't have to be polite with me. I understand that you know what I—what my problem is.

I'm just calling to make doubly sure Miss O'Toole was clear with you about what I want done."

"Right. You mean, no photos, no hard evidence. Just a verbal report."

"Exactly. You see, I . . . Well, this is embarrassing to say to a stranger, over the phone, but I love Cheryl very much. She's that important to me, Garnish. And if she's doing anything, I don't want to frighten her away. I just have to *know*, you understand? So I—so we can work things out."

I couldn't help it. I was beginning to like him. Especially I guess since I seemed so good at frightening people off myself these days.

"No problem. I understand, Mr. Howard. But I've got to tell you, sir, that this is a hell of a way to use a private detective. I mean, God knows we can use the business, but haven't you thought about just *talking* to your wife? Maybe you could see a marriage counselor . . . I don't know. A priest, a rabbi, whatever—"

"No, no," he interrupted. "Look, I *can't* confront her with something like this. Not until I *know*, damn it! I mean, if I was wrong, I could ruin everything!" The poor guy sounded close to tears. I began to murmur something that I hope sounded sympathetic, but he went on, getting more agitated by the word.

"Please, Mr. Garnish. I know you can't . . . You don't know Cheryl. But whatever she's doing, whatever she's involved in, she's a very special person. Look, I didn't mention this to Miss O'Toole, but for years I had a drinking problem. Oh, shit"—and he laughed—"I was a *drunk*. And it was Cheryl who helped me put myself back together. I mean, she saved my life. I never imagined I could be as happy and—yes, as proud as I was with Cheryl. It's just that in the last few months, there's been a—a coldness with her. I don't know, times when she's not home when I get there, phone calls she seems embarrassed about, a lot of little things. And they all frighten me. Can you understand that? I feel like I'm drowning. I'm afraid of what might happen, what I might turn into, if she—if she stopped loving me."

Enough, I thought. You step out of character for a minute because somebody seems troubled and fairly decent, and what happens? What happens is he goes all dorky on you, thinks you're father confessor, and starts showing you all the appendix scars on his shriveled little soul. What I suddenly felt like saying to Mr. Thomas Howard was "Look, Jack, at these prices don't do me any favors, okay?" But a client is a client, so what I did say was "Yes. Of course, sure Mr. Howard. Look, why don't you just try to relax for a while, huh? I know what you want, and I'll make sure you get just that and nothing else. The customer is always right, right?"

"And, Mr. Garnish," he went on, "one more thing. The most important thing. Cheryl must not know she's being watched. I mean, if she's—innocent, and if she found out that I suspected her for nothing, well, it would"—and here I could hear him gulp air—"it would hurt her so much. God, it would even be worse than if—"

I cut him off. "Yes, sir." Hell, it's bad enough talking to a plate of Jell-O. I draw the line, however, at having to talk to the Jell-O while it melts. "No problem. I can assure you she won't suspect a thing. I'm good at my job."

Right. Any PI will tell you you can't assure anything of the sort. But if real estate salesmen and muffler shop owners can get away with bullshit like that, why not us wee folk?

"Well. Thank you, Mr. Garnish." He seemed to have calmed down, at least a little. "Look, sorry to have bothered you like this on a Saturday."

"No problem. I wasn't doing much," I said—an understatement.

And he hung up. I took another look at the photo of Cheryl McLean Howard. That picnic smile was still there. And this time I noticed a shaggy dog in the background, staring at the photographer too. And noticed that Cheryl Howard was wearing what looked like a thin gold necklace inside the collar of her flannel shirt, and that her cute nose had just the smallest sort of twist to it; a little off center, maybe, but having an effect that somehow made her even prettier.

Hell, I thought, Mr. Thomas Howard of Wilmette *was* a dork, maybe even an Olympic-class dork. With a lady like that, a lady who looked like that much fun and who could bring out the kind of love and loyalty I'd heard over the phone, who would or should care if she enjoyed a little occasional action on the side? Not me, I can guarantee you. I've run down a lot of cheaters in my shining career, and I'll tell you something. Damn few of them, men or women, *feel* like cheaters. And damn few of them, as far as I'm concerned, deserve the kind of treatment they usually get once I've developed the film and delivered it to their concerned spouses.

*Tout comprendre, tout pardonner,* Bridget is fond of saying, which, she tells me, means to understand everything is to forgive everything. Of course, if people really believed that I'd be out of a job. And anyway I'm just in the *comprendre* end of the business, though sometimes it can get to bother you.

I noticed I was getting a little sentimental. And I also noticed that while I was talking to Howard I'd put away two more cans of ale. And I was still in my pajamas, and it had been a large fart of a Saturday so far, what with my two phone calls and my growing mood. All of a sudden, the idea of driving to Lake Manitonaqua Resort didn't seem as dreary a prospect as it had yesterday. The woods were still the woods, and I still hated the woods. But Cheryl Howard would be there, and whether she was fooling around or not, I wanted to meet Cheryl Howard. She deserved more than old Tom, I told myself slyly.

Meanwhile, there was still nothing to do till tomorrow. I thought about opening ale number four and decided against it. I thought about going out for an early dinner: nice chiles rellenos at El Tipico on Dempster, my favorite cheap restaurant. But I wasn't hungry, and besides, I had four beef pies turning into large hockey pucks in my freezer. I even thought about visiting Madame Flora's, the best little whorehouse in Skokie. But my bank account was low, and that's always a pretty depressing way to have fun anyhow (I wondered if Saint Thomas had understood *that* when he stiffed the medieval merchant for the overdue bill).

So I decided to do something really constructive. I propped the photo of Cheryl up on the arm of my sofa, kicked back, and thumbed on the cassette of Paul Desmond's lovely, sad last live concert (he died before it was released). And I noticed that in my mind I was already addressing Mrs. Thomas Howard by her first name.

Desmond was playing "Here's That Rainy Day." Tell me about it, Paul.

# 3

THE NEXT DAY, Sunday, I took off for Lake Manitonaqua at about one o'clock in the afternoon. It looked like the place was around a five-hour drive almost due north of Chicago. But I drive a 1969 Duster that's more rust than anything else, and that I get serviced about as often as I have brain surgery. And I drive nervous. So I figured with luck I'd probably roll into the resort by eight or nine that night.

I was right.

But you don't want to hear about my flat tire or my dirty air filter (can they *really* cost that much?) or about the approximately five thousand slow-moving north-bound trucks I met and tried to pass and didn't, on two-lane Wisconsin highways. You want to hear about Lake Manitonaqua, a.k.a. Blood Lake.

Well. Some millions of years ago, it seems, a lot of glaciers came crunching down the top half of the planet like a growing crack on a hard-boiled egg. They were racing like hell for the equator, the silly bastards, and of course they didn't come close to making it. But before they got forced back to the polar cap (where, I hear, they're brooding, waiting for their next attack) they left scars. And especially they left scars—*big* scars—the farther north you look; big hollows in the earth that became lots of lakes, lots of mountains and ravines populated by lots of ferns, and providing lots of the most beautiful sunsets you can think of.

That's how you get Wisconsin. And that's how you get one of Wisconsin's major industries: looking beautiful. The state is just about the same size as Illinois, its southern neighbor, it's got about a third of the population of Illinois, and it's got nearly the same gross annual revenue.

How come? Tourism is how come. All those bored industrialists from Illinois—and from Michigan, and from Ohio, and from Indiana, and even from southern Wisconsin—who spend their lives piling more concrete and plastic on their own countryside, all those Tupperware barons (it's all Tupperware if you think about it) get tired once in a while and feel like they need a vacation. And so they come to Wisconsin, to the Land of a Thousand Lakes, as the board of tourism likes to call it. And there they spend a few days basking, at one hell of a price, in the unspoiled nature they spend the rest of their working year spoiling. It's good for everybody concerned, it makes money, and I'm sure Madame Flora would approve.

As I say, I don't enjoy nature all that much myself. I like cities. But I like cities that are honest about being cities, and cityfolk who are honest about what they are. Or, as my old man used to say, "You make a mess, boy, if you gotta make a mess. But you be by God sure you can look at it after you done it." Pop was never grammatical, but he was usually crude.

Not that I was thinking about geology or my father while I drove north. I was thinking about Cheryl (what the hell, *call* her by her first name), about Marianne, and about the cabin that had been reserved for me. Would it have snakes or other forest dwellers? Muskrats? Frogs? I prefered honest urban cockroaches.

Anyway, I watched the sun go down on my left as I straggled up the map. And finally, after shelling out a couple hundred bucks on my credit card and after passing God knows how many other inviting resorts ("Cocktails—Dinner" they all flashed in neon seductively), I came to the resort.

The approach road, to the right off the main highway, was one of those half-mile dirt affairs that, since they seem built mainly for half-tracks and mobile artillery, feel like five miles. All of it downhill on a two-for-one-grade. It gave on to a large asphalt parking lot. The whole place was laid out like the top half of a pie, if you cut it across the center. Near the middle was the lodge: reception, cocktail lounge, connecting restaurant. Scattered around the semicircle of the crust were the thirty or so individual cabins—less than half occupied, I figured, this late in the season, and all bordering on the lake itself. The lakeshore curved around to embrace almost the entire compound. One road in and out, surrounded by water and dense forest: you couldn't ask for a better place to get away from it all, or to get away from it all with somebody you shouldn't be getting away with.

Even though it was August, there was a nighttime chill in the air as I walked up to the lodge. I had my suitcase, my Ben Gross championship tennis racket and fishing rod, which I had no intention of using, and my new, leather-case traveling bar—a present from Marianne—which I had every intention of using.

The reception desk was about as wide as a kitchen sink. Behind it was the manager's office, and when I rang the little bell the door swung open to reveal a broom closet with a desk and a tin filing cabinet. It also revealed a cowboy striding toward me who made the whole damn room smaller. And I *mean* cowboy: six two if he was an inch, flannel shirt and jeans, and one of those cracked, handsome faces so tanned and with so many crinkles that it looked like a landscape photo from *Arizona Highways*. His wavy, long gray hair matched the nest of grizzled thatch peeking out from the open top third of his shirt. I fought back the urge to say "Howdy, pardner" and just gave him my name.

He didn't have to check the register; business must be slow. "Ah, yes, Mr. Garnish," he said in a surprisingly soft voice, and smiled an instantly likeable smile. "Welcome to the lodge. I'm Ross Connors. I sort of own this ol' place, and I surely hope you'll enjoy yourself here." He held out a big hand.

"Thank you kindly, Mr. Connors," I said, taking the hand. "I reckon I surely will." I couldn't resist it; how often do you get to speak John Wayne to a native?

Connors laughed, and his laugh was as surprisingly hearty and genuine as his voice was soft. "Please, call me Ross, Mr. Garnish. And you don't *have* to talk like *Stagecoach* unless it comes natural, or unless you feel like it."

I laughed back. The guy was not only for real, he was quick. "No offense, Ross. Does the city mouse stick out that far? The air around here must be getting to me. And call me Harry—unless you think Dude is better."

Again he smiled—it looked like the natural position of his face—and leaned toward me like a conspirator. "Harry," he said, "if it wasn't for you dudes I'd be broke. So don't let it worry you. This place is *for* city folks to have a little country fun in. Hell, boy, on *my* vacations I check into the Palmer House in Chicago and try to score for tickets to the Lyric Opera. And down there, I'm the dude."

I was prepaid for the week, and Ross Connors told me I was assigned cabin 12. He looked at the bags I'd piled against the counter. "It isn't far," he said, giving me the key, "but I'd be glad to help you tote your gear down there. There's not a lot goin' on here, and I could use the fresh air."

"Well, actually," I said, glancing toward the brightly lit bar at the back of the lodge, "I thought I might . . ."

"Oh, hell, yes," he cried. "You been driving all day, you must be good and dry. Hey, dinner's over. We close it up around six on Sundays. But I can rustle up a sandwich or something."

I told him not to worry. Just a couple of quickies and I was going to turn in.

"Sure thing," he said. "Just leave your bags here." We stacked them behind the desk, and as I turned to walk to the bar, he shouted, "Hey, Harry. As country mouse to city mouse, tell Michelle behind the bar that you're on my tab tonight."

"I think I'm in love," I grinned. "Join me?"

"Love to. But I'm gonna be working on the books, so I better keep a clear head. Maybe tomorrow. And Harry." He looked wryly at my gear.

"Yeah?"

"Looks like you forgot the middle section of your fishin' rod, Dude." The guffaw couldn't have been friendlier. To my laughing "Aw, shit" he turned back into his office.

The bar was one of those circular things that drive bartenders crazy. The glasses, the water spigot, and the cherries and olives and such are all impossibly far from one another, and the booze is stored under the bar, so you have to bend to get at it. In other words (and I've held the job myself a lot of times), to make something as simple as a Manhattan or an old-fashioned you have to run and stoop twice as much as you really should, and on a five-hour shift you get very tired. Scattered around the small room were about ten tables, each one big enough for a solitaire game. Four or five people were in the bar, and the jukebox was playing, predictably, "The Shadow of Your Smile."

But there was nothing predictable about Michelle behind the bar. Most Wisconsin resorts use college kids for their summer help, and it's what Bridget O'Toole would call "axiomatic" that there are a lot of pretty undergraduates out there in Universityland. But this one was—well, the only word I can think of is *heartbreaking*. She was so slim she was almost skinny, but she wasn't skinny. With *really* honey-colored hair, more than shoulder length; and with breasts that were both small—compared to the Himalayan fantasies of *Playboy* and

*Penthouse*—and absolutely impossible to ignore. Her forehead glistened with little beads of perspiration (those goddamn circular bars) and the smile she turned on me as I slid on to the bar stool and the glitter in her pale blue eyes made me sorry (I think for the first time) that I hadn't gone to college.

"Sir?" she said.

"Uh." I gulped. "Uh, Mr. Connors told me to tell you to put this on his tab, okay?" And I swear to God I blushed. Why hadn't Connors gone to the bar to tell her that himself? I felt like a South Side wino trying to cadge a pint of Thunderbird.

Michelle just smiled, though; a little warmer, if anything.

"Oh, sure. You must be a new guest. What would you like?" So the free-round routine was standard drill for new arrivals. I felt a little less embarrassed, and a little disappointed. I thought *I* had charmed the big man into the freebies.

"A martini would be nice," I said, trying to keep my eyes focused above her neck. She laughed a little laugh—I think she could see how hard I was trying—and turned to make it.

"Hyeugh!" boomed a voice in my ear. "Crazy Sam Two Feathers!"

With pantherlike private-eye reflexes I jerked around, and damn near fell off the bar stool. A hand the size of my tennis racket was being shoved in my face.

"Wha," I said.

"Crazy Sam Two Feathers!" the voice exploded again. "Craziest goddamn Indian you ever met, I bet! Full half-blood Dakota! Madison! Videotape machines, games, TVs, whatever! Welcome to the camp, fella! Name?"

I'm five seven, so I had thought Ross Connors was pretty impressive. But Crazy Sam Two Feathers (if that was his name and not some weird password) made Connors look downright ordinary. I think I would have come up to his tie clasp, if he had been wearing a tie. But what he was wearing was a red Dacron shirt that would have outfitted two jockeys, black polyester pants that would have draped both their horses, and enough gold, silver, and turquoise around his neck and on his hands to finance the pot for a match race. When I finally found his face—I don't usually bend back that far—I saw a brown expanse of meat, a grin that could have chewed up Cleveland, and two black eyes so small and so sharp that they looked like they'd been borrowed from somebody else's head.

Oh, yes. His long black hair had been braided into two pigtails, each one held in a silver and turquoise ring.

"Uh, Harry Garnish," I said, watching his hand swallow mine. "Chicago." If you say "Evanston," they always ask you how far from the Loop you live, anyway.

"Yeah? Hot damn! Great town! Some of my best jobbers down there! Hey, Harry, your firewater's on me!" Michelle was just putting my martini down in front of me. I caught her eye and saw that she was trying hard not to giggle.

I explained to Crazy Sam that I was already on the house, and then something odd happened. He stopped talking in gunshots and began talking sentences.

"Well, okay, some other time then. Listen, Harry, meet some of the other campers. It's late in the season for a really big crowd, but we've all been having a hell of a time up here."

When you talk as loud as Crazy Sam in a bar that size, you don't keep a lot of privacy. I glanced around and saw five faces, some amused and some bored, waiting to be introduced. Three kids, about Michelle's age, sat around one small table: a pretty brunette (though not in Michelle's take-your-breath-away class), a young white man, and a young black man. Across the circular bar, staring at me, sat an obviously married couple, the woman in a tennis dress and with a nervous, uncertain look in her eyes, the man with a shaggy beard and a calm, self-satisfied air about him. I noticed with relief that the husband looked shorter than I. After Ross and Crazy Sam, I was wondering if I'd stumbled into the Land of the Giants.

I also noticed that Cheryl Howard was nowhere in sight.

"Hyeugh!" grunted Crazy Sam, regaining some of his steam. " 'Pears as though we got as many em-ploy-*ees* here tonight as we got payin' guests. Well, hell. Why not? Okay, Harry Garnish. These three kids at the table work here. Kerry"—the brunette smiled sweetly and nodded at me—"she does the beds and everything. That blond kid beside her is Danny. Danny *Bernstein,* can you believe that name and that face?" Danny, who looked like a fugitive from a Southern California travelogue, did his best to blush and grin. "And this boy"—I winced as Crazy Sam indicated the black kid at the table—is Byron. Byron, he's the lifeguard. Swims like a goddamn fish." Byron didn't smile and didn't look embarrassed. He just looked, and nodded shortly.

"And here's Doc Logan," Sam began, indicating the couple across the bar. But Logan interrupted him, rising from his chair. "Pat Logan," he said, smiling through his beard. "Not a doctor exactly, a resident. From Milwaukee. And this is my wife, Pam." Pam didn't say anything and didn't smile at all. And I got the quick impression—probably unfair, I thought—that she was too used to being "my" something: daughter, secretary, wife, piece of furniture.

I nodded at all of them, pronounced my name again, and waited for somebody to begin a conversation. Nobody did. They all just unfocused their eyes while the jukebox switched over to something by Barry Manilow. I never can tell what it is, exactly, by Barry Manilow; just something by Barry Manilow.

While we were all rushing not to talk to one another, lovely Michelle came over to ask me if I'd like another martini. I nodded gratefully, not even minding that she called me "sir."

"Well," I boomed at the group. "Not a real large bunch, are we?" H. Garnish, life of the party.

"Ah, hell," boomed back Crazy Sam, and treated me to another bear hug around the shoulders. "Like I say, buddy, we have enough fun for twenty more folks." He looked around the room for agreement, and since nobody disagreed violently, I suppose he took it for enthusiastic confirmation. "Besides," he roared on, "we got some more people here you haven't even met yet. "Hey! where *are* the damn Schneidermans and the goddamn Krugers? Michelle, darlin', you want to fix me another old-fashioned? Boy! Crazy Sam likes his firewater!"

The jukebox—somebody must have stuffed it full of quarters—clicked from Barry Manilow to Tony Bennett. I sighed inwardly with relief. The company wasn't getting any more interesting, but at least the music was getting better. At the same time, Dr.—or not-quite-Doctor Logan—spoke.

"The Schneidermans said they were going to bed right after dinner, I think. And the Krugers were going to take a short stroll by the lake when I saw them last. Mr.—Garnish, is it? Chicago is my hometown. What part are you from?"

"Well, Evanston, really," I said. Real Chicagoans always let their faces fall when you admit that. But it's okay—we don't pay taxes as high.

Logan's face did fall, but just a little. He was a gentleman.

And where, all this time, was the lady I'd driven up here to track? Where the hell was Cheryl Howard? I'm a sucker like everybody else, I guess. I assume that when you bother to disguise yourself as a simple tourist, when you borrow a ratty tennis racket and a fouled fishing pole from your dry-cleaner friend, on purpose to make yourself invisible to your prey, your prey ought to by God *be* there when you get to the stalking place. But suppose, came the thought to me, suppose that Cheryl Howard and her suspected boyfriend didn't know they were required to behave like characters in a TV show. Suppose they'd gone somewhere else for their fun and games. Suppose they hadn't gone anywhere at all, but decided to call this weekend off.

Well, wasted time and missed appointments are so much a part of my business that after a while you don't even get mad about them anymore.

But, damnit, I *was* getting mad about this one. Maybe because I'd driven so far, and wasted so *much* time, just to come up zero zero zero on it. Maybe because I was pissed off about being robbed of a weekend by Bridget O'Toole. And maybe because I really wanted to see Cheryl Howard.

Anyway, we all sat around as before, just a bunch of late Sunday drinkers waiting for an excuse to go back to our cabins. Ever notice that? Birds on a telephone wire, dogs in an alley, and drunks in a bar: they all have this secret radar that tells them when it's time to split— in a flock, a pack, or a stagger.

My own radar was giving me that warning beep—have one more quick one and get ready to go—when Cheryl Howard walked in.

Remember how Ingrid Bergman walked into Rick's Place in *Casablanca?* Not like she owned the place, but like the place ought to stop in its tracks for a minute, just because she was there. Well, nothing stopped in its tracks when Cheryl came in. Crazy Sam was still grunting to himself, the Logans were still sitting and not talking, the way married people do, and the three kids were still rapping (if they still called it that) about whatever kids just past the legal age rap about. But I stopped.

She was wearing a tennis dress, with a green sweater tied around her neck by the sleeves. Her hair was in the same ponytail she'd been wearing in the picnic photo. She was laughing with the man beside her at some joke, whose punch line must have been delivered just before they opened the door to the bar. And her eyes had that same flash, that same sexy smartness that I had seen in the snapshot. Yep, no doubt about it, it was Cheryl Howard, and I was being about as professional about her as a salmon is professional about swimming upstream to spawn.

"Hello, Michelle." She smiled at the other lovely thing behind the bar, a genuinely sweet smile. "Two Scotch and waters, please."

"Hey!" shouted Crazy Sam—who else? "Hey, Krugers! Say hello to a newcomer. This here is Harry Garment—"

"Garnish," I corrected him.

"Yeah. Whatever," he said. "So. These are the Krugers, Mike and Elaine. And ol' Elaine here"—indicating Cheryl—"is a killer on the court. You folks enjoy your walk?"

I was smiling at Cheryl, trying to think of an unforgettable opening line. Naturally, I said "Hi." She held out her hand and said, "Hello." And then my stomach tightened up like a fist.

Trained observer that I am, I hadn't pried my hawk's eye away from Cheryl since she'd come in, but as I took her hand I glanced at Mike Kruger. Only he wasn't Mike Kruger. He was Richard B. Schwartz, a sleazebag lawyer from Chicago whom I'd run across a few times on cases, and whom I'd played poker with a few times, and whom I once got piss-faced drunk with at a Christmas party.

Dick Schwartz wasn't smiling. He said, politely, "Hello, Mr. Garnish." But his eyes were saying something else, something along the lines of "You've been made, asshole, and if you try anything to blow this for me I'll nail your butt to the wall and split it six ways from Sunday."

At least, that's what *I* think his eyes were saying. And, considering the circumstances, I couldn't have agreed more.

# 4

MARTIN O'TOOLE, BRIDGET'S father and the man who taught me the business, used to say that the only real talent you had to cultivate to make a living as a detective was how to lie.

"Harry, my lad," Martin would say, grinning at some private joke and playing with his pipe, "Harry, all this movie crap about reasoning and clues and billy-be-damned what else isn't just blarney: it's three-day-old, flyblown blarney. Rancid blarney. Blarney fit only for the consumption of the beasts of the field. Learn to *lie*, boyo"—and here he would always lean across his desk toward me, whispering the word *lie* like he was imparting a secret formula. "Lying is our vocation and our trade. The world is full of liars, you know. And for a modest emolument you and I agree to separate some of the liars from some of the others. That's all. 'Tisn't a noble callin',' if you take my meanin"—old Martin's brogue always got thicker the more he enjoyed hearing himself talk—"but it's *our* callin'. Now your amateur liar, your garden variety liar, thinks that it's simply a matter of fabricatin' a—a fabrication, and then putting the brazen face on it. Nothin'—*nothin'*, lad—could be further from the truth of the matter. Because that brazen face, don't you know, will always show a crack, no matter how hard you try to keep it perfect. Always. Always." And he would look into the bowl of his pipe, as if it held some special message for him, like tea leaves at the bottom of a cup, you know?

"Now you and I, Harry, bein' as it were freemasons and high priests of the craft"—he pronounced it, of course, "crahft"—"we know better. Indeed, indeed. We know that lies *are* baloney—they spoil quickly. But the trick is to make your lie last a little longer than it should; just a little longer, if you follow my meanin', than its shelf life. When the brazen face begins to crack, well, then you just show another brazen face beneath it. It's a waitin' game, laddy buck, and if you got the stuff to stick it out long enough, the other fellow's mask will always crumble before yours does. And there's no feelin' in the world like that one. No. Nothin' like watching the other fellow's mask crack and crumble."

And then he would sit back in his chair—now Bridget's chair—and light his pipe, blissful at having once again summarized human nature in five minutes. He was a cynical old bastard, was Martin O'Toole.

Well, I tried to think myself into Martin's frame of mind as I sat in the bar, made pointless talk, watched Cheryl Howard and Richard Schwartz finish their drinks, and watched Richard Schwartz watch me. A really *good* liar, a Martin O'Toole-class liar, wouldn't let himself be disconcerted for a second because Richard Schwartz had recognized him. Nope. He'd just find himself another brass face underneath the one that had got cracked and go on peacefully drinking his martini like nothing had happened at all. A piece of cake.

Except it didn't feel like a piece of cake. It felt like a crock of crap, and the devil's motorboat was coming straight for my head. Know that joke?

Luckily it was late enough that I knew I wouldn't have to stay there that long, although I also knew I couldn't do what I really wanted to do and get the hell *out*. It was a funny, disturbing, kind of middling situation. If I didn't brass it out at least a little with Schwartz, I might as well fold up my tent and drive back to Evanston tonight and report to Bridget and Mr. Thomas Howard that our elaborate and subtle surveillance operation had been blown out of the water before it even got started, because the investigator of record (me, that is) had, at least figuratively, dropped his pants.

I tried to concentrate on what Martin O'Toole had told me about the brazen face. And the harder I tried, the harder it got. Maybe it was that I'd driven all day and was tired, maybe it was the two martinis I'd already put away, or maybe it was just the situation. Anyhow, I felt like a fool—a fool with his pants down, as I think I've said.

Crazy Sam at least saved me from having to think of anything clever to say. He could probably have run a conversation all by himself in an empty warehouse if he'd had to. Anyhow, he kept on making remarks loud enough to scare the fish in the lake, and dumb enough to stun the ones he couldn't scare. Cheryl, whom I watched furtively while I fiddled with my drink, kept up her end, laughing gracefully at the bellowing and the har-har comments about her legs.

I couldn't bring myself to look at Schwartz, because I was sure he was looking at me. He hadn't said a damn thing since we'd been introduced.

After a few minutes—Crazy Sam was just beginning a joke about a tennis player with hemorrhoids—two of the kids, Danny Bernstein and Kerry, got up, smiled good night all around, and headed for the door.

Sam interrupted himself to shout after them, "Hey, Bernstein! It's still Sunday, you hear? You let that little Christian girl get some sleep, now. No nookie tonight, right?"

Kerry turned, grinning nervously and blushing like a stoplight, to say, "Oh, Mr. Two Feathers, you're *terrible!*" Actually, I thought she was right. And so, I guess, did Danny; he didn't stop, didn't turn around, and Kerry had to skip to get through the door he shoved open.

At least the kids saved us from the joke. "Ah, what the hell," said Sam, turning back to us. "I guess I've had about enough for a night, too. See you all tomorrow, right? Hey, Michelle, honey, put it on my tab." And he lumbered, a whale in Dacron, to the door. But not before throwing one unmistakable glance and sigh at Michelle, and growling on his way out, "God *damn.* With all these tight young pieces around here, how's a horny redskin supposed to get any sleep? Hyeugh, hyeugh, hyeugh."

No doubt about it, the man left a wake behind him. Like a motorboat, or maybe like a garbage scow.

In the silence I fumbled off the bar stool. "Well, I guess I ought to turn in too. Good night, Mrs. Kruger, Mr. Kruger. I left my gear at the front desk." And I turned toward the lobby.

No such luck. "Here, Mr. Garnish," said Kruger-Schwartz. "I'll help you carry your things to your cabin. Honey," he said, briefly taking Cheryl's hand, "you can find your way in the dark, can't you? I won't be long."

Cheryl, looking puzzled, said she'd be fine. I thanked Mr. Kruger for his kind offer—no nice folks like the nice folks you meet in the woods—and we walked to the lobby.

I mean, sooner or later Schwartz and I were going to have to go around and around, at least a little bit, about this business. And though I would have been happy as a clam to put it off till tomorrow, when I'd be awake and sober, there was really no point in trying. It would be just as bad then. And if I haven't learned to lie like a pro, at least I've learned that when the shinola hits the Mixmaster, you can duck or you can take it in the eye, but you can't ask it to wait a second.

The quickest route to the cabins would have been back through the bar at the rear of the lodge. But as we picked up my stuff—hardly enough for two people to carry—Schwartz said quietly, "Let's go around the front of the building, Harry." I lit a cigarette and nodded.

It felt chilly after the heat of the bar. And the cool air must have been good for me, because I surprised myself by taking the attack.

"Schwartz, Richard B.," I said as we walked. "Attorney at law, current residence, Chicago. Married, fair poker player, worse lawyer, and, I guess, ladies' man. How do we want to play this, Dick?"

He stopped walking, put down my tennis racket and fishing pole, and reached inside my shirt pocket for my cigarettes. When he got one to his mouth, I lit it for him.

"Harry," he said, looking up at the clouds and the moon, "you've been around long enough, you know I know a few leg-breakers."

"I know, Dick," I said.

"No. I mean real South Side types, Harry. A couple ex-Blackstone Rangers, like that. And I helped a lot of them, right? So a lot of them think they owe me a favor. You don't want to be a favor, do you, Harry?"

"Believe me," I said, "I've no desire at all."

"Okay. Good. So. You don't want me calling in old markers on you, you tell me what the hell you're doing up here. And spare me, please, the bullshit about the great outdoors and the sports and all." He looked at my—and Ben Gross's—aged racket. "Christ, you probably wouldn't even know which end of this son of a bitch to grab. So I figure you're working—hey, you still working for what's-her-name, O'Toole? Yeah? Well, tell you what. I'm not gonna ask you what you think you're working on—you'd only lie, right? But I'm telling you, my friend, that it better not have anything to do with me or that lady back in the bar. Because if it does, your best bet is to keep on driving till you hit Montreal, you follow?"

In my heart I blessed old Martin O'Toole. By God, Schwartz *didn't* know I was there to keep tabs on Cheryl. Or, better yet, he didn't *want* to know. He was nervous. And when you hang around liars, cheaters, and weasels as much as I have, you learn that a nervous liar will *help* you lie to him, if his choice is that or being caught out. And that you can use.

"Hey, Dick. Look, man, I'm not going to lie to you," I lied. "Of course I'm working up here. Hell, I hate the woods." We were strolling toward the cabins again, smoking and looking around like two old pals. "And," I went on, "I can promise you that I don't want to mess up your action at all. That's some pretty lady you got there, by the way. Kruger her real name?"

"Harry," said Dick Schwartz, "go fuck yourself."

"Yeah. Right," I said. "Anyhow, I'm not about to lay my hog on the table where I'm not paid to, and *you've* been around enough to know that about me. But I'll tell you the truth, you could be some help to me. See, I need to know something about this Indian. You know—Sam. There's this videotape distributor, very big, in Evanston, who would like, a *lot*, to find out about the guy's rental and sales procedures. You had a chance to talk to the Indian at all?"

"That guy, huh?" he said, a little grudgingly. "No. No, I can't say I've had a lot of talk with him, except if you count listening to his goddamn jokes. But look, Garnish, you ain't shitting me?" And he stared at me; even in the moonlight I could see him convincing himself to believe me.

Good old Crazy Sam, loudmouth enough to announce his business to anybody in the first two minutes of conversation. And good old me, knowing just enough about business matters to think that "sales and rental procedures" sounded like something a videotape retailer might be interested in.

"Hey, Dick," I said. "Would I shit you? Seriously. Hell, you're the guy knows all the leg-breakers."

"Yeah. So I am. But look, let me do you a favor. You want to know about Sam Two-Whatsis? So I'll put some people on it, look into it, right? You know, guys who know how to look, so if they look, they find. Dig?"

I dug. If they look, they find; it's an old slogan at the IRS, among other grafters. And it means, basically, that there ain't no justice. If they—whoever the hell *they* are—try to find out what they can about your past, about your most secret fears, then they'll find. It's why you always tense up just a little when you're called for one of those telephone surveys.

They look, they find. Not that everybody is guilty; everybody may be, but that's not the point. The point is that everybody thinks they *must* be guilty of something, and the really cagey cats know how to work on that. Bridget, who likes to use words like *inauthenticity*, calls it "the despair of inauthenticity" and tells me what all the Super Bowl–class philosophers have said about it. I call it "the sense of schmuckness," and I've got enough of it myself; I don't need telling. Ever have somebody at a party or in a bar ask you, "Do you *really* believe that?" And what do you say? You say, "Well, not *really*, you know, but . . ."

But I also dug that Richard B. Schwartz had just told me he was scared, and scared enough to dangle some raw meat in front of my nose. I was very happy. Gosh oh golly, I *had* weasled my way into the saddle.

"Hey, Dick," I said, "thanks a lot. That would make my trip up here a real vacation, you know? And, look, about this Kruger woman"— damn it, I was enjoying myself—"not to worry, okay? I'll stay out of your way—just sit in my cabin and drink and wait for the sunsets. I can use the rest."

"That'll be just fine," he said. "I'll get the stuff on the Indian to your office when I come up with something." In a pig's ass, I thought. Schwartz might know some leg-breakers, but if he knew anybody who could run a decent cash-flow check on *anybody,* he wouldn't be representing leg-breakers, junkies, and little old ladies whose cats got julienned by Chicago street cleaning machines.

Actually, though I wouldn't want my sister to share a 747 with him, I had always admired Schwartz (a little) for being at least forthright about being a bottom-dwelling slug. I don't know how it affected his clients, but on his desk he had only one ornament: a fake bronze ashtray in the form of a shark.

Besides, I don't have a sister.

We had come to my cabin, number 12. There wasn't much else to say, and if Schwartz was bothered by the fact that I just happened to be right next to his and Cheryl Howard's cabin, he didn't let on; just put my sports equipment on the ground, turned on his heel, and walked off. I'm a convincing cringer—people have told me it's one of my best things—and I'd given him a carrot and a stick he thought he could use on me. Swell. I hoped the son of a bitch slept like a baby, because I sure the hell was going to pull his chain tomorrow.

It was while I was thinking that and looking around cabin 12—a bed, dresser, john with shower, and that's it—that the reaction hit me. Damn it, so Cheryl Howard was fooling around, after all, and fooling around with a guy I *knew* could take home a gold medal if they ever held a pig Olympics. I was disappointed, even if her husband had been assigned permanent wimp status in my mind. Dick Schwartz? *Dick Schwartz?* Tall and, if you like oil and hair dye, good-looking, okay; more than me on both counts, I gave him that. But that was, like, *all*. The guy was hopeless any other way, and could Cheryl really be silly enough to get silly over someone whose whole personality was between his legs?

I don't know. Maybe if you spend enough time in any racket, eventually it gets to be sour and smelly, like when you wear the same shirt three days running. And God knows my racket was already smellier than most, and God knows I'd seen enough cheap cheating —I had eight-by-ten glossies, for Christ's sake—to make me used to it. But I'll tell you, lying there on the bed, trying to sleep with all my clothes still on, it bothered me. And tomorrow I was going to call Bridget O'Toole, collect, and make sure that not only Cheryl and Schwartz and I but Mr. Thomas Howard and as many people as possible got to look at their fair share of the ugliness. I wished I'd been a bartender, or maybe a priest: they got paid to listen to your stupidities, but they didn't have to draw pictures.

What was it Bridget had said about Saint Thomas's whore—I mean, the whore who had taken her beef to Saint Thomas? Oh, yeah. Even the sinful deserve justice. Well, I thought, I knew as much about justice as I did about nuclear fission; that is, I could spell them both. But I decided I would go back to the cocktail lounge, and if Cheryl was still there, I would give her a chance to bail out of things before I called the office.

Don't bother telling me that's unprofessional, sentimental, and frog-brain dumb. I told myself all of that all the way back to the lodge.

Well, almost all the way. I was still a good ten yards away when I saw I was too late. The place had a big bay window in back and it was still fully lit up inside, so I could tell from that distance that Cheryl, and Dr. and Mrs. Logan, had left.

I could tell because Michelle and Byron, the black kid who hadn't left with Danny Bernstein and Kerry, obviously had the place and the world to themselves. Byron had walked behind the bar—hell, he was younger and wirier than me, maybe he'd jumped the damn thing. Anyway, he had both his arms shoved up under Michelle's blouse, and she had both her arms down below where the bar cut off my vision, and they were both trying to smile, talk, and eat one another's ears at the same time.

I stopped, sighed a little, and reached for a cigarette. Okay, kids, I thought. Have a good time—especially you, Byron, you lucky bastard. At least I don't have to report on you. Maybe in a few years; I'll still be around, or somebody like me will. For now, enjoy.

As I said, I'm not exactly a frontiersman, and I hadn't taken any pains walking there to avoid stepping on twigs or spooking jackrabbits or any of that other nonsense Clint Eastwood always does when he sneaks up on Eli Wallach. But I must have been better at it than I thought. Because as I lit my cigarette I saw in the flare of the match that I had company. Ross Connors hadn't heard me approach, probably because he was too intent on the scene in the bar. He was crouched a few feet ahead of me, and when he heard my match strike he sprang to his feet, glared at me, said, "Good night, Mr. Garnish," and strode off rapidly into the darkness.

Well, that wasn't my business either. I left Byron and Michelle to their midnight snack and Ross Connors to whatever was twisting his face all to hell and walked back to my cabin. I was going to have to try, at least, to sleep; I'd need all my energy to blow the whistle on Cheryl Howard tomorrow.

# 5

As THINGS TURNED out, Monday took more energy than I'd thought.

I woke up at about six A.M., which is a lot earlier than I like to wake up. Lake Manitonaqua advertised in its brochure that, because of the prevailing winds, it was "largely insect free": that meant either that large insects came free with the rooms, or that the only two mosquitos in captivity thereabouts had picked my bed to dive-bomb all night long. And then at six half the birds in Wisconsin decided that this was the perfect time and place to scream their fuzzy little heads off. When you're hung over, the collective noun for birds isn't *flock*, it's *insanity:* an insanity of birds.

The lodge, I remembered, didn't start serving breakfast until seven. There was no instant coffee maker in the room. There was no TV; therefore, no Jane Pauley (the lady I most usually wake up with). There probably would have been hot water in the shower if I'd waited long enough, but I wanted to get back to Chicago in time for the Bears' opening game. And I realized I'd been so proud of myself for remembering to pack my toothbrush and my razor that I'd forgotten to pack my toothpaste and my shaving cream and—ah, hell—my blood pressure pills.

So there I stood, outside the lodge doors, at six forty-five, shivering, face cut, mouth tasting like Ivory soap (ever brush your teeth with Ivory soap?—don't) and, for all I knew, pumping blood like a racehorse. Call me superstitious, but I didn't think it was going to be one of my more stellar days.

I didn't feel any happier about the state of the universe when Ross Connors, passing through the dining room, caught sight of me. He stopped in his tracks for the shortest of instants, and I thought I saw his face freeze in that same panicked, hurting look I'd seen a few hours before. But then he relaxed into his big, warm smile and strolled over and pushed the door open.

"You're up early, Harry," he said, grinning. "Anxious to get out and do some fishin', huh?"

Yeah. Well. If he wanted to make believe it hadn't happened, that was okay with me. I always follow suit, and I never play a trump unless I have to. I lose a lot of bridge games that way, but I also keep my thumbs.

"Right," I said, walking into the lodge and grinning back. "I figured maybe I'd bag me a poached salmon with rice on the side. What do you bait those with, anyhow—hollandaise sauce?"

Now he laughed outright. "No," he said, "for that particular game I think you're best off using a Visa card. And, Harry, by the way—you *bag* things you hunt for; things you fish for you *land*. Look, breakfast won't be ready for another few minutes, but you look to me like you could use a cup of coffee. Come on out to the kitchen."

I told him it sounded better than driving a nail through my foot, and followed him into the kitchen. Michelle and Kerry, looking fresh and cheerful as a pair of sunnyside-up eggs—okay, *two* pair—were mucking about with dishes and cups and breakfast rolls. Michelle was wearing one of those white things, I think you call them peasant blouses, pulled down from her bare shoulders; I wished again I hadn't forgotten my blood pressure pills. There was also a woman, or maybe a mummy in an apron, bending over the stove and stirring a couple of smoking skillets that looked about as big as the rims of a Peterbilt. Ross introduced her as Winifred, the cook. She turned halfway around and grimaced at me, and I decided I didn't want any breakfast.

After Ross poured me a mug of coffee and I took it out to the dining room, he pulled out a chair and sat across from me, still with that big damn, friendly damn smile on his face. He sat down the way they do in cowboy movies, reversing the chair and folding his arms over the back. On him it looked good.

"Harry," he said after a couple of beats, "I guess you're a little curious about last night."

Oh Christ, I thought, trying to sip coffee without burning my lips. A confession. And, since I *hadn't* become a bartender or a priest, it wasn't really in my job description.

"Look, Ross," I began. "It's none of my business—"

"No, it isn't," he interrupted me. "But I don't like you to think I spend my evenings spying on the hired help. See, these are all good kids. I mean, I don't hire kids to work here summers unless they come in with recommendations, character references, *you* know. All four of them are college kids."

He said that—"college kids"—with real pride, the way a guy will say "My boy's in medical school." You couldn't help liking the man.

"So," he went on, "you understand, while they're here, I feel kind of responsible for them. What's the phrase—in locus parentis?"

It was in loco parentis. I'd listened to enough Bridget O'Toole dialogues—or monologues—to get my Latin straight. I didn't correct him.

"Yeah," he said, "that's it. In locus parentis. I mean, I don't want these kids getting messed up in anything that's going to—well, going to mess them up. Oh, *hell*. I'm not making any sense!" And he slapped the table.

I thought he was making a lot of sense, but probably not the kind he wanted to make. Ross Connors wasn't the sort of man you could imagine being ill at ease. But he *was* ill at ease, and watching a man like that acting nervous makes *you* nervous. There was nothing I could say, though. He had to get it out all by himself, and we both knew it.

"Maybe this will make sense," he said after a moment. "I know I'm not anybody's guardian. But, you know, sometimes you see things that you know are going to be trouble. And look, I've got nothing against Negroes—black people, I mean."

I'd been waiting for that one. But I was surprised that, the way he said it, I actually believed him. Usually when somebody says that you assume that what they're proudest of is not having said "niggers." But however strained he was, he still sounded honest.

"But you have," I offered, trying to help him out, "got something against kids making damn fools of themselves while they're under your roof."

"That's right!" he said, and looked at me gratefully. No, really—gratefully, like I'd just patted him on the shoulder. I *hate* it when people do that.

"That's exactly right, Harry. I mean, look, I know what kids are supposed to be up to nowadays. Hell, you know"—and he relaxed into a chuckle—"they even deliver *Newsweek* all the way up here. And let's face it, it really isn't all that much different from what we all did at that age, is it? Except there's a lot less unwanted babies to be abandoned or beaten up by parents who hate them for being there."

The chuckle had gone out of his voice. "Yet and still," he went on, "I worry. Despite the pill, despite the—what do they call it—the 'new mortality' and all that, I just don't want anybody getting—ah, *hurt* while they're here."

"Sure, Ross," I said. "I know what you mean. But look, man—"

"No, you *don't* know what I mean." And he laid his big hand on my arm. I damn near jumped.

"Harry," he began. And then he froze. Just stopped, like snapping your fingers.

Michelle was standing at our table, smiling down at me like my half shaved face was the nicest thing she'd seen all day (and, remembering Winifred in the kitchen, maybe it was). "Hi," she said. "I can bring you some breakfast now, if you'd like me to."

She was stunning enough, and knew she was stunning enough, that I didn't even have to try and tell her what I'd *really* like her to bring me. Those eyes and that smile did it all; held an offhand invitation and an amused turn-down all at once. Really beautiful women can do that. So I just grunted a drowsy, early morning no thanks, and watched her dance back to the kitchen.

She and Connors hadn't exchanged a word.

He looked at me with the look men will share after someone like Michelle passes through the room.

"*That's* what I mean," he said. "Harry, I've been running this place twenty years. Don't know how many kids I've had working for me in all that time, but I can tell you I've *never* had the likes of Michelle up here. She's—what? She's older than she ought to be, and she's younger than she ought to be, too. Believe me, she drives the men around here crazy. And I mean the guests, too, not just Byron and Danny. You ought to see the looks she gets from some of the wives. And you know, I don't even think the poor kid *knows* what she does to people."

"Ross," I said. "Take it from a fresh victim. She knows."

He laughed and looked down at his hands, spread flat on the table. "Well, okay." He sighed. "Maybe she's gotten to me a little, too. But, see, a girl like that—I mean, summer crushes, they're part of what these kids come up here looking for, huh? But this girl . . . I'm really scared she could do some real damage, to herself, or to whoever she—ah, chooses."

I thought about asking him why he didn't just fire her on grounds of sexual teasing without a license. But he really *was* worried, and I liked him too much to smartass to him.

I figured, though, that I'd taken up enough of my time. While he'd been talking Dr. and Mrs. Logan had walked in for breakfast, both as quiet and solemn-looking as last night. They were followed by a man and a woman, fat gray twins in sky blue jogging suits, who joined them at their table: the not so mysterious missing Schneidermans, I assumed. Anyway, I wanted to get out before I ran into Cheryl and smiling Dick Schwartz.

"Ross," I said, rising and lighting a cigarette, "I'm really sorry, buddy, but I don't know what the hell to tell you. Anyhow, the season's almost over, right? So you might as well just let things ride, right?"

Wrong. If he had looked at me a few minutes before like I'd patted him on the shoulder, he looked at me now like I'd just pan fried his parakeet. If he had a parakeet.

He rose with me. "Can I walk along with you for a bit?" he asked.

A very bad headache, that's what I was getting.

I mean, what would *you* say to him? "Sorry, fuckhead, but I'm here on assignment and I don't have time to float around in your smelly little problems and obsessions." Or, maybe, "Gosh, Ross, I'd sure like to help you out, but see, I've got to make this call to Chicago to tell a guy that his wife has been screwing around behind his back." Or something else along those lines. Go ahead, make one up yourself.

What I said was "Oh. Sure." And I shrugged.

I had planned to go right from breakfast to the nearest pay phone and call in my good news to Bridget. But I was still wondering if I couldn't, maybe *say* something to Cheryl Howard to get her out of trouble before I put her deeper in it myself. Maybe, who knows, I even welcomed Ross and his goddamn child care problems, just as a way of or an excuse for putting off the phone call a little longer. At any rate, much as I hate getting involved in other people's problems, I didn't really mind all that whole hell of a lot his walking along with me back to my cabin, taking me farther and farther away from the nearest phone.

It was a sunny morning, crisp, with just enough of autumn in the air to make the summertime feel all the more valuable. In the Midwest you learn to hoard your summertime.

Ross walked silently alongside me till we were about halfway to the lakeshore. Finally he spoke. "Harry," he said, "I ain't a fool." I noted that it was the first time he said "ain't," and I couldn't figure out if it was for effect, or because he really was agitated. But I didn't say anything. It was his party.

"I mean," he went on, "you come up here with your week prepaid. Money order. And, till a couple days ago, I didn't even know your name—just knew I was to keep a cabin free for a week for *somebody,* name to follow, you know? And—excuse me, Harry—you show up, and you really don't look like a fellow wants to spend a few days fishin' or soakin' up what sun's left this time of year. Fact is, Harry, you don't really *belong* here, you know?"

I thought maybe I could joke my way out of it. I always think I can joke my way out of it, and I'm always wrong.

"Hey, Ross," I said. "You caught me. I'm just a Chicago Czech impersonating a jock. Never even go out-of-doors in Chicago, if I can help it. You want me to pack up and get out now, or can I stay for lunch? I mean, you can keep the deposit on the cabin."

It not only didn't work, it was what some of my pals in advertising —they love to talk like this—call "counter-productive." That means it was a fuckup.

He stopped and stared at me. "You don't have to help me if you don't want to," he said. "But I don't see any reason for you to go on like that, like I'm just ignorant. Do you?"

I don't blush a hell of a lot, so I remember it when I do. I did.

"No," I said. "I'm sorry." And I meant it.

He put his hand on my shoulder. "It's okay," he said. "I know I'm asking a lot of you, just to listen to me. But, see, if you hadn't showed up at breakfast, I was going to look you up anyhow. The thing is, Harry—ah, hell, I *know* you're not here for the fun of it. And that means you're here for some sort of job, right? And *that* means you must be some kind of investigator." I started to mumble a denial, but he cut me off. "No, no. I don't give a damn about what you're here to check on. Though bein' in the motel business for twenty years now, I got a pretty good idea it ain't national security, right?"

I stared at the burning end of my cigarette.

"Okay," he said. "Like I say, I don't want to mix in your affairs. But hell, in your job you know that a lot of hanky-panky"—so help me God, he said "hanky-panky"—"goes on in places like this, just like in motels. Except my clients have to be a little richer." He smiled and grimaced at the same time. "Well, I can't rightly mind that," he went on, "but I can't rightly approve of it, either. Anyhow, for the last few months some of this—ah, hanky-panky's been backfiring on my customers, and that means it's been backfiring on me."

"I don't get it," I said. I got it.

"Blackmail, Harry!" he said, proving that I'm not as stupid as I look. "I don't know how they're doing it, but somebody's blackmailed at least two of my customers this summer for coming up here with people they . . . they weren't married to."

"Right," I said. "I didn't think it was for cheating at backgammon. But how'd you come to find out? You mean the marks *told* you?"

"Marks? Oh, yeah. Yeah, Harry, they did. You see, these guys were both old friends of mine, and when they got the grip put on them they got mad at me."

"Can't blame them, Ross, I'd get mad at you too, if I was lucky enough to be in that position. But you know that means there's probably a lot of non-old buddies who got caught in the shit too."

"Exactly!" he said. "Listen, it's not just that it's an ugly business, though God knows I hate it. But it's damn bad for my lodge, too. You know, word gets around about places that are safe and places that aren't. I don't know how—there must be some kind of underground railroad for folks who want to fool around. And I've known a few fellas who've been put out of business by stuff like this."

I raised my eyebrows. All these years, I hadn't thought about that. Imagine! A secret underground of adulterers, one-night stands, and assorted kinkos who knew just what motels to hit for a secure—well, a secure hit. Hell, maybe they even had a journal, and secret decoder rings and such. But then, my end of the business was more the keyhole-and-camera part than the room key-and-ledger end.

I also wanted to ask Ross what this had to do with last night and our tag-team Peeping Tom contest, and with his worry about his summer help's purity, or safety, or whatever. But it didn't feel like the right question. And besides, I already knew the answer. He was half over the gunwale about Michelle. Hell, who wouldn't be, after a summer in the woods with an ass that could launch a thousand quips? And even if he *was* too Red Ryder to do anything about it (except, of course, think), he could still be jealous of her—especially if he thought the dude she was playing ten-finger poker with was a blackmailer.

Anyway, it wasn't the time for the question. Especially since I didn't give a rat's gonad for the blackmail problem at Lake Manitonaqua. I do what I get paid to do, and this time around I was being paid to ruin Cheryl Howard's life, Thomas Howard's life, and maybe Dick Schwartz's, too—though *that* would be sort of like trying to redemolish a building.

With practiced, and earned, boredom I explained to Ross what they always explain about blackmail on *Ironside, Kojak, CHiPs,* and other TV versions of *Gidget Goes Metro:* the best solution is to go to the cops, the blackmailer only has the whip hand as long as he/she can scare you into secrecy, once you start paying you keep on paying, and blah blah blah.

But Ross had been around too long. He knew as I knew that it was all at the very best rancid guacamole. Think about it. They (you know who *they* are, don't you?) find out the worst thing you ever did or ever were. And you're going to let everybody know the bad news just so you can screw the evil extortionist and reestablish truth, justice, and the American way? Tell me more. And then tell me the one about Tinkerbell and the Tooth Fairy Go to Mars.

He didn't even bother to tell me he knew it was all bullshit. He just said, "Harry, I can give you a retainer if you want."

I told him we'd have to go through all kinds of contract signing nonsense before I could accept a retainer on behalf of the agency—that's the truth, by the way—and that I would think long and hard about suggesting that O'Toole Investigations take the case. That was a lie. But he looked like he needed to be reassured.

And I saw a way to use him.

"No problem," I said as he began thanking me. "And, look, I can use a favor from you. Can I use your office phone in a while? There's a couple of confidential calls I've got to make."

He was assuring me that I could direct-dial Cambodia, for Christ's sake, if I felt like it, when the morning quiet of the woods was shattered by a loud "Hyeugh! God-damn! Any tennis players around here?"

Now, I don't know if you've ever seen three hundred pounds of Indian rolling at you in nothing but orange tennis shorts—I swear to God, orange—and a yellow tank top with CRAZY SAM'S, MADISON, WISC. across the front. But let me tell you, it's the kind of thing that could give flesh a bad name.

Ross relaxed into his usual grin as Crazy Sam intercepted us. "Well, it's a little early, Sam," he said, "but you might be able to scare up a match back at the lodge."

Sam swung a backhand with his racket. In his hand, it looked like a Ping-Pong paddle. "Early, my ass! Hell, if you palefaces *always* laid in bed smelling your farts so goddamn late, you wouldn't *never* of taken our land away. Hey, Garner, how about it? You wanna go a couple sets?"

"Garnish," I said. "No, thanks, I'm going to try some fishing. It's more in my line."

Ross looked at me sharply. "Fine, Harry," he said. "Thanks for your time. And remember," he said, smiling, "what you fish for, you *land.*"

"Gotcha," I smiled back. "And what you hunt for, you *bag.* See you guys later." And I walked the rest of the way to my cabin, while Ross strolled and Sam bellowed back to the lodge.

Hello, cabin; hello bed, toilet, dresser. Hi there, traveling bar. It was only about eight-thirty, but, thank God, the sun's always over the yardarm *somewhere* in the Czechoslovakian Empire. And the way my day was going so far, I figured a mild buzz couldn't possibly make matters worse. So I poured two fingers of Walgreen's best Scotch, and lay back on the bed to consider my options.

I still had to make my phone call, that much was certain anyhow. In fact, there was no real reason for me to stay up here, now that I had found out what Mr. Thomas Howard was paying me to find out. Mission accomplished. Bloody hooray for me.

Plus, I didn't seem to be doing all that well in the business of concealment and infiltration: I'd been at the place twelve hours, and so far two people had made me for a PI. If things went on this way, I figured Winifred the cook would be down in the next hour asking me to track down something for her—a new face, maybe. Best to call Bridget, get it over with, and see what was planning to fall out of my car's chassis on the drive back to Chicago.

And guess what. The more I argued myself into making the call, the less I felt like doing it. I fumbled around in the bottom of my suitcase and brought out the photo of Cheryl Howard.

A crush. Son of a bitch if that wasn't what was ailing me. At forty-four, with enough adulteries in my casebooks that Reno ought to give me the key to the city, and with a few notches on my own Barcalounger, for crying out loud, what I had was a crush on a lady I knew one sure thing about, and that one sure thing was that she fucked around. It was so damn adolescent, I wondered if I should check in the bathroom mirror for zits.

It was just, I thought, looking at her photograph, that there was something—ah, hell—*nice* about that face. I mean, remember when *nice* meant something? Not "cute," you dig, not "sweet," or "safe." Not even "innocent." *Nice.* Like the first time you made out and discovered to your surprise not only how easy it was, but how much fun it was. Cheryl looked like that: something you remembered, something you *missed.* Maybe even something you'd never had as much as you should have had it.

So I was going to put her through the process, right? "The process" is what everybody in my business calls it when we're talking shop over beer and chips. It begins with a report and a dossier and usually with candid Polaroids, and it moves through divorce court, and it winds up with a lot of kicking and hollering and crying and everybody loses money and self-respect except the lawyers and the guys in my business, and we just keep the money. A thousand times a day, folks.

Process, my ass, I thought. I remember once walking into the office and having Brenda, our secretary and one-woman distillery, leer at me over the *Tribune* crossword puzzle. "RRRy," she gulped at me, "didja know that *dung* can be used as a trans as a tansitive *verb?*"

That was the kind of thing that Brenda could sit and meditate about, blinking and shaking her head, until lunchtime. But I remembered it now because that's just how I felt about this job. I was going to *dung* Cheryl Howard: I was getting paid to, in fact. Jesus Christ.

I was convincing myself that a little more Scotch would be a very bad idea, when there was a knock on my cabin door. Damn! I thought, Winifred the cook already?

Worse, I saw: Michelle, looking quizzical, but still smiling. "Mr. Garnish?" she said. "Ross—Mr. Connors—said you wanted to see me?"

Dung, I thought, as a transitive verb.

# 6

WELL, BUCAROOS, IT was the kind of situation that called for quick thinking and fancy talking, as Hopalong Cassidy used to say in all those old movies I watched on TV when I was a kid.

The problem was, I didn't feel quick and I didn't feel fancy. I felt tired, grungy, and a little dizzy from the breakfast Scotch—and more than a little pissed off at Connors for shoving the girl off on me. Damn it, I'd told him I would *think* about it. That didn't mean he was supposed to send the little twit to my cabin for counseling as soon as she'd scraped the leftover egg and ham into the garbage.

Oh, yeah, that was another problem: the little twit didn't *look* like a little twit. She looked like a beautiful woman who was asking to come into my room. Since I'd seen her at the lodge she had tied her long hair back in a ponytail—like Cheryl, I realized before I could stop myself—and changed her skirt for a pair of what are called "designer" jeans, which I guess are called that because if the right girl is wearing them you find yourself making designs.

Michelle was the right girl.

So Hoppy, I thought, why the hell didn't you tell me how to handle this one? But I did my best anyhow. When she smiled up at me and said "Hi. Could I talk to you for a minute?" I didn't hesitate more than a split second. This was beginning to sound like her own idea.

"Oh, yeah," I said. "Come on in."

Quick-draw Garnish, that's me.

Is there a word that means something like "skipped," "danced," and "floated" all together? Anyhow, that's just what she did, right to the bed, where she planted herself, crossed her legs into a sloppy and wonderful version of the lotus position, glanced at my open bottle of Scotch, cocked a sardonic eyebrow at me, and said, "So. Okay, what can I do for you?"

Just like that. Like turning on a light switch, *click!* and she was in control of things. That kind of assurance, I thought with admiration and a little bit of wariness, only comes with a *lot* of practice.

"Ur," I urred. "Ur, well, the fact is, Michelle—hey, what's your last name, by the way?"

"Hill," she said. "At least, that's the name they—my foster parents —gave me. I'm an orphan, you see."

"Oh. Sorry," I said. She shrugged. "Well, ah, what was it you wanted to see me about?"

"Oh yeah," she chirped. "Well, Mr. Garnish, it's just that you're new at the lodge, and us kids like to help out newcomers if they, like, want to know where the good places are to eat around here, or go for a drink and dancing or stuff. Mr. Connors doesn't tell us to do it, but we kind of got in the habit, you know? So—anything I can tell you?"

And I felt old, old, old. When I was a kid, we called ourselves kids and didn't think anything about it. I mean, dig, if Wally and the Beaver could do it, it was okay. But when Michelle said "us kids," I knew she was pulling my chain with that Judy Garland let's-put-on-a-show-in-the-barn blarney, and my intelligence (it surfaces once in a while, like a groundhog) was insulted. I go to my share of Brooke Shields movies. "Mr. Connors doesn't tell us to do it, but we kind of got in the habit, you know?" Come *on*. She might as well have handed me a card, like the guys who stand outside the massage parlors in Chicago: Nobody Has To Know.

I'd known she was sexy (did they still use *that* word?) and smart enough to know she was sexy. I hadn't until now known she was precocious enough to be a businesswoman.

Ever been in a strange town and wondered where the whores were? *Sure* you have, even if you never did a damn thing about it. But, if you did do a damn thing about it, what you'd do is, you'd ask the nearest cab driver where was the best place to—uh, to eat, you know, and have a drink, and . . .

"And get laid?" the cabbie, bored—he's heard this a thousand times—says.

And "Yeah," you say. You're the customer and the meter's running (read: You're the mark). So you're entitled to sound as eager as you do. Innocent, even, if you like.

Michelle was my cabbie. And like I say, I felt old looking at that much experience making out to be innocence. Old and tired, as tired as one of the wheelchair entrants finishing the Boston Marathon. No —those guys train. Tireder.

Don't tell me I should have tossed her out the door then and there, and don't tell me I'm an asshole for doing what I did. And don't tell me that granite is harder to sculpt than cream cheese. I *know*, dig?

But she was there, and I was thinking—as I should not have been—about Ross Connor's problems, and maybe I was just a little interested in how far my young businesslady's impulse was to carry things. So I did my best combination yawn, shrug, and inquisitive shoulder-hunker.

"Something around here besides restaurants and bars?" I said. "I mean, Michelle, the restaurants and bars are all listed in the travel folders. Do you mean something else?"

"Oh, come on. *You* know what I mean. God-*zooks!*" And her smile turned into a pout, and her pout, if you can believe it, was even more inviting than her smile. "Mr. Connors is—well, you know. He's old-fashioned, and I dig you might be a little shy talking to him. But, you know, like, really, there's nothing you should get uptight about. Hey —listen, you mind if I smoke?"

It sure the hell wasn't my show, so I just gave my clever shrug again.

She sent another arch glance at my Scotch (I'd never really understood before what *arch* means—it means pissant-nasty and superior). She fished in the pocket of her blouse—How could something that sparse have pockets? I wondered—and brought out a cigarette.

Surprise, surprise. It wasn't factory made.

I was supposed, I supposed, to be shocked. Or scared or something. The devil's weed, the first step toward heroin addiction, all that. *You* know the clichés as well as I do. There was real defiance in her eyes as she took the first ritually long and loving drag and looked at me.

It just made me feel old. Again. Jesus, I thought, that's what you call rebellion, is it, little girl? I didn't realize that, after all, you're such a *little* girl. So, screw all. Enjoy your joint, and let me know how stoned you get. I'll be waiting here, ready to talk, when you get back from Disneyland, where all the rides are safe and none of the animals really bites.

"Wow," she gulped as she let the smoke out—really, folks, she said "Wow"—and held the joint toward me.

Maybe she was puzzled when I accepted it and had a toke myself. Forty-four-year-old farts, after all, are supposed by the young to have scruples about their drugs of choice. I hope she was puzzled, anyway, because grass bores me and surprising her was the only reason I toked. Anyhow, as my eyes watered and I let the scent of incense settle to the back of my throat, I decided it was time to pounce, leopardlike, to the attack. While I could still focus my eyes.

"Michelle," I said. Or coughed. "Michelle, are you saying that you can direct me to—ah, to—brothels in the area?"

She was smoking happily away, but at that she burst into laughter.

"Jesus!" she gulped, trying to get her voice back. "Brothels? I mean, you really still call it—them—that? I mean, god-*zooks!*" And she giggled: unconvincingly.

You see, pot smokers giggle a lot; not because anything funny is going on, and not even because they think anything funny is going on. They giggle a lot because they've been told that when you're stoned you giggle. So you protect your investment—you prove that your dealer didn't stiff you with a lid of catnip and parsley—by chortling your ass off as soon as you take your first drag. If you're an amateur doper, that is.

Michelle was and always would be, God help her, an amateur. Most of them are. It's how your average dealer stays in business these days: no enlightened consumer advocacy.

"God-*zooks,*" she said again, staring at her joint. "Oh, boy, Harry— can I call you Harry? I mean, there's no, like, official *houses* around here. But there is a restaurant and bar up the road, just a mile or so north on the main highway. The Bayou North, it's called. From what I hear, anyhow"—and the smile got sly—"there's a lot of action there, most nights." She took another deep drag. The stuff she was smoking was first cousin to crap, but she was bound and determined she was going to get wrecked on it.

Or hell, I don't know, maybe the stuff was stronger than I thought. I'd had one, count it, one toke—granted, with a Scotch appetizer. And I was discussing the local screwing scene with a kid half my age (giving me the benefit of the doubt) and what was worse, I guess, getting hornier the more we talked. Ross, Ross, I thought, you've got more to worry about than you even imagine.

"Uh, right," I muttered, glad I was sitting. "The Bayou North. Look, Michelle, I don't know how we got on this topic, but maybe we ought to, ah . . ."

"Stop?" she interrupted me, and tossed her head, flipping her long blond hair over her shoulder. I got gladder I was sitting. "Well, sure, if you want. But, like, you know, it's not all that unusual, Harry. I mean, for God's sake, this isn't the Middle *Ages*. You don't have to feel uncomfortable about—well, about expressing your sexuality."

That last phrase, I figured, had to come from a college lecture somewhere. Or a textbook. You could almost hear the quotation marks around it.

"And," she went on, "you might not even have to look as far as the Bayou North." *Warm* smile.

I mean, remember *Planet of the Apes?* Charlton Heston is trapped on this world of talking gorillas, right? And there's a scene early on in the film where, surrounded by them, he looks into the camera and shouts, "What the hell is going on?"

So here I was, as far as I could tell, trapped on the planet of the goats. As Crazy Sam had remarked last night, there was enough firm young flesh on the old campground to open a musk factory. In the immortal words of Charlton Heston, what the hell was going on?

One thing going on, I thought, was that I wasn't in any real condition to decide what *was* going on. But then, I didn't really have a hell of a lot of choice, did I? Maybe Michelle was trying to seduce me ("seduce"—Christ, I was sounding like Bridget O'Toole!) or maybe she was just telling me that she knew, and could tell me, where I could get seduced. The "kids"—if there was more than one kid involved—had invented themselves a very nice scam. Nothing but hints until the COD and then . . . well, what? Maybe nothing, if you looked like the type to blow the whistle. Or maybe pig heaven, if you looked like the type who carried credit cards only for emergencies.

You've been there. Do the signals mean what you think they mean, or are you reading the wrong code? Sure, sure, you always read them right the morning after—with a grin or a groan. But when you're *there* it's like bullfighting in the dark, and you don't even know which side of the cape you're on.

One thing, I decided, that *wasn't* going on was any more of this. Not that Michelle wasn't worth a couple of broken teeth (where *was* Byron, by the way?). But nobody is worth being a hockey puck for; that is, worth letting them slap you around in a game where you don't even know the score. So I did the honorable, moral thing. I shaved my bacon.

"Michelle," I said. "I hate to ask you this—believe me, I do—but how old is your father?"

She shook her head, amused. Her eyes were *very* blue.

"Okay, I get it," she said, coming off the bed and standing over me (damned if I was going to get up). "Harry, you ought to understand that age doesn't mean anything anymore. It's a new day, haven't you heard? And you're an interesting guy; I thought so last night when you came into the bar. But"—sigh—"if you're uptight, you're uptight. Only"—and she reached out and, for Chrissake, tousled my hair—"remember, I'm around and free most of the day. Nothing is *wrong*, you know." And she was out the door.

Hi there, traveling bar.

Whatever that had been about, it was time to make my phone call and think about getting my ass back to Chicago where, as a public service to aging lechers, they kept the prowling coeds isolated on game preserves called campuses. Good old Chicago. Goold old House of Walgreen's. I took a quick and pretty respectable swig, waited for the kickback shiver to work all the way up my spine to the top of my head, and walked out into the—thank God—fresh air.

It was about eleven by now, and the air did, I hate to admit it, taste better than the coffee, Scotch, or grass I'd had. In fact, it's only in the woods that you notice that air *does* taste; sort of like a brew of pine needles, brook water, black earth—like that. In the city, I realized, you spend most of your time deliberately not noticing the air. It's the same habit of mind that lets you survive YMCA locker rooms. I even found my Michigan Avenue, get-the-fuck-out-of-my-way pace slowing down as I walked toward the lodge.

Yeah, I thought, taste. There's something to be said for it. And that, naturally enough, started me thinking about Michelle again.

"Bullshit," I said to nobody. The place was getting to me, and I had a phone call to make. And, speaking of quick minds, it came to me that the last place I wanted to make it from was Ross Connor's office. One thing I didn't need was a bout of lying to him about how I'd had a nice long chat with his summer help about her gland problem, and how I'd convinced her that sanity demanded she keep her pants on part of the time, anyhow.

So. Where had Michelle said the Bayou North was? It ought to be open for lunch by now, and I was suddenly hungry enough to eat broccoli, if need be. And they had to have a pay phone. So I turned toward the parking lot.

The Bayou North was easy to find. Not many places in northern Wisconsin have an oversize Mardi Gras float on their marquees, or a sign advertising in foot-high hand painted, crimson on black letters CRAYFISH. JAMBALAYA. WORLD'S BEST GUMBO. HEINEKEN. Inside it looked even friendler than its billboard. Small, with no more than ten or twelve tables, and a bar about as long as a Volkswagen. But all paneled in wood, and wood that somebody obviously polished regularly, and with photos of famous jazz musicians all over the walls. As I walked in I recognized Basie, Sarah Vaughan, Lionel Hampton, and Charlie Parker, among others. And I noticed that a lot of the photos were autographed.

Behind the bar stood a black man in a silk paisley-figured shirt, washing cocktail glasses. He was shorter than me—and I'm short— with frizzled gray hair and a beard even grayer that looked like it could be trained to attack. The place was empty otherwise.

"Hi," he said, smiling, as I entered. "We just opened, so the oven's cold. Get you a drink while it fires up?" I swear to God it looked like his beard nodded separately.

"Thanks," I said, sitting at the bar. "Maybe just a glass of soda water. You really serve gumbo here?"

He chuckled. "Man, *you* saw the sign out front. Gumbo, ceviche, any New Orleans specialty; we do it and we do it right." He pronounced it *Nor*leans, and the rest of his accent was just as legit. "I mean, of course, the okra and the shrimp I got to import frozen, but the crayfish, I dig 'em up right back of here, on the lakeshore. And the filé powder—that, my friend, I make myself."

He put my soda water on the bar in front of me and with a flourish peeled a razor-thin slice of skin off a fresh lime and plopped it into the glass. After my own last few hours, it was nice to watch a man who obviously enjoyed what he did for a living.

"Now," he went on, "your next question is going to be, How the hell did you and all this fine Louisiana cuisine get all the way up north —ain't that right? Well, sir"—not dropping a beat—"the answer is simple: rock and roll."

I cocked an eyebrow. It was the time, I could tell, when people usually cocked an eyebrow at the story.

"Yep," he said, drawing himself a beer, "rock and roll. See, I used to be a musician. Played with a *lot* of bands, played all the *hell* across this country. And then, guess what? The Beatles, that's what. And the Rolling Stones, and I don't know what else, and all of a sudden I couldn't play a high school dance if *I* paid *them* to let me take the stand. So I hung up my ax and I figured, hell, I'd open up a place where I could serve what I like. Oh, yeah. My name is—"

"Elliot Andrews," I said. "You played alto sax in a Howard McGhee quintet for a while, and you did one album under your own name for Prestige Records, and the last time I heard you, in Chicago in sixty-seven, you sounded as mean as Sonny Stitt."

Truth to tell, the last time I had heard him he had sounded godawful. But life is short, am I right? And it was worth it to see the expression on his face.

"Well, gawd-*damn!*" he crowed. "I don't *believe* it! Chicago in sixty-seven, huh? Sure, that would have been the old Hole in the Wall Club, and I was sure the hell there. I used to do that Cole Porter medley as a set-closer, you remember that?" I nodded. I didn't. "Aw, Jesus," he went on, "I haven't thought about that gig in I don't know how long. Hey, listen"—picking up my soda water—"you don't really want to drink this stuff, do you? What do you like—on the house, dig? Hey, what's your name, anyhow?"

I shook his hand, told him my name, told him that a Heineken and a dish of gumbo would be great—maybe a couple of Heinekens and a couple of dishes of gumbo—and asked him where the pay phone was. It was out back, in an old-fashioned booth like the ones Clark Kent used to use.

Now, it isn't hard to call O'Toole Investigations, Chicago, collect. Brenda, bless her pickled little heart, accepts any and all collect calls as a matter of course. I've told Bridget I don't know how many times that we ought to try to help Brenda break this costly habit. Because after she accepts your call, you see, she has a tendency to put you on hold and forget why you're there. Brenda isn't real good with buttons.

But today I was in luck. Maybe there was a bourbon embargo against Chicago, or maybe it was Polish Lent. Anyhow, it wasn't too long until I heard Bridget's familiar raspy-gentle voice over the wire. "Harry," she cooed. (Ever hear a pterodactyl coo?) "What do you have to report?"

Or course, she would say it like that: What do you have to report? Just like we were in the secret agent business, and I was on assignment in Dakar or Calcutta and not three hundred miles north outside a roadside bar-and-grill phoning in on a sleazy adultery. She'll never learn.

"Bridget," I said. "What I have to *report* is this. I checked in last night, and I've seen Cheryl Howard—not to mention a whole lot of crazy types who don't concern us—and so far I've got nothing to tell you except that."

Oops. I hadn't meant to say that. I had meant to tell her all about Cheryl and Dick Schwartz, and tell her also that I was on my way back to Chicago that afternoon.

So why didn't I? Go figure. Maybe I wanted to talk to Cheryl Howard again. Maybe I wanted to spend some more time tasting the air in the North Woods. Maybe I was just getting stupid in my middle age. Whatever the reason, I'd said it, and there we were. Dumb, I told myself. Dumb, dumb, dumb.

Bridget couldn't possibly have known what was going on. Nevertheless, her voice got . . . well, *different.* "Harry, are you sure you're all right?" she asked. And before I could assure her that I was (I wasn't, I was beginning to think), she added, "Well, dear, I think you'd better stay for a few more days—just to make sure of things."

"Yeah," I said. Damned if I didn't get the impression she was suggesting I stay up here for my own sake.

"And, Harry," she said, "if you would like some—well, some help, dear, I would be glad to drive up there. I could be there in a few hours, you know."

Now, dig. Nuns or ex-nuns never drive anywhere. They get driven there, kind of the way pilot fish never have to swim because there's always a passing hammerhead shark going their way. So that meant if Bridget came up to help, dear, it would sure as hell be Knobby, my co-worker and king of the swine people, who would be driving her. Not to mention that I wanted her moral support the way a goldfish wants a walk in the open air. I was doing so great by myself, wasn't I?

"Hell, Bridget," I said. "There's nothing out of shape up here. And there's got to be some business you ought to be taking care of down there. I mean, we're not that damn strapped for customers, are we? Just give Knobby my cases and make sure he doesn't steal the cloth towels from the men's room, okay?"

She—you guessed it—sighed. "Oh, all right," she said. "It's just that you don't sound like yourself. And you know how I worry."

Swell. A Czechoslovakian mother I've got; so an Irish Catholic mother I need? When they have a garage sale on guilt, man, I'm going to clean up. Anyway, with the renowned Garnish courage I stuck to my guns and told her not to come up. She told me in a voice like an abandoned baby walrus that she wouldn't, but that if I needed it, help was as near as the nearest phone. Reach out and put the touch on someone, right?

"Right, Bridget," I said. "Call you tomorrow." And hung up.

Well, I might be a lousy private detective, but I was sure as hell a first-rate teenager. I'd just falsified information and cost our client several days extra expenses, and all for the sake of a crush that didn't even make sense to me.

I was congratulating myself on my silliness as I stepped out of the phone booth. That's when I got my skull cracked.

Well, not my skull, at first. Something hit me from behind, square in the middle of my back, and as I pitched forward I watched my glasses sail ahead of me, toward the gravel of the parking lot. I think my face and my glasses both hit the ground at the same time—didn't Galileo or somebody do an experiment about that? Anyway, *that's* when I got my skull cracked. Something—a boot, a club, a Greyhound bus—came down and came down hard across the back of my head.

They call it "losing consciousness," but when you're hit like that you don't lose it; you let it go, because you know how bad it's going to hurt if you don't. So I watched the world turn gray and fuzzy and then go away altogether, and I heard a voice saying, "Just keep your dirty hands off Michelle, old man."

I tried to turn over to see who was giving me this very good advice, but my body didn't seem to feel like taking any order from my brain, such as it was. I lay there on the ground, thinking about that curious fact, for what felt like a long time.

Then Elliot Andrews, ex-jazz musician and gumbo chef, was bending over me. He and his beard both looked very worried.

"Hey, man, you all right? Are you all right?" he kept asking. And when I managed to mumble that I thought I would live, he said something I couldn't, fogged as I was, entirely believe.

"Well, we better get you inside. Your gumbo's getting cold."

# 7

THERE'S A DRINK called a kamikaze. I think they call it that because you have to be one to order one, since it's equal parts tequila and vodka; maybe *kamikaze* translates "fool." I only had one once, on a very weird night in Chicago (ever have a *very* weird night?)—actually, I had three—and the last thing I try not to remember is picking a fight with a lady at the next table and being asked nicely but firmly by the management—six inches taller, forty pounds heavier than me, and oh, so polite—to leave.

Well, the point of all this is to tell you how I felt as I walked back into the Bayou North. *Walked* isn't really the word, because what I was doing was leaning on Elliot Andrews and trying to watch my feet move without getting dizzy. And *felt* isn't the word either, because I felt about as much as *you* would feel after four—check that, five kamikazes.

Anyhow, after six months or three minutes I found myself sitting at a table—how *nice* to sit down, I thought—being leaned over by Elliot and a large lady who could have been a black Bridget O'Toole if only she had been ugly.

"Man," Elliot was saying, "somebody did a *job* on you, baby! You got blood all the fuck on the back of your head. Wha'd you do, mess with somebody's chick, or what?"

It's one of my great gifts, folks: even when I'm dying I can always be entertaining.

The non-Bridget saved me from having to respond. "Elliot," she said. "Don't you see this poor boy's in pain? Now you stop pestering him with dumb questions and go get him some brandy. And maybe you better call a doctor too."

But as they say, Mrs. Garnish didn't raise any idiots. "No doctor, ma'am, thanks," I said. "But the brandy sounds just fine."

"Oh, yeah," said Elliot. "Harry, this is my wife Eleanor. She does the real cooking and such here." I'll bet she did. Dazed as I was—and I've been less dazed at the end of a Chicago Saint Patrick's Day—I could see the authority and the confidence radiating from her. The cooking, I thought, and probably the books and the grocery orders, and a hell of a lot else. She was being a nurse right now, and a damn good one, smiling reassuringly down at me and mopping the back of what used to be my head with a big towel.

"You just sit and be quiet, son," she was saying. "Elliot will be back with a nice brandy for you soon. You *sure* you don't want a doctor, honey?"

I choked back the urge to call her Mom and bury my head between her breasts (a Volkswagen could have parked there without a hell of a lot of steering), and just told her I was feeling a lot better already.

Eleanor cooed and I moaned until Elliot came back with a water glass and a full liter of Christian Brothers. And suddenly I understood why Saint Bernards always look like they have such kindly eyes. It's because you always imagine even if you don't see the cask tied around their necks.

Now, the thing about booze is it doesn't make you feel better, but it does make you *think* you feel better. Ben Gross, who drinks hardly at all, calls it a *mitzvah*—whatever that is—whenever we share a glass of (too sweet) wine. I'm sure I had a concussion; couldn't even put my glasses on, because whenever I tried to, the room began to swim like at the end of a Vincent Price horror film. But be that as it may, after my second glass of brandy I was ready to referee a mongoose-and-cobra fight and was chatting away happily with Mr. and Mrs. Andrews about the golden days of bebop. Who played guitar behind Charlie Parker on "Relaxin' at Camarillo," what was the order of solos on Woody Herman's "Four Brothers," whatever happened to the great white tenor saxophone player Allen Eager—you know, stuff like that. It's what my generation has instead of sitting around finding the hidden meanings in *Sgt. Pepper,* and a hell of a lot more productive, if you ask me (I know, I know: you didn't).

"Dead," said Elliot Andrews. "Dead, every god-damn *one* of them, except of course for Dizzy and Max." (That's Gillespie and Roach, respectively, for those of you who've just arrived from Venus.) "Bird, Bud Powell, Fats Navarro, Tadd Dameron, Wardell Gray, Serge Chaloff, Monk. All *way* before their time." His eyes were watering, and mine began to, too. Probably it was the brandy. "All those poor great sons of bitches," he went on, "dead years before they had to be. And you know *why?*"

"Now, Elliot," said Eleanor. "Don't you start in on that again. Can't you see this boy is sick?" Graceful people that they were, neither asked me again why I was left in their parking lot with the back of my head bleeding. We were just old pals, talking on about the one thing that mattered: jazz.

"No, honey," said Elliot, waving a hand at his wife. She sighed again, and I got the distinct feeling—you get it, sometimes, with married couples—that I was about to hear a line Eleanor had heard too many times to count. "Now, really, Harry," said Elliot, "you know *why?*"

"Ah," I articulated. "Drugs?"

It was like I'd said the secret word on the old Groucho Marx show; I could almost see the magic duck coming down.

*"No!"* Elliot said. Or shouted. Or table-thumped. Anyway, it was how I knew I'd made the right, dumb, response. "No," he went on. "Hell, man, if it was drugs, I'd be one of them too. You know I did powder for six, seven, maybe eight years? And I took my *self* off it. None of that Synanon shit. None of that I-found-Jesus crap, neither. I just *did* it, you know? Drugs ain't what was so fucked about those guys. So, now, you know what *was?*"

The brandy was wearing off and the concussion was marching on, so I didn't even try to think of the right answer. I just stared at Elliot, the way you used to stare at Sister Mary Godzilla or Miss Peach while you waited to be told in which hemisphere Paraguay really *was*. Or is.

*"Belief!"* Elliot said, or nearly shouted. "Belief, damn it! That's what killed those poor dumb motherfuckers, those great cats. See, they thought—they *believed* that if only you could play good enough, fast enough, strong enough, then you could make the world pay attention to you like you were a *man*. No—they really believed that, they really believed in music. Hell, man, you should have heard Bud Powell talk about what his music meant to him; I mean, it was like listening to a preacher. And how did he die? Drunk and broke, and he couldn't even get a decent gig anymore. Music's going to change things? *Shee*-it. That's why I got out of the business, Harry."

"Oh, lord," sighed Eleanor to herself. She knew the next line, obviously. But much as my head hurt, this fascinated me. Both that he was so passionate about this—I mean, ever listen to a guy *really* try to talk out his own sense of failure?—and also, there was something in what he was saying that reminded me of something else. Maybe of something in one of Bridget's endless lectures? I wasn't sure.

"That's what I got out for, Harry," he repeated, and leaned toward me, breathing beer and gumbo into my headache and about to impact a secret along with the aromas. "Because I found out it don't *matter* how good you play. Don't matter at *all*. It matters how good you *are*—that's all. And once you know that, you don't have to prove it by playing anymore. Can you dig that?"

Eleanor had by this point left the table in the friendly despair of the very married; she would give him hell for this speech in a half hour or so, but it wouldn't really mean anything between them. And I was beginning to wonder if the brandy had been such a good idea after all, since passing out was beginning to look like a pleasing as well as distinct possibility.

But he was the guy who had picked me up from the parking lot, and he was also a guy who seemed to be trying to tell me something not just for his own sake but for mine, and Czechs never really pass out anyway, we just glaze over a little. So what the hell, I told him I could dig it.

"Good," he said, pouring me another tumbler of brandy. "Now, here's why I'm telling you all this. Because, my friend, you were nice enough and hip enough to remember me from my playing days, and because you obviously got some trouble of your own, I'm giving you some good advice with your fuckin' gumbo. And that is, my man, don't try to *play* your way out of it. I mean, don't try to dance or smartass or talk or think or lie your way out of it. It ain't gonna work, boy. You *be* your way out of it, if you can find out the way. There. I never met you before in my life, and I just gave you the advice it took me fifty-five years to learn. Generous son of a bitch, ain't I?"

I was too sick, and wouldn't have had the heart anyway, to tell him that he had picked exactly the wrong man to give the advice to, since I got paid to dance, smartass, talk, think, and lie my way out of situations. Advice kindly given is always something special. It's like when you're in the line at the grocery, you've got a quart of milk and a pound of bologna, and the lady ahead of you has ten items—usually all cat food—and nevertheless she notices and says, "Oh, you go on ahead." Of course, you're always a lot more grateful than you really need to be. But then, you don't run into really *nice* all that much a day, am I right?

So what I did was, I smiled at him, and said, "You know, you *were* meaner than Sonny Stitt."

He threw his head back and he and his beard, I swear to God, laughed separately. "Aw, *shee*-it," he crowed. "You don't think I'm really dumb enough to buy that bullshit, do you?" Now we laughed together. "Look, baby, I got to go tend bar and such. We got other customers. But you stay cool, okay? And just sit here as long as you want. I'll check back on you in a while. And, Harry—"

"Yeah?"

"Thanks for remembering."

He strolled out of my cloudy field of vision while I fished in my pocket for a cigarette and stared at the third glass of brandy he had poured me. I decided yes on the cigarette and no on the brandy and wondered when I'd be able to ask him for a cup of coffee. Remember the words, I mean.

And, dazed as I was, I was also getting worried about what I was going to do when I got back to the lodge. Before, the worry had just been about whether or not to confront Cheryl Howard, warn her about who I was and what a swine (the word had never come so suddenly to my mind before) Dick Schwartz was, and suggest she get her lovely ass out of the situation as quickly as possible.

But now there was something else to worry about, and something a lot more important to the Garnish sense of self-preservation—which, I don't know about you, but I've always regarded as one of the prime laws of the universe. Who the hell had tried to give me a Stone Age lobotomy when I left that phone booth?

Byron was the obvious nominee, at least since I'd watched—or seen—him playing four-handed zumba with Michelle last night. But that didn't exclude Danny Bernstein (kids, I'm told, trade off a lot more than in my Jimmy Stewart—June Allyson generation) and, for that matter, didn't exclude any of the grown-ups at the camp—except, I assumed, Dick Schwartz, whose heart and whatever else was functional belonged to Cheryl. I remembered that Ross Connors had gone out of his way to mention to me that Michelle was driving the daddys as well as the sonnys out of their skulls—or out of her Calvin Kleins—that summer.

Don't tell me—a really tough private eye wouldn't have given a damn about all of that, would have just considered it a minor annoyance, and would have gone back to Lake Manitonaqua Resort and done what he had to do in the matter of Cheryl Howard. I watch television too, you know?

Except I'm not that tough. Somebody had just thought it okay to dance on my head because I'd spoken to Michelle for, what? Twenty minutes? I was dazed, maybe a third drunk, and worried about whether I even wanted to do the job I'd been sent here for. My blood pressure was up (they call it a symptomless disease on TV, but when your head starts to pound and your hands start to shake you know you can't trust those commercials any more than you can the ones about the world's best fabric softener).

I was thinking about all these things when I heard some conversation close to me. Very close, like right above me. If you've ever been really concussed you know what that feels like, that scary feeling that there's a real world out there, somewhere, but you just can't quite manage to let it in.

I concentrated real hard, and finally got the voices to come in. "Mr. Garnish? Mr. Garnish?" a male and a female voice were saying—if not in chorus, then in counter-point. I forced myself to look up.

Elliot Andrews had said there were other customers in the place, but I hadn't really been paying attention. The other customers, it turned out, were Dr. and Mrs. Logan, from the bar last night when I'd first arrived. She still looked tense, and he seemed now to be tense at how tense *she* was.

"Ur," I said, in what I hoped was my least hospitable style.

But it didn't work.

"May we join you?" said Dr. Logan, grimacing politely at me and looking, I thought, disapprovingly at the cigarette still smoldering in my ashtray.

"Ur."

They sat down gratefully—no, really, gratefully—and then did something that surprised the hell out of me, semiconscious as I was. They smiled at one another, took each other's hand, and turned back to me in consort.

"Mr. Garnish," Pat Logan went on, "we know you're on vacation and we know you probably don't want to work on vacation, but we surely would like to ask you for a little bit of help."

"What?" I said. One-syllable words were getting to be a heroic effort.

"Well," said Pam Logan, and it was the first time I think that I'd heard her talk, "excuse us for being so nosy, but we hear you're a marriage counselor."

I drank the rest of my brandy. Wouldn't you?

# 8

SO. INNOCENT, WELL-MEANING snitch that I was, in the last twenty-four hours I'd been threatened with having my legs broken, had my head danced on, been damn near seduced by a twenty-year-old, and now I was being mistaken for a shrink.

When I was in high school, Brother Declan forced us to read a book called *Walden*. If you've never read it, don't; it's about as exciting as watching the pine cones grow. But anyway, it's all about how peaceful life in the woods is after the hustle and bustle of the city. I was thinking, as the Logans smiled nervously—hopefully?—across the table at me, that if Thoreau had just come to the woods with *me*, Jack, I'd have showed him a time that would rattle his gonads.

Another confession, that's obviously what I was going to get. And by now you know how much I love hearing confessions, right?

"Uh, look, folks," I said—or tried to say, since a very tiny bird was evidently building a nest in the bottom of my mouth. "I'm sorry, and I don't know where you got that idea, but I'm afraid you're wrong. A marriage counselor I'm not."

Ever notice how in a symphony orchestra the violinists' bows always go up and down, up and down, in exact synch with one another? That's just how their faces fell, and how they both reddened.

Mrs. Logan spoke first. "Oh," she said, "but Michelle said—"

"That's all right, Pam," interrupted Dr. Logan—obviously meaning "Shut the hell up, my dear." And his tone of voice and her expression told me why they'd come to my table in the first place.

"Mr. Garnish," he went on. "This is an embarrassing situation for all of us, and we're sorry to have bothered you"—the proprietary "we," I noticed. "I hope you'll accept our—say, are you all right?"

I must have been looking as woozy, with a capital Wooze, as I felt. Because all the anxiety and blush left Logan's face, and he was looking at me with that attentive fix-you-like-a-butterfly-on-a-pin stare that doctors reserve for patients, teachers reserve for students, and lawyers reserve for the unlucky.

I was thinking *Michelle? Michelle?* Why the hell would she want to lie about me and get me involved with, of all people, the Logans? And then I understood. Of course, the young lady didn't like being said no to, so this—pretty sad—joke would be her way of letting me know that she was pissed off. Never mind that other people got embarrassed in the middle of things, it was her own kind of greeting card. Well, well, I thought. Twenty, sexy as all hell, and vicious to boot.

See, as my old man used to say, there's no experience you can't learn from. (I know, I know. I always thought it sounded like bullshit too.)

And while I was thinking all these profound things, Logan was doing what he, I supposed, did best: being a doctor. You know, things like asking me if I remembered where, exactly, I'd been struck, looking around my head for bleeding places, holding up two fingers (I hope it was two) and asking me how many fingers I saw. He may have been a rotten husband, I remember thinking, but he was very good at what he got paid for.

After about ten minutes of this song and dance—Pam, I noticed, was sitting perfectly still and perfectly in awe of her competent husband—he sat down across from me again with a sigh and a professional, self-congratulating look on his face.

"Well, Harry, you're definitely concussed," he said. I noted that since I'd been demoted from marriage counselor to assault victim I'd also lost my last name and my "Mr." "But it doesn't look that serious to me. I'd recommend that after you file your report with the local police you just go back to your cabin and stay in bed for a day. And no drinking or smoking," he continued, glancing accusingly at the array on my table, "for at least twenty-four hours."

No doubt about it. I didn't like this guy at all.

Well, okay, you caught me. I *did* like him. I mean, doctor or not (and I *hate* doctors), the son of a bitch had seen that I was in pain and had snapped into his doctor mode, all professional and all helpful, in spite of the fact that he and his wife had just inserted both feet in both mouths in front of me. Or is it all four feet?

He was still giving me good advice, and I was still trying to think of a way to thank him, when Elliot came—no, *exploded*—back to our table.

"Hey!" he hey'ed. "I see you folks found one another. Harry, you feeling all right? Ah, folks"—turning to the Logans—"your order's at your table now. Would you like me to bring it on over here?"

I think the Logans were just getting ready to leave and go back to their table when I insisted that they stay here, and that their lunch bill be put on my tab. Pat Logan, of course, objected, but not too much. He saw that I felt like I owed him, and he was gentleman enough to let me act the feeling out. Like I always say, if you want to find somebody you can deal with, find somebody from Chicago. Who knows? Maybe it was even a gesture of friendship.

Elliot brought two bowls of gumbo and two—surprise, surprise—glasses of soda water to the table, and I tried to focus my eyes.

"So," I said, "Michelle told you guys I was a marriage counselor? How the hell did that come up this morning?"

"Oh," said Pam Logan. "We were just chatting with her by the lakeside—it's so nice there, you know—and she happened to mention that she'd heard that's what you were. So when we came in to this place and saw you here, we just naturally . . . I mean, we just—" And she broke off, looking at her husband nervously with what I can only describe as the patented Sandy Dennis lip bite.

That must have been about the time, I thought, that my head was sailing toward the gravel in the parking lot. Our Michelle, heartbreaker that she was, really didn't like to hear no, and really didn't lose any time getting even for hearing it.

But it was a nasty joke on the Logans. How had Michelle known that that particular lie would be the one to find them where they tied their goat? Most of us get pretty good at hiding the goat, which is how come I make a living. But Michelle—well, hell, she seemed about as good at it as I was. Maybe, I thought, I ought to suggest hiring her for the agency.

Remember, I was concussed.

The Logans and I made polite conversation—or as polite as we could make, given the circumstances—till it felt like that magic moment when you can get your ass out of an uncomfortable scene without showing anybody that you're as uncomfortable as you know *they* are. (If you've been there, you won't have to ask me to explain that last sentence. If you haven't, just wait.) I rose to go, Doc Logan insisted that I shouldn't drive in my condition, I assured him I was okay, Pam Logan clucked, and so forth. As I was pushing the door open, though, I felt a hand on my arm. It was Elliot Andrews and his beard.

"Hey, man," he said. "You sure you can make it? I mean, baby, you can leave your car here and I can give you a lift back to your place. You don't look so good, you know?"

I told him what I'd told the Logans, and he let me go, but only on condition that I come back soon and listen to some rare tapes of Howard McGhee that he had in his back room.

"Deal," I said. "But only if you let me guess who's playing alto."

He laughed. "Ah, *shee-it,*" he said. "You ain't hurt at all, you just a natural-born asshole, is all. Now get out of here, and come back soon."

Truth to tell, I *was* sick, and the drive back to the lodge felt, inside my head, about as long as one of the voyages of the starship *Enterprise*. Funny, on TV they get snorked on the head from one Pepsi commercial to the next, and then they bounce right back and beat the living shit out of all of Fort Wayne, Indiana. But the guys I know, if you give them a good shot to the skull, might not be able to focus their eyes for a couple of days. I don't know, maybe I hang out with sissies.

Anyway, my head was pounding bad enough by the time I parked my car (all the parking lines looked double), and my legs were Gumby-toy rubber enough, that I decided Doc Logan was part right and part wrong. So I staggered across the gravel parking lot toward the lounge, looking like something that had spent the last week crammed up a camel's armpit. Logan was right: I should take better care. Logan was wrong: I needed a drink.

And there, behind the bar, was Michelle. And there, alone at the bar, was Cheryl Howard.

# 9

SHE WAS SITTING at the bar drinking soda water, and I, as I sat at the bar, was thinking, So what?

I think So what? a lot. As in: they refuse to accept your check at the grocery the one week you know you're *not* overdrawn. So what? Or: the bus pulls up to your stop just after you've lit your last cigarette, or maybe the expensive cigar a friend just gave you (in this case, of course, it pulls up faster). So what? Or: they call to tell you your old man's had a heart attack at two in the morning, after you've finished the Scotch and can't even find yesterday's socks (which are always, damn it, *somewhere* on the floor). So what? You expected, maybe, better luck?

So what? in other words, is the only defense we have against Murphy's Law. Murphy's Law says that anything that can go wrong will go wrong.

Bridget O'Toole says (and I quote) that Murphy's Law says the perversity of the universe tends toward a maximum.

I say that Murphy's Law says that the earthquake always hits when you've got your pants down. So you shrug and say—you guessed it— So what? (Except of course if you're Ben Gross. When you tell him that the jacket you gave him to be dry-cleaned came back with one pocket ripped, he joins his head to his shoulders and says, *"Nu?"* which I think is the Yiddish translation of So what?)

Anyway, this particular So what? had to do with the fact that I looked and felt like horseshit from hell and that Cheryl looked like a horny Boy Scout's dream and that Michelle behind the bar was smiling at me the way you smile at your cat after you've caught it using the litter box. I'd more than half decided to blow the whole operation and, hero that I was, tell Cheryl to get her (heavy sigh) ass back to Thomas Howard before any more shinola hit the Mixmaster. And here was my perfect chance (where was Dick Schwartz? I wondered). And I just wasn't up to it. At least not before I'd had a beer or two.

"Heineken," I said to Michelle as I took my stool, with what I hoped was my best we'll-talk-later-and-if-you-say-a-word-now-I'll-break-your-face grimace. I don't know if it worked or not, because she just smiled that over-the-rainbow smile and put the beer down in front of me.

Cheryl had a smile of her own for me as Michelle turned back toward the cash register. "Mr. Garnish? Hello."

"Hi, Mrs.—Kruger," I said, and congratulated myself on remembering her entry (that's her motel name, if you're not in my racket; only cops and feds call it an a.k.a.).

But I didn't congratulate myself long. As soon as I called her Mrs. Kruger, she blushed and even spilled a little of her Perrier on its way to her very nice lips.

Christ, I thought. She knows, too? She was, at least, at least as nervous as I was tired. And Michelle kept humming, her back turned to us, over the cash register. Had Cheryl, it suddenly crossed my mind, been looking for me?

"Actually, Mr. Garnish," she said, putting down her glass, "I've been looking for you."

Again, Christ. When did I get to play secret agent and *win?*

"You see," she went on with a quick glance at Michelle, still bent over her receipts, "I think I know some other people named Garnish from Chicago. And I was wondering if, auh, if they were relatives of yours. Maybe we could take a walk around the grounds and talk over, auh, the Chicago Garnishes?"

Now the Chicago Garnishes, folks, are not what you'd call real numerous. And those that there are, if I knew any of them, are probably not the sort of people I would care to know, but I don't anyhow. And I doubted that Cheryl had ever met a Garnish in her life before yesterday. But this was my chance, and Murphy's Law or no Murphy's Law, I was going to take it.

"Sure," I said. And turning to Michelle, "Hey, honey, give me another for a traveler."

Believe me, there's nothing a waitress hates more than being called "honey." When I used to tend bar in Chicago, we had a game: anybody who called the waitress honey asking for seconds got a leftover olive in their martini or a leftover orange peel in their old-fashioned. The customer never knew, but I got some good dates out of it.

Cheryl nodded so long to Michelle, I picked up my Heineken, and we made our way into the breast of Nature.

Actually, we just walked toward the lake. And she was nervous as hell. So nervous that I could almost have taken her for a client. So nervous that I almost wondered if she wasn't trying to look nervous. Crazy thought, I thought. But as my eyes began to focus again—hooray for Heineken—I looked at her and realized with a kind of shock that there was more of the real Cheryl Howard, my Cheryl Howard, in the lady in the Polaroid back in my cabin than there was in the scared lady walking beside me. Ever have that feeling—that the people you care about are somehow more real in their photos than they are when you meet them? Oh, well. I swigged my warm beer. The hell with Michelle, I thought. The Heineken's label says to serve it at room temperature and she, just because I'd called her honey, actually had. Take it from me, Jack, there's a traitor lurking around every corner.

We were halfway on our rambling mumble to the lake before she talked about anything but how pretty everything was. Then she stopped in her tracks and asked me for a cigarette. I gave her one, and after a long amateur's drag on it she looked at me and coughed. It was her moment. I let her take it.

"Mr.—Garnish," she said. "I really don't know any other people named Garnish in Chicago. But I thought . . . I thought you and I should have a private talk." And she dropped her eyes shyly—just like Jennifer Jones in *The Song of Bernadette*—and dropped her three-quarters unsmoked cigarette on the ground.

"Yes?" I brilliantly suggested.

"I know what you are, Mr. Garnish," she said. Imagine my surprise. By this time I figured even the chipmunks were lining up to hire me to track down their lost nuts, or whatever it was chipmunks lost. "You don't need to call me Mrs. Kruger anymore. Mr. Schwartz told me last night what you are and what you do."

I liked the "what." "Who" would have been polite, but I gave up expecting polite a long time ago. The thing that bothered me wasn't that, but why Dick Schwartz had blown the whistle on me, when I thought I'd convinced him that I wasn't up here on his or Cheryl's trail.

She didn't keep me in the dark about that for long. "Dick—Mr. Schwartz," she said, "told me that you two recognized each other, and also told me that you weren't up here to spy on us. I hope that's right, Mr. Garnish."

Well, what would *you* have done? Here I had spent damn near twenty-four hours trying to talk myself into chucking the job and forgetting about everything I'd learned about the business, and here was my perfect chance to do it, to let her know what she was in for and tell her to get the hell out while there was still time.

And I couldn't do it.

Maybe Martin O'Toole trained me too well, or maybe I just have a higher weasel quotient than most people. Anyhow, I just stared and waited. Staring and waiting will take you a long way in life. Try it the next time a cop pulls you over for speeding or your girlfriend wants to know where the hell you were last Tuesday night.

When you stare and wait, dig, they always feel like they have to say something more. And that something more is usually just what you're waiting for.

"My real name is Quill. Mary Ellen Quill," said Cheryl Howard finally.

"Nice to meet you, Mrs. Quill," I said. "I assume it's Mrs." She did her best to blush, but she really wasn't very good at it. I pretended not to notice.

"Yes, it is," she said. "And—Oh, I suppose I shouldn't be talking to you at all, but Mr. Garnish, I'm frightened. I'm frightened about what might happen if my—my husband ever found out. He's a very fragile man, Mr. Garnish, and I do love him. If he thought I was . . . well, carrying on, I just don't know what he might do to himself or to—other people."

"Carrying on" I liked. It had the same nostalgic ring as Bridget's line about "being unfaithful." Sort of like hearing the Tommy Dorsey band, you know? And I guess I shouldn't have been angry that she'd lied to me about her real name. But, damn it, I was.

"Mrs. Quill," I said. "Don't worry. Like I told Schwartz last night, your business is no business of mine, and I don't intend to make it mine, either."

We'd come to the pier at the lakefront. The two mosquitos I had spent the night with had, I guess, decided to invite their relatives over for a picnic with us as the main course, because the rest of the conversation took place in between us slapping or scratching ourselves. From a distance we must have looked like entrants in a Three Stooges look-alike contest.

"Oh, thank you," said Mrs. Quill–Mrs. Kruger–Mrs. Howard. "And Mr. Schwartz assures me that you're a reliable man." Dick Schwartz, I figured, was a bigger liar than I'd thought him to be. "But, Mr. Garnish, I want to tell you that I really, I *really* don't want anyone to find out about me. I mean, it's worth a great deal of money to me." She slapped a mosquito on the back of her neck—did I mention that she was wearing a halter, shorts, and no shoes?—and dropped her eyes to where I'd dropped my beer bottle. (You're into ecology? So sue.)

I'd been stunned enough recently in the parking lot of the Bayou North that I won't say I was stunned now. But I sure as hell was *interested,* if that's the word. Within a half hour Cheryl Howard had insulted me by telling me she knew "what" I was, had lied to me, and here she was baring her neck to the knife.

"Mrs.—uh, Mrs. Quill," I said. She raised her eyes, and for a moment I saw the face I'd seen in the picnic photo. "Mrs. Quill, I don't think you know what you're doing. At least I hope you don't. I mean, blackmailers approach the mark—the victim, not the other way around. But you're practically begging me to bleed you."

"Oh, no, I didn't mean that," she said, and now she blushed. "It's just that—"

"It's just that *nothing,*" I said, cutting her off. "If I was more of a weasel than I am I could whipsaw you seven ways from next March, and I wouldn't even have to feel bad about it, because you came to me with the whipsaw. God damn it, where have you been living, Mars?" I was madder at her than I'd meant to get; but she *could* have been skewered, if she'd met up with a bigger weasel than me. Like I said, I can do without polite, but I hate dumb.

She was scared. Good. "Mr. Garnish," she said, blinking back tears, "please. I didn't mean that I thought you could—would—blackmail me. I only wanted to make sure that . . . Oh *damn!* You must think I'm so silly."

I did think she was silly. Silly enough that I wanted to hug her, and maybe take her back to my cabin and explain to her the ins and outs of the snoop business—very slowly, and at great length. But it wasn't the right time (when is it ever the right time?), and besides, out of the corner of my hawklike private eye I could see a sixth of a ton of orange cotton and American aboriginal flesh slumping in our direction.

"Look, Mrs. Quill," I said, "you don't need to worry about me." That was a lie, but I already told you I'm good at that. "But," I went on, "you might want to think about—well, you know. About getting out of here, maybe keeping things cool for a while, you get me? I mean, you *are* pretty visible, and not everybody is as much of a prince as I am."

What the hell, I might or I might not tell Bridget what I knew about Cheryl Howard. But I was thinking about what Ross Connors had said about the lodge being a summer camp for blackmailers, and I didn't want her, whether or not I blew the whistle, to be blood in the water for some other school of sharks.

Wonderful, isn't it, when ethics and good business sense point in the same direction like that? Saint Thomas would have been proud of me, not to mention his whore.

She was just beginning to stammer thanks, agreement, and blah blah blah, when Crazy Sam lumbered within hailing distance—which, you understand, was about twice as far away as hailing distance would be for any normal-size human being.

"Gawd-*damn!*" he gawd-damned. "Little girl, I been wondering where you got off to. Where's that no damn good husband of yours? We was supposed to play tennis this afternoon, but I figure he must've gone all chicken-shit out on me. Not that I blame him," he said, swinging a backhand that looked like it could have decapitated Mr. T. "Oh, hi, Garment."

"Oh, Mr. Two Feathers." Cheryl half laughed, with a cautious glance at me. "My—my husband drove in to town to take care of some . . . business. I'm sorry he broke your tennis date." And where *was* Dick Schwartz? I wondered.

"Oh, that don't make no never mind." Crazy Sam shrugged. "Hey, listen! You want to play a set? Court's all empty."

"Mr. Two Feathers," she said, "you know I couldn't give you a decent game. Why, I—"

"Why, nothing," he interrupted. "Christ, this ain't no money game I'm talking about. I just want some *fun*. Listen, I tell you what. Garment?" He turned to me.

"Garnish," I said. You get used to it.

"Yeah, right. Garnish. Anyhow. *You* had a tennis racket with you when you checked in last night, didn't you? So why don't I play you and Mrs. K here two against one? Come on, how about it?"

Now, I know this is going to surprise you, but I'm not a jock. And especially then I didn't feel like a jock. My head was trying to decide how many parts to split into, I didn't know what I was going to do about, or with, Cheryl Howard, and besides all that, Crazy Sam Two Feathers looked like the kind of guy who played tennis as a blood sport. You know; every serve is a one-hundred-mile-per-hour insult and every forehand smash is aimed at the bridge of your nose. Wise words of my father came back to me. "Boy," he said, "when you see an asskicker, don't think and don't talk. Just grab your ass—with *both* hands—and run. Backwards."

Thanks, Pop, I thought. "No thanks, Sam," I said. "I'm kind of tired, and I thought I'd take a nap before dinner, okay?"

Ever see a walrus look hurt? Well, neither did I, but Crazy Sam did a pretty good impression. "Aw, shit," he said. "Anyhow, Garner, I'll walk you back to your cabin. Catch you later, Mrs. K."

I was about to tell Crazy Sam that I didn't really need any help getting back to my cabin and what was left (I hoped) of my Scotch. But then I thought what the hell, there might be more mad muggers in the woods, and Sam could make an Israeli commando flinch.

So we strolled back together. Kerry, the kid who made up the beds and such, was just leaving the cabin and gave us a wide, bashful smile as she saw us coming.

"Hyeugh! I don't know about that girl," said Sam. "You know, Garnish, I get the feeling she might be—what do you white folks call it—randy."

I didn't answer. I was concentrating on my bed, and how nice it would be to get back to it. I was too tired to be horny, and, Jack, that's *tired.*

And then, as I had my hand on the screen door, Sam's voice changed. No more bellow, no more bark, just a soft, persuasive tenor.

"Mr. Garnish," he said, getting my name right and putting his T-bone hand on my shoulder. "Can we talk? I understand you're a private investigator."

"Private," I thought, was by now stretching things a bit.

# 10

SAM FOLLOWED ME into the cabin and glided for a landing onto the one chair in the room. I settled on the bed and, heroically, didn't lie down.

He cocked an eye at the Scotch bottle—a third full, maybe there *is* a God—and then at me. "Mr. Garnish," he said, "you don't look so good. Would you like me to pour you a glass of Scotch?"

I was surprised at the new tone in his voice, but more than that, at the new tone in his self, if you get me. "Thanks," I said. "If you'll join me."

He smiled and shook his head. "No, thank you, sir. Drinking with me is strictly a business expense. You see, everybody wants to deal with a drunken Indian. What was the list price on Manhattan, twenty-four bucks worth of earrings? So naturally, in my line of work it helps if people think I'm Crazy Sam, who's had maybe a couple of snorts over the line. But you and I don't have to play that round, do we?" He sighed, sank back in the chair, and lit a long expensive-looking cigarette. And handed me my drink.

"My name is Samuel White—ironic, huh? Actually, Samuel Morse White, if you want to check out the birth certificate. Bachelor of arts from the University of Wisconsin, master of business administration from Cornell. Oh, yeah—the part about my being Dakota is true, just bent a little bit. Like, I was never on a reservation. Mom lived in Milwaukee and ran a grocery store most of my life. And I don't think I know a hell of a lot more about Indian lore than you do—unless, of course, you're addicted to cowboy movies."

I sipped Scotch and wondered how soon I could get him out of my cabin. "And Mr. White," I said, "you think I'm a private detective?"

He laughed, throwing back his head and slapping the arm of the chair—which I hoped was insured. "Hell, man," he roared. "I know you are! Look, you come up here, single, mind you, with a load of sporting gear that hasn't seen the sun in fifty years and with the complexion of a fuckin' cave fish. What am I gonna think about you?

And then this morning I see Ross Connors talking to you like he's telling you he's pregnant. Mr. Garnish, please believe me; I'm not a stupid man."

I believed him. I just didn't want to talk to him. "But *you're* up here alone," I said. "That doesn't make you a private eye, does it?"

"Come on, Mr. Garnish," said Samuel Morse White. "You wouldn't even have let me in here if I weren't right about you. And besides"—he leaned toward me, and when somebody Sam's size leans toward you, you jump—"my being here alone is mainly what I would like to talk to you about. You see, I've never been married. But I've got this little girl back in Madison, and she'd just be all hurt as hell if she thought I was— Well, if she thought I was fooling around on the side. You get me?"

I got him, oh yeah. Like the way a mechanic gets your blown head gasket or the way a chiropractor gets your pinched vertebra. Our lad was in trouble and was willing to pay a lot to get out of it and stop hurting.

"Who's shaking you down?" I said.

"I don't *know,*" he said—and he *did* go red. "Look, all I know is I got this a couple of days ago." He fished in the pocket of his shorts and came out with a piece of typing paper folded in four. I took it, a little reluctantly, and opened it to see—surprise, surprise—a message made up of letters clipped from newsprint, a strip of tape over them to form a skewed sentence. It read:

We KNoW WHAT your doIng UP heRe with alICE WaNt us to TELL sherrY? WAit for next MESSage.

I looked at Crazy Sam. "Who's Alice?" I said. "And who's Sherry?"

He shrugged. (They always shrug, minimizing the importance of it all. I bet they do that in IRS audits, too.) "Oh, you know," he said. "Alice is, like, a code name for this lady I meet up here sometimes. I don't think you really need to know her real name, do you?"

"Sam," I said, "so far I don't have to know anybody's real name, not even yours. If I am a detective, which I haven't told you, and if I am available for consultation, which I also haven't told you, all this could still be just a random conversation between two friendly drunks who meet in the woods. As I understand the detective business, things only get serious when there's some money on the table. But let's, just for argument's sake, say I'm offering you a free sample—you know, like in dishwashing liquid? So you tell me you want to talk. So, you want to *talk?*"

Don't ask me why I did it. I should have just told him to get the hell out of my cabin and leave me alone to photograph the squirrels or bomb the minnows or whatever it was you did in a place like that. But there was something engaging about the guy when he wasn't in his loudest-man-in-the-zoo mode. And besides, I'd heard now from Ross Connors, Cheryl Howard, and Crazy Sam that blackmail was one of the less advertised but most popular sports at Lake Manitonaqua. I was getting interested.

And before you jump to any dumb conclusions about me as a dedicated crime fighter, let me tell you about blackmail. In the first place, it's money in the bank. I mean, if you can track down a blackmailer and nail him, I mean really nail the bastard, then you've got yourself a credit card for at least a year. Figure the mark is going to pay you because you've got him off the hook, and you know he's *going* to pay you because you know what he knows (take it from me, grateful marks never tell you the check is in the mail). But the *hook* will pay you too; you're saving the son of a bitch, after all, from the one rap in this country that's as hard to beat as kidnapping. I know, I know. It's blackmailing the blackmailer. But I told you I loved capitalism, didn't I?

I began to see, in other words, the possibility of turning a few shekels on this trip even if I decided not to pull the chain on Cheryl Howard.

Sam just sat there, looking like a very unhappy master's in business administration.

"Okay," I said. "Who is Alice? I'm asking one more time, and that's all I'm going to ask."

"Oh, hell," he said. "Alice is a—a married lady from Madison. I meet her up here every once in a while. She was here just a few days ago, and now I can't even call her on the phone. I'm afraid somebody might be checking her calls, you know? And . . . Well, all right, Mr. Garnish, I'll come clean with you. She's sort of—her husband is kind of a business partner of mine, and things could get really messy if anything came out."

I tried not to swallow my tongue in sheer astonishment. "And Sherry?" I said.

"Sherry—ah, Sherry is only twenty-four."

"Marvelous," I said. "Any other distinguishing characteristics?"

"Well, she—she sort of wants to marry me. And I've sort of told her. Told her yes. You understand?"

Understanding, as I said, isn't really in my line of the business. But maybe sympathy is—at least, for someone almost as dumb as I am. We were coming full circle: Thomas Howard wanted his wife watched but not blackmailed, Ross Connors was having his guests blackmailed and didn't want them watched, and now Crazy Sam was about to be blackmailed, and wanted me to watch over him.

"Sam," I said, finishing my Scotch, "I won't shit you. I could take a retainer—yeah, damn it, I am a PI—and I could get a lot of bread out of you and find out who's giving you the cramps, and you'd be happy and I'd be happy and the cramper would be CLF—"

"What?" he said.

"Cold, lonely, and fucked. Trade term," I said. "End result of messing with professionals, ask any lawyer. But the thing is, dig, I'm not going to do any of that. I'm tired, I'm more than half drunk, somebody decided to fricassee my head this morning, I've got another job to do up here, and besides all that, you look like too nice a guy to have as a client. So I'm going to tell you the truth. No charge, no tip, and then you leave. Okay?"

No doubt about it, I had his attention. He reached the Scotch toward me, and I shook it off. The most important word in Czechoslovakian is *enough.*

"The truth?" he asked.

"The truth." I sighed. "It comes in two parts. The first part is this. You're scared and you're not thinking clearly, but you've got to have realized that whoever sent the note knows all there is to know about the situation. When did you first suspect that maybe Sherry or Alice was your gremlin?"

I've never—and never would—hit a guy as big as Sam. But if I did, and hit him right (that's why I never try), he'd look about like Sam did. I told you he had tiny black eyes. Now they were trying hard to be big black eyes.

"No," he said. "They couldn't do that. I mean, Garnish"—I noticed I'd lost the "Mr." again, which happens a lot in these situations—"I mean, Garnish, these are two fine, loving women. Why would either of them want to shake me down?"

Since he was red in the face and on his feet as he said this, I didn't think it was a great idea to argue the point.

"Sam, sit," I said. Sam sat. "You wouldn't have gotten that pissed off if you hadn't at least thought it yourself. But if you're satisfied it's out of the question, *sei gesund.*"

"Sigh what?" he asked. I forget that everybody doesn't have daily conversations with Ben Gross.

"It means forget it," I said. "But I haven't told you the hard part yet. The hard part is that you can do whatever the hell you want to do about this note, but I'll tell you, man, the best thing you can do is nothing."

"Huh?" he said.

"Read my lips. Nothing. Blackmail is a strictly horse-shit business, and only members of the loyal and ancient order of turkeys tumble for it. Go figure. The guy who thinks he's got you by the short hair only has got you by the short hair as long as you agree to be afraid of him. But what if you decide to admit the truth, along with the fact that you were being squeezed? Man, you're a fucking hero. Or better yet, what if you let the squeezer release the bad news, and you lie your ass out of it? Either way, pal, he's up shinola creek with a lot of hard-earned information he can't make a dime on, and that can buy him five to ten, hard time. Do yourself a favor, okay? Burn the goddamn letter and anything else you get from this wuss. You don't answer him, he don't spit in the soup. That's the trade secret I'm sharing with you because I'm so damn tired. Now, you said something about leaving?"

If I'd just told him he had won the Nobel Prize for videotape selling he might have looked more satisfied. Or he might not.

"Mr. Garnish," he said, "I can't thank you enough. I *will* take your advice. You're right. There's nothing he could really do to me or to— to Alice that could really harm us. Thank you."

I noted that Alice, but not Sherry, had entered into the no harm equation, and thought to myself that there was one twenty-four-year-old back in Madison who would not be marrying any videotape magnates real soon.

And I hate it when people thank me, especially when they thank me for advice that could cost them their buns. Poor Sam was being ding-donged, and I'd just told him not to feel any pain. Like the old joke about the guy goes to his doctor, raises his arm, and says, "Doc, it hurts when I do this." The doctor raises *his* arm and says, "So don't *do* that."

Three times out of five—okay, maybe two—the advice I gave Sam would work. But on the other two or three flips of the coin, he could find himself waist-deep in what they grow rice in. Anyhow, the squeezer would give him plenty of chances to back down, think things over, and pay through the nose. And then he could call O'Toole Investigations again.

I stretched out on the bed, ignoring Johnnie Walker whispering my name across the room, and thought about what I was going to do.

I was worried about leaving Cheryl Howard to the sharks. But apparently there were enough sharks up here to shoot *Jaws IV*. I mean, a little action on the side is always a relief. But oh, what a tangled web we weave when first we labor to relieve, no?

I remembered asking Bridget once if she wasn't bothered by how much of our business had to do with the sleazier part of sex. It was one of my many pathetic attempts to get her out of the business so I could take over. So call me Alf Landon.

Bridget smiled. "Oh, Harry," she said. "No offense, dear, but only someone with a Hollywood idea of nuns would ask that question. Seriously, now, do I *look* like Audrey Hepburn in a wimple?"

I did not—*not*—say she looked more like Rod Steiger in a snood.

"The center of loving is forgiving, Harry. But the center of forgiving is understanding, and not being frightened by what may have to *be* forgiven. Do you know how Saint Augustine begins *The City of God?*"

"Gurgle?" I gurgled, rising to leave.

She held out her hand, palm down. I sat. Old habits.

"He begins," she went on, "not by discussing the political significance of the sack of Rome but by reassuring the good Roman women raped by their barbarian invaders, telling them to feel no shame at their misfortune—not even for any inadvertent pleasure that may have accompanied the act." She beamed. "Now, isn't that a marvelous, humane thing to come from a man so often maligned as a crabbed, malicious puritan?"

I guess so. I guess it's what old Martin O'Toole had told me, years before, sitting in the same chair that Bridget now, damn it, occupied.

"Harry, lad," Martin said. "You find me a cure for gonad-itis, and I could close down our business—and the bloody United Nations—

within the week. So don't ever do it, honey boy"—smiling the way wolves must smile—"we need the revenue, don't you know."

Anyhow, I drifted to sleep thinking profound thoughts like that, not having decided a damn thing about what I was going to do. And then I dreamed about invading the United Nations and terrorizing all the lady simultaneous translators. Some of them even spoke Czech.

A few hours later, the dinnertime buzzer sounded in my room. Might as well feed, I thought. I hadn't had anything all day except Elliot Andrews's gumbo. And Elliot's gumbo was indeed the real thing. Talk about "Midnight Express."

I combed my hair, brushed my teeth (Ivory soap again—don't *ever* do it), and hoped there wouldn't be cauliflower on the table.

There wasn't, as it turned out. But there was an hors d'oeuvre.

Ever have a bottle thrown at you? Don't. I mean, *don't,* as in if you get the choice, brush your teeth with Ivory soap instead.

I had just stepped out of the cabin when the bottle hit, on the wall to my right, with a loud and scary *pop!* I threw my arms over my face in the patented Garnish cringe. I *like* my eyes.

I also scuttled like a lobster on amphetamines around the corner, just in case my attacker had brought a six-pack. My cheek was bleeding, and I pulled a six-inch (okay, half-inch) sliver of brown glass out of it and tried hard not to gag.

My assailant (isn't that a *nice* word?) was nowhere in sight. That didn't mean he didn't have four or five bottles waiting for me, but it did mean that he—or she—was cautious enough not to try a frontal attack. And, given my own wimpy stature, it also meant that my glass-throwing friend was at least as scared as I was. Besides, I figured, it had to be the same cat who had hit on me at the Bayou North. Somebody who just wanted to scare me away from Michelle. I nominated Byron. The motion was seconded and passed by acclamation.

I stood up. Poor bastard, he just wanted to intimidate the hell out of me, and he didn't realize how easily I intimidate.

No more bottles came flying out of the trees. I strolled toward the lodge and promised myself that if Michelle came within fifty yards of me, I'd call a forest ranger as a chaperone—for me, I mean. I also promised myself that later on I'd have a private conversation with young Byron about jealousy, hospitality—things like that. It would start from behind his back.

Everybody was there, including Dick Schwartz, sitting with Cheryl at a separate table. The gray Schneidermans were sitting with Dr. and Mrs. Logan, and Crazy Sam was sitting with Ross Connors, yawping away like he didn't have a care in the world. He must have been one hell of a salesman. They both waved me over to their table.

Dinner was about what you'd expect, if you've ever been to a summer resort at the end of the summer. No cauliflower, but lots of mashed potatoes, salad as limp as a cat in the rain, and what we used to call in boot camp mystery meat. I glanced quizzically at Ross, who grinned and shrugged. What the hell, late August we break out the Spam.

He caught more than my look. "Harry," he said, "what the heck did you do to your cheek?"

I mumbled something classically stupid about shaving, and of course neither Sam nor Ross bought it for a minute.

Michelle and Kerry were serving dinner. I didn't know where Danny or Byron were, and given the quality of the food, I didn't really want to know where Winifred the cook was. It was one of those evenings when you figure nothing, and I mean nothing, is going to happen.

I was wrong.

Ross and Crazy Sam were chatting about the best bait to use for trout—or grunions, some damn fish, I don't know. I was half listening and trying to catch a glimpse of Cheryl across the room. I was falling asleep with my eyes open, which is not a bad way, by the way, to spend most of the parties I've been to. And then I heard a too familiar, gravely voice and started to choke myself awake—especially because I couldn't believe what the voice was saying.

"Oh, yes," it was saying. "I remember the Stan Kenton orchestra very well. You know, Mr. Andrews, one of the sisters on my first post was Gerry Mulligan's aunt. And when young Gerry was arranging for Kenton, he used to send Sister his records. We all loved them. Do you remember his marvelous arrangement of 'Young Blood'? Oh—are you Mr. Connors?"

Yep. She was at my table, and she was Bridget O'Toole, and she was wearing, I swear to God, a sweatshirt and jogging slacks.

I hoped for a brief moment I had been hit by the bottle and was hallucinating. No such luck.

# 11

NOW, THE THING you do when your cover is blown is you try not to blow it any worse. Lesson fourteen from the Martin O'Toole Academy of Finking. If Bridget wanted to let on that she knew me, that was her business. (I know, I know, it *is* her business. Don't remind me.) I just sat and glared, sure that I would have a chance to talk to her later and that she would convince me she was right to come up here and I was wrong to be pissed off. It always works out that way.

Ross rose, smiling, and Elliot did the honors. "Yes, ma'am," he said, "this is the fella you're looking for. Ross, this is Miss O'Toole. She says she talked to you today. Hey, Harry! How's the head, man?"

I nattered something about feeling just fine while Ross did his welcome-to-the-lodge thing with Bridget, who in turn insisted that Elliot join us for dinner.

"Mr. Andrews," she said as she sank into her chair, "was kind enough to pick me up at the Whitebait Airport"—which I knew from my Mobil road map was thirty miles away. She smiled warmly at him. "Before he was a famous musician, you know, he was a student of mine."

I was past surprise. She had told me, I remembered, that she knew some people nearby. But Elliot was the last one I'd have expected to be one of her pupils. But I told you, do you know a nun who has to drive herself anywhere? Or one who doesn't have ex-students peppered strategically all across the country? God, they could probably have transcontinental free-ride rallies, if they wanted to. Part of the Vatican Olympics, maybe.

"That's right," Elliot said, smiling. "Fifth grade, Saint Joan of Arc, Baton Rouge, Louisiana. But you wasn't *Mizz* O'Toole then. Sister Mary Juanita, right?"

It went like that. I was introduced to Miss O'Toole and growled politely. As it turned out, Miss O'Toole, a.k.a. Sister Juanita, a.k.a. the pain in the ass of the known universe, was a passionate outdoorsperson who had found herself with some free days and decided to visit

Lake Manitonaqua, which her dear friend Leslie Cheek had told her was one of the most charming places in Wisconsin.

Of course, I'd never heard of Leslie Cheek. She could be a figment of the O'Toole imagination, sure. But she could also be a U.S. congresswoman upon whom, when Bridget was assigned to the Navy Medical Corps, she performed an emergency appendectomy, thus cementing a lifelong debt of gratitude. One way or the other, I really didn't want to know.

What bothered me more was that, all through dinner, she chatted with Ross Connors about wildlife and with Elliot Andrews about jazz. She seemed to know as much about one as about the other, and I was getting pissed off. I don't really give a rat's ass or a deer's dork about the great outdoors, but jazz I *know*, you know? And then comes the mention of the great quintet that Tadd Dameron led in the late forties, so naturally I pipe into the conversation, saying, "Oh, yeah. Wardell Gray on tenor and Fats Navarro on trumpet. What great stuff they did."

Elliot looked at me strangely, and Bridget looked at me like I'd forgotten my homework assignment. "Well, yes, Mr. Garnish," she said. "It was a wonderful group. But I believe the tenor was Allen Eager, not Wardell Gray."

Elliot nodded silent consent, and of course they were both right. I made a mental note never to speak to Bridget O'Toole again and to trash all my jazz tapes as soon as I got back to Chicago. Michelle and Kerry served us our coffee, and Michelle, smiling, told us she'd be in the bar soon, awaiting our pleasure. Kerry just sniffed and kept on collecting plates.

"Hey, Garner," walrus-barked Crazy Sam. "You didn't buy me no drink last night. How's about now?" Sam had his mask safely back on, I was glad to see. And even though I was dying to get Bridget alone (Christ! had I ever thought I'd say that?) Sam's offer was hard to resist. A guy able to keep up the bullshit under that much pressure must have something going for him, I figured.

Bridget solved my problem for me. "Oh," she piped, smiling around the table. "A nightcap sounds like the very thing to complete the evening. May I join you and Mr.—Mr. Garnish, Mr. Feathers?"

While I tried to remember if there was a crime on the books called "nun strangulation" as opposed to simple murder two, Mr. Feathers announced to everyone within earshot, and maybe also to some passing aircraft, that having Miss O'Toole join him at the bar would make him happier than winning two Cadillacs and a weekend at Disneyland with Dolly Parton. Ross, just like last night, begged off, and Elliot, the gumbo chef, who had struggled like a hero through the mystery meat, excused himself too, after a couple more fond reminiscences about Saint Joan of Arc in Baton Rouge.

Everybody was straggling toward the bar. Even the Schneidermans—they looked about as exciting as twin aspirin tablets —had decided to take a wild fling and have a couple of beers. Monday night madness, you know? Danny Bernstein and Byron Wilson were sitting in a corner nursing Cokes, and I fought back the urge to go over and ask them if I hadn't seen one of them already a couple of times today. Their double glares in my direction helped a lot in the fight.

Crazy Sam waved us to a table and stalked off to fetch our drinks. Then I did my cobra impersonation.

"Sister Mary Juanita," I hissed. "What the *hell* are you doing up here? Don't you know you could foul up the whole operation?"

She didn't even sigh—and she *always* sighs. She just looked at me. "Harry," she said. "Please don't be angry, but after our conversation this morning I just knew something was wrong up here—with you, or with the situation in general. And  . . ." And she blushed. "And I felt responsible for putting you in a position that seems, now, so riddled with complications. It's—what do those children call it?"—looking at the college kids in the corner. "It's *bad vibes.*" And now she did sigh, and smile, satisfied, I guess, to have used at least one phrase belonging to the twentieth century.

"Bad vibes, Bridget?" I hissed again. "And who, if you don't mind my asking, appointed you guardian angel to my bacon? Hell, this is a bad vibes business we're in."

She looked hurt. "Harry, dear," she said, "you know how I worry." Remember your mother when you got in at four A.M. from the junior prom? Feels great, doesn't it? "And besides," she went on, handing me a small vial from her very large purse, "you forgot your blood pressure pills."

Crazy Sam saved me the trouble of gargling in exasperation—and gargling in exasperation is hard—by coming back to our table with the drinks. "Hyeugh!" he hyeughed, looking at the bottle of Inderal. "Garment, don't tell me you're on drugs, too?"

"Sure thing," I said resignedly. "I mainline Alka-Seltzer four times a day, and Miss O'Toole here is my Chicago connection. Isn't that right, Miss O'Toole?"

Bridget smiled and said something almost as stupid, Sam laughed like we were Martin and Lewis, and we all settled down to our drinks. Actually, I settled down to quite a few drinks. Remember, I had had one hell of a Monday. And Bridget drank like a nun—how *do* you make an old-fashioned last that long? And Crazy Sam, who probably had the capacity of Moby Dick, drank *like* Moby Dick, sucking the ice from each glass like it was plankton and not showing a bit of it, except that occasionally he forgot himself and completed a grammatical sentence.

But not old H. Garnish, no sir. Somewhere along the line I'd decided to carry on the grand tradition of Chicago drunks, which meant that by nine o'clock I'd forgotten how many Scotches I'd had, or whose round it was (Bridget, of course, was not allowed to buy) and had to take off my glasses to read on my watch that it *was* nine o'clock.

People were gradually filing out of the bar, including Cheryl and Dick Schwartz. Schwartz, I figured, must have recognized Bridget, but he was maintaining his cool—I mean, at least he hadn't come over to our table and offered to have her legs broken. A real gentleman. The Schneidermans had left long since, and the Logans were sitting nursing their drinks and not talking to one another. At least they were married, for sure. And the kids were waiting for the departure of the old farts, a.k.a. paying customers, so they could put on that devil's music, rock and roll, and go wild.

Bridget heaved—levitated?—herself from her chair after a while. "Mr. Garnish?" she said, "would you be kind enough to walk with me to my cabin. Mr. Feathers, I'm very glad to meet you, and I hope I see you again tomorrow." Sam looked at us both, and at the bottle of pills between us, and grunted politely. Another cover blown, I thought, and tried to get to my feet, both of which seemed to have decided to go on strike.

As we walked, or wobbled, toward her cabin, Bridget looked at the sky and said almost to herself, "A ring around the moon."

"Aar?" I articulated, trying to find the ground.

"Oh," said Bridget. "Sorry, dear. There's a ring around the moon tonight. See it? That means rain soon. And notice that the crickets are chirping more slowly than they were earlier this evening; another reliable sign. Why didn't you tell me that Mrs. Howard was up here with Mr. Schwartz?"

I started to stumble but from years of practice turned it into a graceful Fred Astaire (okay, Ray Bolger) two-step. "Bridget," I said, finding myself facing her at the end of my pirouette, "I just didn't think things were, well, firmed up enough to call in a final report. I mean, there could be a lot of reasons for them to be up here, you know?"

Even in the moonlight (with a ring around it, by God) I could see the look on her face. They must issue nuns bullshit detectors. Zippos, probably.

"Harry," she said. "Remember what I told you about Saint Thomas and the prostitute? Our task is to tell the truth as we see it, not to reason about the motives behind what we see. We can not afford the —the moral arrogance of appointing ourselves judges. Now, tomorrow you and I will drive back to Evanston and will report to Mr. Howard precisely what we have discovered, which is precisely what he has retained us to do. To do any more, or any less, would be a strict violation of our proper role."

Well, hell. Never argue with your boss, especially if your boss has medieval theology on her side, and most especially if you know she's right. I remembered the dumb reassurance I'd given Cheryl Howard that afternoon and was sorry that she was going to be burned after all. But the fire was out of control now that Bridget was on the scene, and the best I could do was make sure that the Garnish came out on the right side of the burning barn.

"Bridget," I said, "you're not only right, you're downright upright. And I'm dog tired. So I'm going to turn in. I'll see you at breakfast, and we'll drive back to Chicago and pull the chain on Cheryl—on Mrs. Howard. You can find your cabin from here."

She gave me her fourth grade look. I've learned to rank her looks by what grade they're appropriate to, and the fourth grade look is the one that tells you she's sorry you made an ass of yourself but it isn't entirely your fault, as in "Harry, you should have held up one finger even if it *was* during the geography lesson." I was glad it wasn't the eighth grade stare. That's the one that says "Harold Garnish, how could a boy your age *do* such a thing?"

Anyhow, she let me schlepp to my cabin and sink into sleep. At least, I tried to sleep.

For a long time, I tried to sleep. My cabin was warm—no, it was hot, and it stayed hot no matter how many windows I opened. And the moon, reflecting off the lake just outside the cabin, was like having a light in the room. So I tossed, turned, and thought those crazy thoughts you think when you can't fall asleep. And still I was awake.

I had turned in at twelve o'clock; nothing to do but drink some more down at the lodge, and I had already drunk more than I liked. The last time I looked at the watch on my bed table—I had already looked at it ten or twelve times—it told me it was two in the morning. Bullshit. I don't like to sleep in the nude, but I had already stripped my pajama top and I was still sweltering. So I got up, pulled the string on my pants, went to the john, and fell back onto the bed.

And then, I guess, I finally fell asleep. Or I fell somewhere between sleep and waking, anyhow, with sights and sounds and feelings that were sometimes feverish, sometimes lovely. You'd probably like to hear about the lovely parts but I don't remember much about them, and what I do remember is my business. There was a woman involved, I can tell you that much.

And then I woke up again. I'll never know what did it. It could have been a scream, it could have been a gust of wind, it could have been just the creaking of the cabin. Probably the last; at least, I hoped it wasn't a scream.

I swore out loud. The Scotch I'd consumed made my mouth feel like the bottom of a birdcage, and I knew I'd never get back to sleep now. Might as well take a short walk around the woods and maybe examine the cabin next door where, I was sure, my mark was sound asleep. But what the hell, no harm in checking. I was a highly paid professional, wasn't I? I pulled on my pants and a shirt and fished in my jacket for a cigarette. The pack was empty. So it was going to be that kind of night, I thought as I stepped out the door.

The Wisconsin woods on a full-moon night look unreal to a city boy like me (especially if, like tonight, the sky is also full of glowing, fast-moving clouds). It's a brightness like the lighting effects you get in those glossy, black and white films of the forties. Remember *I Married a Witch?* Or *And Then There Were None?* And it's *quiet.* I mean, the crickets or whatever they are, and the occasional fish plopping in the lake, spreading ripples under the light—those things just remind you how quiet it really is. It's not spooky, exactly. But if you're used to traffic noise and the television set from the apartment below and a police or fire siren once in a while, it's damn unsettling.

My cabin was number 12. My quarry was in cabin number 14, about fifty yards away from mine. Just like in elevators and in hotels, they didn't have a number 13. Bad medicine, number 13. Both cabins gave on to the lake in back, and I decided to stroll along the water's edge. Like all nonswimmers, I'm drawn to and a little scared by big bodies of water.

I could see that the lights were out in 14. No surprise there; everybody must have been asleep, I suppose, except me. The water lapped against the shore like a friendly dog's tongue. And it was cold, even in later summer; I hadn't bothered to put on shoes. It was all very nice. I was even beginning to enjoy being awake at this hour of the morning. Maybe I'd misjudged the woods, I was thinking. As the lake lapped the shore it burbled over scattered pieces of wood, beer cans, and other debris that it was trying to spit back to the land. I noticed that I had passed number 14 a while ago. Walking east along the curving lakeshore, I must have been near the back of number 20 or 24 by now. In a little while I would turn back and try to sleep again.

Then I noticed a very peculiar piece of flotsam a little way out in the water. It didn't look like wood or like a mass of vegetation: too big. And it didn't look like anything else I'd seen on my short walk. I decided I'd stroll down to it, and then turn back.

About ten or twenty feet away from it I could see by the moonlight that the debris had blond hair.

I ran the rest of the way, right into the water. And pulled her back onto the shore. I was gasping, as I remember, from the cold water, which I'm not used to. She wasn't gasping. Or anything.

I've been a private detective for a long time, which means I've seen a few corpses and a few ruined bodies, though not as many as you might suspect if all you know about the business is from movies and television. Anyhow, I've never been able to deal with it. There's something, well, *heavy* about a dead body. It's become, you know, a *thing*. And once you've lifted one, you'll never forget that peculiar, special kind of weight.

And the back of her head had been crushed—"stove in," as the country boys say. She was in a black two-piece swimsuit, so maybe, I thought, she'd hit her head on one of the rocks that dotted the shore. But how damn silly, I thought, to go swimming in this cold water in the middle of the night. Anyway, the back of her head was crushed. The lake must have carried off a lot of the blood, but there was still enough there, clotting that beautiful hair, coming off on my hand as I laid her on the grass. Her eyes were still open; I could see, under the moon, that the pupils seemed enormously dilated.

After I'd pulled her all the way out of the water, and after I'd made sure she really was dead, I stumbled back down to the lake and tried to be sick. But it was only dry heaves. I remember thinking that somebody had better be told—fast. I remember thinking—crazy thought—that maybe *this* was the back of cabin number 13, the bad medicine cabin. And I remembered that, when this all began, it had been just the prospect of a week in the country.

Surprisingly, impossibly for such a clear night, the moon began to cloud over, and big, fat raindrops began to spatter. I wanted to brush the drops off her upturned face. I tried to remember how they closed the eyes of the dead in the movies. Did you just put your fingers on the lids and pull them down? But I couldn't bring myself to touch her again. Not that pretty head, with that clotted blood in the hair. The rain was getting heavier, and then thunder broke. It was so goddamn corny I started to giggle. And then the giggle turned into a sob. A week in the country, I thought.

# 12

OKAY. SPOT QUIZ, no credit for close guesses. It's the middle of the worst part of the morning, you've just found a dead body, and the rain is doing those big globby drops that mean that in a few minutes it's going to come down like five sons of bitches. Now, quick—what do you do?

The right answer—remember, *I'm* giving the quiz—is that you run like hell for the lodge and ring the bell until Ross Connors, looking like a soggy mountain range, drags himself out of bed and blinks at you until he digs what's going down. Then you both run like hell, not even caring about the rain, back to the corpse. And then—since Ross Connors, at least, has more than cream cheese between his ears—you slog through the mud (and it's like walking through chocolate pudding) to Dr. Logan's cabin. You wake him up and explain to him at least three times, since he's very sleepy, what's happened, and then the three of you shlump back (by now it's *runny* chocolate pudding) to what we professionals call the Scene of the Crime.

"Dead," said Logan, the rain soaking through his bathrobe and his fingers against her throat. "Dead, God damn it! Has somebody got something to cover her with?"

Ross and I looked at each other, each thinking what a dumb bastard I am for not thinking of that, until Logan did the only sane thing and made us, all three, carry Cheryl's body back to the nearest available cabin, which happened to be mine.

Once we got her into bed—*damn* it, corpses are heavy—Ross decided to go to cabin 14 and tell Mr. Kruger—Mr. Schwartz—the bad news. "She must've gone for a midnight swim in the lake," he said, looking down at her. "Hit her head against a rock. Those waves can be a lot stronger than you think. Poor kid. Listen, can you guys wait here for me?"

We could. And while we waited, we tried not to stare at one another or at the thing on the bed. I fished in my jacket and—maybe there is a God—found a bent cigarette in one pocket and a not too wet book of matches in the other.

"Swimming accident." I coughed. "Can you think of a stupider way to go?"

Logan stared at me, and he was right: it was a dumb bloody thing to say. And he didn't like my smoking. And then he glanced at dead Cheryl. And then he looked at dead Cheryl. And then I watched him while he examined dead Cheryl, checking the back of what used to be her head, her face, and her ankles and wrists.

Never at a loss for words, I said, "Wha?"

He looked at me like he'd forgotten I was in the same room. "Oh," he said, "nothing really. I guess. It's just that there's a funny—a funny trauma here."

"Trauma?" I said. "I thought that a trauma was something that scared you. How the hell can a dead person be scared?"

He smiled, with that pain-in-the-ass, oh-Johnny-did-you-think-that-was-a-chipmunk? condescending smile that every specialist I've ever known saves for nonspecialists.

I don't have a specialty, so I've learned to live with it.

"No, no, Mr. Garnish," he lectured. "Trauma can mean any severe damage to a system, physical or mental. Believe me, I'm no Freudian." He chuckled. I didn't know why he was chuckling. "No, it's just that the trauma here, the wound as you might say"—he indicated the bashed back of her head, which I sure as hell *would* call a wound—"shows some strange characteristics."

I'd seen her smiling in photographs. I'd talked to her, anxious and hopeful, in the pinewoods. So, fine, *tell* me I'm a wimp. I didn't want to look at her again dead. I didn't look.

Logan went on anyway. "See?" he said. "Look at this clotting at the base of the skull. Now, blood clots when it's exposed to air. Of course, it will clot even if you suffer the trauma in the water, but not nearly as much. Now *this* clotting"—and I swear to God, he almost stroked the congealed blood—"*this* clotting is what I'd expect if the wound were suffered in the open air. Yeah," he went on, talking to himself, "there's just too much of it."

I was queasy, getting queasier. "But she's in her swimsuit, damn it," I said. "Are you telling me that this wasn't an accident?"

He looked at me strangely. "I'm not telling you anything of the sort, Mr. Garnish. I'm only telling you that this is a very unusual trauma *for* a swimming accident."

"What's this all about?" said Ross Connors, who had come back while Logan was talking. Logan explained to Ross what he had explained to me, and Ross's color, if I could tell by the bad light in the cabin, turned a whiter shade of pale.

"Oh, shit," he said. "Harry, have you got a cigarette by any chance?"

I reflected that that was the first time I had heard Ross use a dirty word, and the first time he had asked me for a smoke. "What is it, Ross?" I said.

He turned toward the window. "Schwartz isn't in his cabin," he said. "Listen, we'd better get the police in on this right away. I'm going to the lodge and call the Whitebait Station. Can you stay with the—the body just a little longer?"

"I'll go with you," I said before Doc Logan could get his mouth open. "Doc, would you mind? I'm not used to, uh, to corpses."

Logan smiled that condescending smile again and said he wouldn't mind at all. One trip to the dissecting room and they all think they're Charlie Ironballs. We left.

The rain was still pretty fearsome, but after you get soaked enough, they can't soak you anymore. What is that, Gresham's Law? Gresham must have been related to Murphy.

Anyway, we got halfway to the lodge before I sprung it on him. "You said Schwartz, not Kruger," I said. "How come?"

Ross didn't break stride, and he didn't look at me.

"What are you talking about, Harry?" he asked, in a very flat voice.

He wasn't a man I would especially care to annoy, and it wasn't the best time in the world, or of the day, for a confrontation anyhow. But then, what time is? "You said Schwartz," I repeated. "You didn't say Kruger. I don't want to brace you on this, man, but that means you know a lot more about—well, about things—than you're supposed to know. Like, for instance, do you know what the late Mrs. Kruger's real name is?"

Now he did stop, even though the rain was coming down like the Red Sea in *The Ten Commandments*. "Harry," he said, "you sure pick the darnedest time for making problems. But, okay, I'll tell you. I don't know the poor lady's real name. And I don't want to know it, though I reckon I'm going to find out before this is all over. Schwartz told me who he is and what he does for a living when he made reservations up here. Said it was important for some legal reason, I forget what, that somebody have a record of that."

"And you *bought* that?" I said. "Jesus, man, don't you realize that that's asking for trouble?"

"I don't know, Harry," Ross said. "Schwartz even offered me twice the daily rate if I'd take his name and keep his secret. And—hell, I could never take advantage of somebody who told me something like that. Do you believe me?"

I did. I also knew that Dick Schwartz must be as good a judge of character as he was a crummy character himself. Maybe they went together—you know, like it's only when you've got a toothache that you remember what it's like not to have a toothache. But the rain was getting, if possible, worse. And I didn't see Charlton Heston striding from anywhere to stop it. And Cheryl Howard was lying, getting colder by the minute, back on my bed.

"Okay," I said, "I'll bite on that for the time being. But let's get out of this fucking rain."

Back at the lodge, Ross called the nearest police and I decided to go wake up Bridget. I mean, things were bad enough, I figured I might as well make them as bad as possible as soon as possible. Ever stick your finger down your throat? Best hangover cure in the world.

While Ross was still on the phone I waved myself out the door and headed toward Bridget's cabin. The rain was letting up, and there was the damnedest light in the east, sort of a combination of Pepto-Bismol and the color of Baltic Avenue in Monopoly. I guessed it was dawn.

Luckily I wasn't hung over, because if I had been Bridget when she opened her door would have split my headache in six and started my eyeballs waltzing. Did *you* know that large ex-nuns sleep in orange paisley nightgowns?

After the ritual "Harry, dear, what could be the matter?" I told her what the matter was, and that the local cops were on the way. She took it all in without raising an eyebrow—they probably weighed an ounce apiece, anyway—and then she did something that whipped me around as much as anything—well, almost anything—had that had happened so far that night. She turned her back to me, dropped her head for a minute (I mean a full minute), and crossed herself.

"That sad girl," she said, turning back to me. I noticed that Bridget was the one person so far who hadn't called Cheryl a *poor* girl. "Poor Harry," she said, looking at me. "It must have been terrible for you to find her, and all by yourself."

I didn't say anything.

"Well," she went on. "Well. I'm glad you came to me as soon as you did, Harry. We might still be able to make some human sense out of all this. And, of course, there's no need for us to try and retain our—what do you call them?—our covers, is there?"

Now it was my turn to sigh. "No, Bridget," I said. "Not our covers, our bed sheets or even"—with a glance at her robe, getting brighter as the sun rose—"our jammies."

If she got the dig, she didn't let on. She almost never does.

"Yes," she said. "Harry, please go back to your cabin. I'll join you there as soon as I can. And, Harry—" She frowned. "I wonder, is Mr. Connors still at the lodge?"

I told her he probably was, and without another word she threw on a raincoat and without another word slogged off toward the lodge through the mud, in her fuzzy blue slippers. I shrugged, and headed back to the cabin.

It's great how in the movies they always know exactly what to do as soon as the corpse is discovered. You know, everybody splits in five directions on important errands, like in fire drills in seventh grade. The trouble is, I was in a real fire in the eighth grade, and what we did was, we ran around and hollered a lot—Sister Mary Celeste included —until Jim, the janitor, stumped in and announced that all the smoke was from a loused-up waffle machine in the cafeteria.

Same-o same-o now. Logan had dozed off, so I shook him awake and told him to go back to sleep. Then I sat and stared at everything in the room except the bed, and then I sat and stared some more. I opened the window for air.

I was beginning to wonder if everybody had decided to sneak off on me when there was a knock at the door.

Crazy Sam. I decided there was no God.

"Hey, Harry," he boomed as I opened the door. "You wanna come to breakfast, or—holy *shit!*"—as his eyes fell on the bed. "Harry, what . . . what . . . ?"

"Sam, you'd better come in," I said. "There's been an accident."

As usual when he was serious, his voice got lower and his eyes stopped twinkling. I explained to him how I'd found "Mrs. Kruger," and that Ross Connors was calling the authorities. That was as much as he needed to know, I figured.

I figured wrong. Most people, myself included, don't like to look at dead bodies; notice sometime at a funeral how long people stay beside the casket. But not Sam. He stared at Cheryl all the time I was talking. Then he leaned over and stared harder.

"Harry," he said softly, "I think you got something more than an accident on your hands here."

Christ, I thought. First Logan, and now Sam. Was everybody going to get to play Sherlock except me? "What do you mean, Sam?" I croaked.

"Well," he said, thoughtfully scratching his belly, "I ain't no coroner, but look here at the way her bikini top is tied." I looked. It was tied in a double butterfly: remember how they first taught you to tie your shoes? "So?" I said.

"So," he said, "that there is a *tight* knot, the kind you can tie in your shoes because they're in front of you. But you just try tying a knot like that behind your back. Listen, boy, I've untied my share of bikini tops, and I *know*."

"So," I said. "Somebody tied it for her. So what?"

"So what," said a voice through the open window, "is *who* the heck tied it on for her, and did he do it while she was still breathing, and where the heck is he?"

We both turned, and through the door, followed by Bridget and Ross Connors, came a little man in horn-rims, a down jacket that looked like it came from the Smithsonian, and with, under a wig of spiders' nests, a face that looked like a large apple left in the sun for a week.

Oh, yeah. He was wearing a holster, and on the side of the holster, a badge.

"Luther Frost, sheriff," he said. "You must be Garnish"—to me—"and who the heck are you and what are you doing here?"—to Sam.

Sam introduced himself and Luther Frost grunted. "Well, Mr. Two Feathers," he said, "I think you'd best go on down to the lodge. We're all going to have a little meeting there in a spell. Oh, I don't have to ask you not to try and leave the place, do I? No, 'course not. And"—looking at the corpse—"that was right smart about that knot. Yeah, that was right smart."

Sam left and Frost sat in the chair and pulled out a pipe you could have ladled soup with. He lit it and stared at the bed.

"Now," he said. "First off, the medical examiner will be here as soon as ever he finishes his breakfast. He'll be able to tell us whether we've really got foul play here. Though"—waving his pipe at Ross and Bridget—"from what these folks said, it looks fair enough like it. Which brings me to my next question. Mr. Garnish, Miss O'Toole has explained to me why you were up here, and Mr. Connors has told me that you didn't divulge"—he said *die*-vulge—"the lady's name to him, even after you found her dead this morning. Now, what I want to know is, just why is that? And why, being a professional detective, did you help move the body from the place you found it?"

Remember, I was worn out. "God damn it, Sheriff," I said. "I don't see why Ross or anybody but you needed to know her real name. And for Christ's sake, I didn't think about murder when I found her. I mean, we still don't know for sure, do we? And where the hell *is* the coroner?"

He looked into his pipe bowl. "Mr. Garnish," he said, "besides that there's a lady present, I have to tell you that I'm a churchgoing man myself, and I don't appreciate hearing people talk obscene around me."

Bridget coughed. "Yes, ma'am?" said Frost.

"Well, Sheriff," she said. "It's just that Harry's way of speaking is just his *way*, if you take my meaning, and I'm sure he's very tired and doesn't really intend any disrespect. And besides," she went on, "he wasn't really being obscene. He was being profane."

Frost stared at her for a long minute while I was silently obscene.

"Yes, ma'am," he finally allowed, nodding. "Well, anyway, one of my boys will be at the lodge to take Mr. Garnish's statement. And I think now we ought to get on down to our meeting. Garrett, will you come in here?" A tall uniform stepped through the door.

"Officer Stewart here will keep watch over Mrs.—Mrs. Howard," Frost said, puffing his pipe back to life. "Not that I think she's going anywhere."

Swell, I thought. A beautiful and frightened woman had been killed, and the chief investigator was a card carrying member of the Lionel Barrymore–Walter Brennan sound-alike society. I preferred my cops Chicago style: quiet, mean, and efficient. Mean, anyhow.

We had our meeting, with coffee, and everybody was there. Everybody was properly shocked and everybody was also properly pissed off when Luther Frost told them that nobody could leave the lodge until the investigation was, as he put it, "finalized."

Especially the Schneidermans, whom I'd thought to be about as violent as Maalox, took the news really bad. While his wife hyperventilated and held his hand, Schneiderman hyperventilated and rose to his feet. His face had the calm color of a vegetarian pizza.

"Sheriff," he said, "My—my wife and I *have* to be back in Chicago by this afternoon. I don't really see how we can help your investigation by staying here. Is this necessary?"

I was a little surprised—it was like seeing a rabbit turn on you and assume the attack position—till my mind clicked back into gear, and I realized that the so-called Schneidermans, too, were on an a.k.a. holiday, and that some wife or some husband, or one of each, would be getting worried if the Schneiderman couple didn't disappear into thin air by that afternoon. Murder investigations cause the god-*damnedest* problems for adulterers.

Luther Frost, I guess, had guessed the same. He put on a tolerant, kindly, little sweet-old-man smile and assured them that he'd by gum have everybody back home as soon as ever he could, but meanwhile could they please put up with his slow ol' country boy way of doing things as he tried to piece this thing out.

I always thought you tried to piece things together, but then, I didn't know the difference between being obscene and being profane either.

"Now, this Mr. Kruger, as he calls himself," Frost went on. "Anybody here seen him since last night? His car's still in the lot, so he ought to be around here somewheres."

Byron Wilson stood up. His hands looked like they were trying to hide behind his back. "I haven't seen him since last night," he said. "But I'll tell you this, Mr. Frost. He killed Mrs. Kruger."

# 13

NOBODY WENT CRAZY. I mean, you know how in Agatha Christie movies, with everybody assembled in the drawing room of the country house, one guy—I think it's usually Reginald Denny—jumps up and shouts something like "It was Lord Marchmain, I know it," and everybody else bites their teacups in half?

Forget it. Shelve it with the efficient seventh grade fire drill.

Frost stared. "Mr.—ah, Mr. Wilson," he said finally, "that's a most interesting thing for you to say. Would you like, maybe, to come with me and explain why you said it?"

"I don't need to come with you, sir," Byron said. "It just makes sense. I mean, if he isn't here, and if his car is in the lot, then he must have done it and not been able to get away because of—because of the rain or something. Or maybe he had another car hidden somewhere. And besides, I overheard him fighting with the lady last night, just after supper. I couldn't hear what they were saying—didn't want to—but it sounded pretty serious to me. Isn't that enough?"

While he spoke, his hands had found their hiding place behind his back, and didn't look like they wanted to come out. The kid was terribly scared.

"Well, it may be enough, and then again it may not," mused Frost, staring at the ceiling. I promised myself that when they elect me God I'll make Buddy Ebsen films a controlled substance. "Meanwhile," Frost went on, "I'd like to ask all you folks to please go back to your cabins. I or one of my men will be by directly to take statements. And, Mr. Wilson, I really would like to talk with you now, if you don't mind."

Byron trudged off to the office with Frost, everybody else trudged off to their cabins, and Bridget stalked over to me. Yeah, *stalked.* Really.

"Harry," she said. "Can we talk?"

"Only if you can find me a cigarette," I said. "See, I've been awake for a long time, Bridge"—she *hates* it when I call her Bridge—"and unless I get something in my lungs soon besides this damn fresh air, I'm just not going to function a hell of a lot longer."

As Bridget sighed, a skinny hand held out a skinny pack of cigarettes under my nose. "Sorry, Mr. Garnish," said Michelle, "but I couldn't help overhearing. Will these do?"

They were one of those brands that are supposed to sell to women because they're mentholated, have a cover like a Tiffany lampshade, and are about as thick as a swizzle stick. But at that point I probably would have smoked a swizzle stick. I accepted gratefully and introduced Bridget to Michelle. Michelle giggled hello and said she had to get back to her room.

"Nice to meet you, Miss—Hill," said Bridget, as Michelle turned away. "Miss Hill! May Harry and I stop by your room later for a little chat with you and your roommate? Miss . . . ?"

"Madura. Oh, for sure," she said, and flowed out of the restaurant.

And much as I was enjoying my drag on my Georgia Lavender or whatever the hell it was, I coughed.

"Bridget," I said. "You're not going to do this, are you?"

"Why, dear," she said, "do what?"

That—*that*, dig—is when you can always tell that what they're going to do to you is the thing you would most hate for them to do to you. Pick it. The lady at the insurance company says, "Do you really think they would raise your rates for such a little accident?" The guy at the phone company says, "Why should this late bill be a problem?" You've got your own version, I know, but it's always "Why, dear, do what?" I mean, man, they *know*.

"Do what?" I said, fighting down another cough. "Do *what* is get mixed up in the death of Cheryl Howard. Damn it, Bridget, the cops are here. All you and I have to do is give Brother Frost a couple of statements, get the hell out of this place, and forget the whole *mishegoss*—right after we collect our bill from Thomas Howard. Hell, Bridget, unprofessional is unprofessional. But this is *Wisconsin*, for Christ's sake. Let's just go home, okay?"

"Harry, Harry," she said. "I don't mean to interfere with Sheriff Frost's investigation, and I certainly don't want to meddle in the solution, or resolution, of that unhappy woman's death. But—"

"*But*, Bridget," I said, "with you always makes me feel for my keys and my checkbook." She ignored me.

"But we do have an obligation to Mr. Howard, I feel, at least to give him a correct accounting of the circumstances of—Well, of the circumstances. And Sheriff Frost has already told me that he doesn't mind my asking a few questions, just to satisfy my own conscience."

Now when the hell had he told her that? I wondered. Anyhow, Bridget was going to waste some time on an investigation she wasn't getting paid for, and I wasn't getting paid for, and I wished to God that Cheryl Howard wasn't dead.

"Now," she went on, "why do you think that nice young man—Mr. Wilson—lied about Mr. Kruger—Mr. Schwartz, that is?"

I stopped. I stared. I stammered.

"Lied?"

"Well, of course, dear." She smiled. "He seems a pleasant young person, but he was so obvious. Didn't you notice how he hid his hands behind his back as he spoke, and that he only spoke to Sheriff Frost? Such an amateur performance." She chuckled. "And remember that he only mentioned the quarrel between Mrs. Howard and Mr. Schwartz at the end of his story—almost as an afterthought. If he had been telling the truth, that would have been the first thing in his mind. So, why would he have lied?"

It struck me that Bridget might have learned as much about lying in her years of teaching fifth grade as her old man had in his years as a PI.

"All right," I said, "you're probably right. But I don't think the kid's involved in anything bad. I mean, he's young, smart, and black, which means to me that he doesn't want to get mixed up in some scam that could ball up his whole future."

Don't ask me why I was defending him. I was sure he had coldcocked me at the Bayou North, and I was sure he wasn't real fond of anybody at the lodge—except Michelle. But sometimes even I can recognize a decent sort stuck in a bad patch. As a friend of mine used to say, even a blind pig finds a truffle once in a while.

"I agree, dear," she said. "Then, who is he protecting—or who does he think he's protecting?"

As I said, I'd told her everything about the situation as I understood it. But I hadn't told her about my front-row view of the Byron-Michelle four-handed Olympics. And I didn't feel like telling her about it now. Maybe I just didn't want us to get any more involved in things than we already were. Maybe I didn't want the kids involved in what was looking uglier by the hour, if I could help it. Pop used to say, "When you're in the shit, boy, you can reach for a life raft. But if you're a real man, you don't grab nobody's hand." Words to live by.

I said to Bridget, "I don't know."

She looked at me. For a long time. "I suppose not," she said. "And now, shall we go talk to that young woman—what is her name—Kerry?"

Kerry was in her cabin—she shared it with Michelle—and so was Michelle. They both looked like they could use a couple hours sleep, and they weren't thrilled to see Bridget sail in with me in tow.

"Miss Hill," Bridget said, in her you-may-go-to-the-girls'-room voice. "I wonder if I might have a word with Miss Madura." There was no question mark in her tone, and Michelle, with a toss of the head, left.

Kerry Madura sat on the edge of the bed and looked as relaxed as a rabbit caught in the headlights of an oncoming semi. She wasn't the stunner that Michelle was, but then nobody ever said that "mousy" means that mice aren't cute. She was cute. And scared.

"Miss Madura," said Bridget, sitting down, "my name is O'Toole, and I want you to understand that I have no official connection with the investigation of this unfortunate incident—no connection whatsoever. So you needn't talk to me at all if you do not wish to. I am a private investigator from Chicago—"

"*You?*" said Kerry, and her eyes widened.

"Yes, dear," Bridget went on. "I know it seems unlikely, but take my word for it. Now. Would you agree to answer a few questions, just so that I can get this terrible business clear in my mind?"

"Yes, ma'am," said Kerry. "I don't mind at all, except I don't know what I can tell you that would be any help. I mean, I figure it's just bad karma, you know?"

I won't tell you that at the mention of the word *karma* Bridget sniffed the air like a bird dog that's just gotten a whiff of quail. She did, but I won't tell you that because I've never really seen a bird dog at work. Only Bridget.

"Bad karma?" said my boss. "Are you a student of Eastern religions, dear?"

"Oh, for sure," she said. "At Michigan—that's where I go to school, at Ann Arbor—there's this professor, Professor Crews? And he teaches this great course called Ultimate Questions where he talks about karma and Zen and all that. He's my faculty advisor," she concluded, in the same tone of voice you might use to say Reggie Jackson was your batting coach.

"That sounds very exciting, Kerry—may I call you Kerry?" Bridget waited for the nod and went on. "But what do you mean by karma, and why do you say that this poor lady's death was bad karma?"

Kerry looked puzzled, and I didn't blame her. Murder investigations don't often turn out to be midterm exams. Finally, she said, "Well, you know, karma is like, it's like fate, you know? It's like, poor Mrs. Kruger getting drowned, or killed, or whatever, it's just what the cosmic wheel had in store for her. That's all I meant."

"No, it isn't, Kerry," said Bridget as she stood up. Bridget standing isn't very tall, but she is wide enough to be impressive. "No, I think you meant something more than that. Because you're obviously very intelligent, and because you've studied with Clyde Crews—I've read his book, you know—and because that means you know that karma does *not* mean fate. It means the individual destiny that each of us shapes for himself. I think Professor Crews compares it to the picture of Dorian Gray: that painting of our inmost selves that we construct, choice by choice and stroke by stroke. Does he use that example in his classes?"

Kerry gulped. I stared. I didn't know what the hell they were talking about. "Yes, ma'am," said Kerry when she was finished gulping.

Bridget smiled. "Good," she said. "It's a marvelous example. But now, dear, and I don't mean to alarm you, I have to say that if you thought Mrs. Kruger's death was bad karma, you must have some sense that it was a deserved fate."

"I don't know what you're talking about," Kerry said. "It's just a word. Are you crazy or something?" She stood up. But Bridget put both hands on her shoulders; it was partly a reassuring pat, and partly a brace that would have done the Chicago PD proud.

"Of course you know what I'm talking about, Kerry," she said. "Don't you know that I wanted to talk to you first because I saw how agitated you were when that young man spoke back at the lodge? Now, come along, you tell me what it is that bothers you so much. And I promise, your parents will probably never hear of it."

Kerry looked like she'd accidentally stuck her finger in a wall socket, if you can do that. "How did you know about my parents?" she gasped.

"I didn't, dear," replied Bridget, smiling benignly, "but I do now, don't I? So, Miss Madura, why did you say karma, and what do you know that we should know? Really, young lady, you look as if you could use some rest, and lord knows I have a lot to do today." And—you know I never lie to you—she tapped her foot impatiently. I just stood there with my metaphorical finger up my metaphorical nose, hoping that in my next life my karma wouldn't drop me in a Catholic grammar school.

"Oh, it's nothing," said Kerry. That always means it's something. "It's just that since she came up here, Mrs. Kruger spent so much time talking with Michelle. I mean, like, she would take her aside after dinner and, like, talk with her and treat her like she was some-body special."

"But, dear," said Bridget, "why should that bother you?"

"Oh"—Kerry tossed her head—I don't know. It's just that Michelle—well, she gets all the favors from everybody around here, you know? I mean, she's okay, but . . . but . . ."

"But young Byron likes her better than you, doesn't he?" said Bridget. I needed another cigarette.

Kerry needed a heart-lung machine. She actually put her hand to her breast, just like they do in silent movies when they hear that Colonel Culpepper has been killed at Gettysburg. "What are you talking about?" she said. "Do you think I could—could—fall in love with somebody like that, with a—a nigger? Do you know what my parents would— Get out of here!"

Bridget said, "Harry, we had better go." And to Kerry, "Thank you, dear. I'm sure none of this will have to be repeated to anyone. But just one word of advice from an old woman, and not a very bright one. Never be ashamed of loving anyone, and never shame yourself by denying that love. You're not going to like yourself very much, in a while, for calling Byron a 'nigger.' Your mouth said that dreadful word, but your eyes didn't. Just remember, Kerry, that you're not the first person to betray a beloved at a time of stress. Sometimes the cock doesn't even crow three times. And it's *all right.*"

Kerry stared. I now needed a cigarette *and* a drink. We left.

To meet Luther Frost on our way back to my cabin. Spiderweb hair waving in the breeze, he strutted up to us just as I was about to ask Bridget what the hell had been going on back at Kerry's cabin.

"Miz O'Toole," he said, flashing about twelve of the yellowest teeth

I'd seen since my last Polident commercial. "You been conducting your investigation, maybe?"

Bridget instantly shifted into her innocent-dip mode. "Oh, no, Sheriff," she said. "I'd never try to anticipate the authorities. Harry and I have just been talking to some people, trying to clarify our own interest in the case. I hope that's all right?"

"Well, sure." Frost smiled. I didn't like his smile. "We got no call to *in*terfere with you folk, long as you don't *in*terfere with us. Naw," he said. I hate guys who say "naw." "It's just I been looking for you to tell you we got that guy—Mr. Kruger, Mr. Schwartz, whatever."

Bridget, for one of the few times I've seen it happen, looked startled. "You found him?"

"Well, *I* didn't," drawled Frost, obviously having a ball. "Officer Stewart did, though. And he's dead as cat litter. Schwartz, that is. You want to come see?"

# 14

I DON'T KNOW how dead cat litter is. I hate cats. Bridget has a cat, she calls him Me Too because the little bastard always wants to share her dinner, and she feeds him canned salmon and, dig this, licorice. At me, on those rare, thank God, occasions when I'm in Bridget's apartment he just hisses. I hate cats.

So I don't really know how dead is cat litter. But if it's as dead as Dick Schwartz was, it's dead enough. We were standing around the corpse where it had been found, about a hundred yards into the woods (yeah, I know, a corpse in a copse); Frost, Bridget, me, and the apparently deaf-mute Officer Garrett Stewart. I didn't like Schwartz. And after Cheryl Howard got iced I didn't like him even more than I didn't like him before. But nobody ought to be dead: there, brothers and sisters, is the Harry Garnish philosophy of life. Dying is a bitch, any anybody who tries to tell you different is a creep. Take it to the bank.

I didn't like Schwartz, but I really didn't like him with his throat cut. You've heard it before, it was like he had a second mouth, lying on his back in his jammies in the mud. I wished the son of a bitch was on his feet with a Scotch-rocks in his right hand and a bribe in his left, in Chicago instead of Wisconsin, just being the corrupt nerd God or whoever made him to be in the first place.

"Sloppy job," said Luther Frost, looking down. "You can tell from here that the killer missed the windpipe. That's where you want to hit. And he didn't even know about the carotid artery. Yeah. Real sloppy. Just sawed away at the throat and let the poor fella bleed to death. Leaves us in a bit of a pickle, though, don't it?" he asked brightly, looking at Bridget, Officer Stewart, and me.

Well, it left *him* in a pickle. It left me more anxious than before to get back to Evanston, sleep in a room with a TV set—best night-light invented by Western man—and run down a few nice, simple check jumpers. Nobody ought to get killed. Another translation of that is that murder is a pain in the ass in my business. It's a police matter.

Crimes Against People is the category Skokie and Evanston PD use for it, as opposed to Crimes Against Property. Which is real cute, because it means if you're a cop, you don't have to say you're working homicide, rape, assault and battery, or armed robbery; you just say you're in "peep" as opposed to "prop." And if you're in peep, you get hazardous duty pay whether you're checking on a fourteen-year-old girl who got violated by an anonymous, usually transient, wimp, or on a mass murderer who tears his victims limb from limb with his bare teeth.

But me, I hate murder, because nobody ever pays me to solve it. I get paid for finding where Arnold Snarb, after passing five hundred fish worth of bad paper, disappeared to with the cocktail waitress he met at the Skokie Hilton. She's usually, by the way, named either Debbie or Rhonda. That's *my* job. I do it well, and I don't like to do other jobs any more than I enjoy fixing toilets or replacing carburetors.

Murder is boring. Even if I had (fine, you found me out) been more than half in love with Cheryl Howard.

But it wasn't boring to Bridget. She is, as I guess I told you, unprofessional. For one thing, she lets herself care. While Frost sucked on his pipe and Stewart stared at the trees, she was darting glances at the mud as if she was checking equations on a blackboard. And then, with one dart of her eyes, she grunted.

Now when Bridget sighs you figure you're in for a lecture. When she grunts—which is a lot less often—you figure you're in for complications you really don't want to know about.

"Mr. Frost," she said, "would you look over here?" She pointed to a place about five feet from Schwartz's cut throat. "This may be something you can use, but I would rather not touch it myself."

It was a pack of cigarettes, half concealed by the mud but still clearly visible. Frost fished it out, regulation style, with a pencil stuck through the opening.

Highly trained and dispassionate investigator that I am, my first thought was that I'd sure like to light up one of the ones left. Then I noticed that it was the same brand Michelle had given me, back at the lodge. I didn't say anything.

But Bridget did. "Sheriff," she asked, "may I just look at that once?" "Why, sure, ma'am," said Frost, and held it out to her. She only glanced at it for a second. Would she, I wondered, be sharp enough to recognize the brand too? Nonsmokers usually don't distinguish one brand from another, and I wasn't about to blow any whistles.

Bridget just said "Thank you" to Frost, and Frost, with an odd look, passed the pack on to Stewart, who deposited it in a cellophane evidence bag.

"Well," said Frost, "I figure it's time for another confab"—I was grateful he didn't say "powwow"—"down at the lodge. You agree, Miz O'Toole?"

It wasn't really a question, of course. When you've dealt with cops as much as I have, you learn that the only answer to a cop's question is "Of course, Officer."

"Of course, Officer," said Bridget O'Toole, who seemed to know the rules as well as I. "I'm more or less out of my depth, I'm afraid, in circumstances like these. I'm sure you know the right thing to do."

He bought it. He smiled that patient smile men always turn on women who have just snookered them. "I appreciate that, ma'am," he said. "And I thank you for noticing this little bit of information. It could help a lot."

"Oh, I'm so pleased," said Bridget, fooling everybody but me. "And by the way, has anybody been able to get in touch with Mr. Howard? It's awful that he should be kept ignorant of this—this terrible happening for so long."

"We've been trying most of the day, ma'am," said Officer Stewart. "But his answering service says he's out of the office and they don't know when he'll be back. You can be sure we'll get in touch with him as soon as ever we can. Chicago PD's been alerted to find him, too. It is awful, isn't it?"

Bridget stared, and so did I. I didn't know the bastard could talk, let alone say something sensitive.

Anyhow, back we went to the lodge, where everybody was eventually assembled again. It was almost lunchtime now, and I couldn't help thinking that if this kept on we ought to have another dead body on our hands just about in time for the cocktail hour. Ross Connors must have been thinking along the same lines, because he had had Winifred the Ugly make up some cold-cut sandwiches for all of us. I figured Winifred was the only nonsuspect at the lodge, because she was the only one too grungy to approach a victim without raising a hue and cry.

But Winifred did know what sandwiches were all about. I bit into a cucumber, salami, onion, and French mustard on rye with tears of gratitude (chips and sliced tomatoes on the side), and eyed with lust the ice cold, sweating Heineken that had been placed in front of me. Everybody else was munching at leisure on something taken at random—how could you lose?—from the big tray in the center of the room.

Only Luther Frost, nibbling on a stalk of celery and—sorry—stalking among us seemed unimpressed with lunch. (Even Bridget had snagged a Swiss and mayonnaise on white.) But he was having fun, too.

"Folks," he said, alternately crunching celery and sucking his pipe, "sorry to roust you all out again, but it appears we have ourselves a—well, a kind of a larger problem on our hands than we thought. And I surely hope you'll all help me try to figure things out here."

Everybody stared.

"What I mean," he went on, "is that we found poor Mr. Kruger—well, actually, his name was—is—Schwartz—we found him with his throat cut, and that means we have to figure on a killer who's still here."

Everybody stared.

"I mean," said Luther Frost, and he was obviously losing his temper, "I mean that somebody here knows something they haven't told me yet, and by gosh they aren't leaving this place till I find out what it is. You folks know what house arrest means? If you don't, you're gull-danged about to learn."

Everybody stared, and I wished I was back in Chicago—for a lot of reasons, but just now because at least in Chicago the cops said "I'll be goddamned" instead of "I'll be gull-danged," and when they wanted you to know you were going to have your ass nailed to the wall if you didn't come across, they told you you were going to have your ass nailed to the wall if you didn't come across. Give me, if I've got to be jerked around by one of them, Telly Savalas over Buddy Ebsen. Any time.

Then spoke Bridget. "Miss Hill," she said to Michelle. "You were nice enough to give Mr. Garnish a cigarette a little while ago. Could I possibly have one now?" Which surprised hell out of me, because I'd never known Bridget to smoke. Michelle crossed the room and held out her pack to Bridget. Bridget took one, allowed Michelle to light it, and coughed like a terminal patient on her first inhale. And Luther Frost jumped.

Well, he didn't really jump. But for a little old coot with wispy gray hair and not much of that, he gave the best impression of a bird of prey I've seen outside of *Wild Kingdom.*

"Miss Hill," he said, "is this your ordinary brand of smokes?"

"Yes, sir," said Michelle. Bridget was still coughing.

"Well, then, ma'am, I'm afraid I'm going to have to ask you a few questions—in private, if you don't mind."

Michelle stared at Frost and everybody else stared at Michelle. Except me, staring at my fingernails. And Bridget, still coughing and looking for someplace to get rid of her cigarette.

Then Michelle did something that surprised me. She turned on Frost and shouted. "What the hell do you think you're doing?" she hollered. "You hick turkey, didn't you ever hear of Miranda? If you want to question me, old man, you better read me my rights first—in *front* of all these people, dig, old man?"

Frost was maybe the only person not shocked by the outburst. Or if he was shocked, it didn't stop him from sucking his pipe. "Miz Hill," he said, "I've heard of Miranda, believe me. And I don't intend to violate your—your constitutional rights, especially in front of these good folks. I'm not arresting you. All I asked you is if you'd come along with me, friendly like, where we could have us a little chat. And, by the way, I ain't that old—just sixty last June."

Michelle was about to say something but Bridget, her coughing fit over, interrupted her. "Dear," she said, heaving herself out of the chair. You could almost hear the cushions sigh with relief. "Dear," she said, "Sheriff Frost can't say this to you, because of course he is an officer of the law. But I can tell you that the reason for his sudden interest in you is that—"

"Miz O'Toole," said Frost.

"Oh, no, Sheriff," Bridget breezed on, "it's quite all right, and it might even make your task easier, if you'll allow me to finish." Poor Frost, he never went to school with the nuns. He let her finish.

"The reason," she went on, "is that a package of this same brand of cigarettes was found at—or near—the body of Mr. Schwartz. Naturally, Sheriff Frost is interested in talking to you about how that package might have gotten there. And my advice to you—"

"I don't *want* your advice, you bitch!" Michelle shouted. "I don't want it, you hear? You set me up with that goddamn cigarette business, and now you want to tell me what to do. Well, screw it, lady."

"Dear," began Bridget.

"Don't 'dear' me. I know what you are, and who you are. And I'm not going to let you spoil my life."

Everybody else in the room was quiet. Including me.

"You're a detective," went on Michelle. "You're a paid snoop and a paid leech, that's what you are, Miss High and Mighty. People give you money to find out things, and you take the money and you find the things out, even if what you find out hurts other people. Isn't that right?"

*"Sit down,"* said Bridget in her fifth grade voice of command. Michelle sat down. "Michelle," she said, "everything you say is correct. But I was simply trying to explain to you why Sheriff Frost might be interested in talking with you. Now, I suggest that you go with him and try not to antagonize him any more than you already have."

"Why, thank you, Miz O'Toole," said Frost into the silence. And, to Michelle, "Miz Hill, would you please come along with me now?"

"No," said Michelle. "I know what you want to do. You want to make out that I had something to do with killing those people, just because of that fucking pack of cigarettes you found by the body." I couldn't but notice that, coming from her mouth, *fucking* did sound like a dirty word.

There was a bit of to-and-froing between Michelle and Frost, and Michelle got more and more out of control. I wasn't exactly on her side, but if I'd been a lawyer and she was my client I would have told her to shut the hell up.

Luther Frost sighed. His sigh was almost as good as Bridget's, except it had a note of anger in it that made it less a sigh and more a scold. "Officer Stewart," he finally said, "would you please escort Miz Hill here to Mr. Connor's office for a few questions, if it ain't too much trouble?"

And then two things happened that surprised the hell out of me. The first was that Byron Wilson jumped to his feet and said, "You old *fool*—you think this girl could kill her own *mother?*"

The second was that Michelle gasped, and said, "Oh, Byron, *no!*"

Okay, there was a third thing that happened. While the rest of us stared, Bridget smiled and nodded her head.

# 15

As YOU MIGHT expect, both Michelle *and* Byron were carted away to Ross Connors's office. And don't ask me how, Bridget came along, and don't ask me why, I tagged along. If it had been a homicide investigation in Chicago, of course, our being there would have guaranteed an acquittal without even a hearing; in and out of court in ten minutes, maximum. But I guess the good old boys in the country do it different; bad for the law but good for me, because I got to hear what was going on. Though I kept expecting somebody to come by and ask me to leave.

Frost didn't waste any time. It was probably that farmer mentality. You know—if the cows ain't milked by five o'clock, the cows ain't milked.

"Your mother, Miz Hill?" he said. "Why did Mr. Wilson here say that, and if it's true, why didn't you tell us that?"

Michelle bit her lip and looked around. Biting your lip and looking around is a good way, I've found, of stalling and a great way of screwing yourself in an investigation.

Frost waited for her to finish tasting her lip.

"Okay," she said finally. "She was my mother. Nobody was supposed to know because Mom had me when she—she wasn't married. She was like seventeen or something, you know? The guy—I never met him—the guy split as soon as he found out that Mom was pregnant, and she had to farm me out to this orphanage. I never saw her till I was, oh, like fifteen years old. But she'd been keeping tabs on me, knew that the Hills had adopted me and all, and she came to see me, all the way to Ohio, and told me who she was, and that she wanted to help me as much as she could, because she was into some money now, and she felt, like, responsible, you know? And—"

"Excuse me, Miz Hill," said Luther Frost. "You say that your mother got in touch with you when you were fifteen or so. And she said she wanted to help you, yeah?" Michelle nodded. "Well, now," he went on, "how come, if you were getting some money from your mother, and, I guess, some money from Mr. and Mrs. Hill, how come you took a job like this to put yourself through college? I mean, it appears to me like you're sitting pretty high on the hog, if you take my meaning."

Michelle was about to respond after blushing—funny, but I hadn't imagined she *could* blush—when Bridget spoke.

"Excuse me, Sheriff Frost," she said. "I think you may not understand the nearly impossible cost of higher education today. It is not only prohibitive, it is positively mind and back breaking. Parents go into severe debt so that their children can attend college, and even then the children find themselves impoverished, on expectation of an expensive future. What *is* your major, dear?" she asked, turning toward Michelle.

"Uh, liberal arts," said Michelle.

Bridget looked. And nodded.

I knew what she was doing. There's this recording, I think it's from 1954, of Sonny Rollins and Thelonious Monk playing "More Than You Know." It's a beautiful song, but it's also been Mickey-Moused to death by God knows how many third-rate dance bands and cocktail waitresses with beehive hairdos, long fingernails, and pink sequined horn-rim glasses. A good tune gone wrong, dig? Anyhow, what Rollins and Monk do in the simplest way is repeat the tune again and again and again until the sadness in the song comes clattering out of it the way toys and baseball gloves and vacuum cleaner parts come clattering out of your hall closet.

That's what Bridget was doing to Michelle: just by staying to the simple things and coming round to them again and again she was hoping to make her say more than she knew she was saying.

"Liberal arts," Bridget said. "That's very nice. And what do you plan on doing after you graduate?"

Michelle looked confused, and Frost looked miffed. It was his investigation, after all. But the thing about Bridget is that no matter how much of a pain in the neck she's being, people tend to let her finish because she looks so damn vulnerable and so damn *nice*. I got over it years ago, but Frost was new at the game, so he just let her go on, and chewed on his pipe.

Finally, Michelle said, with a little giggle. "Well, I guess I want to go into teaching or something. You know?"

Bridget smiled. "Yes, dear," she said. "I taught for years myself, and

I found it the most rewarding of vocations. But I should warn you that it isn't really very—well, remunerative for a young lady like yourself. And I hope you won't continue to supplement your income by blackmail. As a teacher, you know, you would find yourself in deeper trouble than you're in now."

Don't ask me to describe the way everybody reacted. Like Byron jumping to his feet, Frost nearly biting the stem off his pipe, and Michelle turning a *very* whiter shade of pale. Or me, all of a sudden, feeling the blood pump through my legs.

Bridget, of course, just sat there with her plump hands folded across her lap—which I think they describe as "ample."

The movies are right about one thing, anyhow. After a line like the one Bridget had dropped there's always at least a three-beat pause. Maybe it's built into the genes.

"What are you talking about?" said Michelle. "Blackmail? Are you crazy or what?"

"Michelle," said Bridget, no longer smiling, "we're now involved in a murder investigation, and that is a significantly more heinous crime than blackmail. But, just to keep things clear, I think you ought to help us establish that you have been blackmailing some of the guests at the lodge. I'm sure Sheriff Frost would agree." She looked at Frost, who looked back and nodded. I think he was trying to repress a smile.

It was Byron's turn to say something dumb, and he did. "Lady," he said, "I don't know who you are or what you think you're doing, but I gotta tell you you're coasting pretty close to slander."

"Oh, no, Mr. Wilson," said Bridget. "It would be slander if it weren't true, or if I made the observation with malicious intent. I do neither. I simply remark that, since Miss Hill is clearly a blackmailer, it would be helpful to the more serious investigation now underway if she—*came clean* about this relatively minor issue."

Before anybody could holler that Bridget was crazy, Frost said, very quietly, "Excuse me, ma'am, but could you tell me—tell us—why you're so sure of all this?"

"Oh, certainly." She smiled. "As I'm sure you have heard, Mr. Connors has been troubled recently because some of his clients have been harassed for their—their indiscretions while staying at the lodge. And I have been fortunate enough to examine some of the notes or rather, one of the notes received by one of the victims.

Rather simpleminded stuff, I must say: words or letters clipped from newspaper headlines and such, pasted on to a sheet of paper. And while I was wandering around the lodge this morning, I couldn't help but notice that only Miss Hill, among the staff, subscribes to a daily newspaper. It's the Madison *Chronicle,* and I'm sure that if we compared its typeface to the typeface in the blackmail letter, we would find that they are identical. Also, when I was in the cabin that Miss Hill shares with Miss Madura, I noticed a pair of cuticle scissors on her bed table—just the right size for cutting letters out of a newspaper."

Frost's face fell and my heart sank. And Michelle, laughing, said what we were both thinking. "What a load of shit," she said. "Anybody could have used my newspaper to make up those notes. What do you think, I hoard all my goddamn papers to myself?"

"But," said Bridget, looking flustered. "The scissors, and—"

"And nothing," crowed Michelle. "Don't you trim your nails? This is really an insult. *Everybody* has newspapers, and nail scissors, and Scotch tape. It doesn't add up to a thing."

"Ah, but it does," said Bridget, no longer flustered and with that smile that, if you know her, always means she's going to trump your ace. Or dump your ass. "It adds up, and you did the addition, thank you. I was hoping you would, if you became excited enough. You see, I described the blackmail note as letters pasted on a sheet of paper. I didn't say that they were Scotch-taped on—which, in fact, they were. Now why would you insist that everyone has Scotch tape if you didn't know what the notes look like?"

Michelle stared for a minute. Then, "You bitch," she said. "You think you're so goddamn smart, but you still can't prove a goddamn thing. I know—"

"Now, Miz Hill," cut in Frost. "I have to ask you to watch your language. And you're right. Miz O'Toole here hasn't really proved anything. But . . ."—and he paused to light his pipe and give it a few strong draws—"But I think you got to agree that, just between you and me and the lamppost, she's got you in a vise grip. Now, wouldn't you like to help us all out a little, instead of making things maybe, you know, harder on yourself?"

Michelle treated Bridget to one of those looks that mean If I find you on the street, you'd better have a Doberman and an Oakland linebacker along with you. Then she shrugged.

"Okay," she said. "What the hell. Listen, I'm not going to be prosecuted for this, am I? I mean, after all, I'm helping with a murder investigation, right?"

Frost opened his mouth to speak, but Bridget heaved herself out of her chair and didn't let him get a word in. She glared at Michelle. It was the kind of glare you can almost hear.

"Miss Hill," she hissed. The hiss was like a slap on the wrist. "We've put up with quite enough of your histrionics, your mewling, and your rudeness. And when you tell me that you are 'assisting' in a murder investigation, I, young lady, have *had it.* You are *not* assisting. You have, in point of pure fact, been all but shanghaied into cooperating. You are cooperating only because you stumbled into admitting that your salient talent is not for liberal arts but for blackmail. And, if I may remind you, the murder investigation in which you are 'assisting' is an investigation into the murder of your mother. You horrible child."

"Hey, wait a minute," said Byron, coming to his feet. "You ought to—"

"Now, now, Mr. Wilson," interrupted Frost, coming to his feet the same time. "I don't think you want to make things any uglier than they are already. You don't, do you?"

They eyed each other. As I said, I was sure that young Byron could take me to the mat in record time. But—don't ask me why—I wasn't so sure about the little old man from the North Woods. Neither was Byron. He sat down. Frost sat down.

"All right, Miz Hill," Frost went on. "Now, I reckon Mr. Wilson here knew about your—uh, your little business on the side. Seems like he knows a powerful lot about you."

Michelle was still shaken by Bridget's tongue-lashing. (I know, I know: "tongue-lashing" is a cliché. But you have to see Bridget do it once.) She stammered. "Mr. Frost, Byron is . . . well, him and me are . . ."

In the pause, I knew it was Byron who had thrown the bottle at me. And I knew why, and I knew he had meant to miss. And I felt sorry for him, the poor bastard.

"Yes, dear," said Bridget, "that's obvious. Although you mean to say 'he and I,' not 'him and me.' But I think Mr. Frost wants to know if Byron is an accomplice, not if he is a close friend." Bridget had shifted to her soft voice, and Michelle, off balance, looked at her almost gratefully.

Now, I don't know when Bridget first appointed herself deputy sheriff, and I don't even know if Frost knew she had. But they were working great together. I mean, if you've ever been interrogated by the cops, you know that there are always two interrogators, one tough and angry and one kindly and understanding, right? Wrong. That's what you read somewhere. The way they *really* whipsaw you is they keep switching off roles, so you don't know which one is your pal. Believe me, it works—unless you're smart enough to remember that neither one is.

Michelle wasn't that smart. It takes a lot of practice, and a lot of busts. "Oh, no, ma'am," she said. I liked the "ma'am." "Byron kept trying to get me to stop. He even threatened to tell Mr. Connors if I didn't, and if I didn't return the money. But—"

"But nothing," growled Frost; his turn to be the mean guy. "I don't give a pint of cowflop if he's a nice man or not. Fact is, Michelle"—no more "Miz Hill," I noticed—"you just told us your boyfriend here is an accessory. Now if you want to save what's left of your bacon, you're going to tell us everything you know about your mother being up here."

That did it. She couldn't tell the red team from the blue team anymore, so she spilled.

"Okay, okay," she said. "Like I say, my—my mother had been sending me checks every month, you know? But it wasn't enough, you know? Like, college is expensive. And honest, that's the only reason I started doing—what I was doing up here. And, like, my mother was getting worried that her husband might find out about those checks she's been sending me."

"Excuse me, dear," interrupted Bridget. "I assume that Mrs. Howard had a private checking account?"

"Yeah. Yeah," Michelle said.

"Do you remember the name of the bank?" asked Bridget.

"Yeah," said Michelle, "Evanston Federal Savings and Loan." No hesitation. You had to hand it to her, the kid had an eye out for the real things. I'll bet she could have recited the account number.

"Anyway," she went on, "she came up here to talk to me with her lawyer, Mr. Schwartz, about some kind of final settlement. I mean, she wanted to see if there was some lump sum she could come up with so that—"

"So that you'd stop blackmailing your own mother," said Frost. "Ain't that it, Michelle?"

Michelle jumped. "What?" she said.

"Come on, girl," said Frost. "You mean, you hadn't threatened your mother that you would tell her husband about yourself?"

"No! No!" she said. "I didn't! I didn't!" Four nos, in my experience, usually add up to one yes.

"Hey, man," said Byron, and now he *was* ready for a fight. "You know this whole piece of shit violates Michelle's constitutional rights? She told you about Miranda, man. You haven't got a damn thing on her you can use in court, so what the fuck you think you're doing, anyhow?"

Frost smiled, and as he smiled I noticed that he shifted in his chair so that his holster was free. I tensed.

"Mr. Wilson," he said, "I'm afraid you civilian folks don't have a real good idea of what Miranda is. I think it's all those movies you watch—you know, Dirty Magnum or whatever his name is. Anyhow, all I've done is have Miz Hill here in for some friendly talk about some material facts in this case. And we got two nonpolice witnesses here who can testify that this couldn't have been an interrogation, because no policeman worth his salt would *let* civilians sit in on a formal investigation. And besides, whatever Miz Hill said, she said in conversation with Miz O'Toole."

Damn. *That* was why foxy grandpa had let Bridget and me sit in. Not that it would all hold together very long in court. But it would hold together long enough to confuse hell out of your ordinary dumbshit jury, and tie up Michelle in mistrial motions for a good few years. Her life, at least as she'd known it, was over at that moment. And Bridget just smiled at her lap. A very tiny smile, though a very big lap.

Michelle was frozen. Byron wasn't. "You son of a *bitch!*" he shouted, and damn near flew out of his chair toward Frost.

Before I could move, Frost had his pistol out of his holster and, as Byron sailed into him, caught him on his right temple hard enough that the kid just crumpled. Frost still had his pipe in his mouth.

"Now, that was really kind of foolish, don't you think?" he said, puffing on his pipe while Byron held his head, moaning. "I don't think you want to be charged with assaulting a police officer, and this is kind of an informal little chat, so we'll just all figure you fell out of your chair. But now"—turning to Bridget and me—"I'm going to have to ask you folks to leave, and to send in Officer Stewart. He's just outside the door. We're going to make this an official session, and naturally, no offense, I can't have nonofficers present. Oh, yeah. Would you see if you can find the good Doctor—what's his name?—Logan, and send him by here. Looks like this lad might've hurt himself."

As we opened the door Frost, relighting his pipe, was already beginning what, since they banned school prayers, was probably the best-known ritual in the U.S.A.

"Now, Miz Hill," he said. "You have the right to remain silent. You have the right, don't you know, to a lawyer. And, why, if you can't afford a lawyer, well, the court will provide one for you . . ."

Stewart was stepping in as we stepped out. You can't, you know, Mirandize a suspect without a witness. It was all very legal.

Then why did I feel like hell?

# 16

AS WE WALKED toward the dining room to fetch Doc Logan, Bridget stopped and put a hand on my arm.

"Harry," she said, "would you please go and fetch Dr. Logan? I have to make a phone call."

"Oh, sure, Bridget," I said. "A phone call. A *phone* call? Christ on a crutch, Bridget! Don't you realize you just did everything but tie those two kids down on the operating table—and all on the basis of some lucky guesses? I mean, guilty or not, they just got themselves good and sliced up, and you know as well as I do that it's all illegal as hell. And now you want to make a phone call? I hope it's to a lawyer, kid. Because we could find ourselves neck-deep in gorilla snot for what went on back there."

Okay, okay, I know I overreacted. But I was up the hoo-hah with the whole business, I didn't want us—that is, the agency—to get any more involved in it, and I recognized—boy, how I hate it—that special crusader's gleam in her eye. And I was still out of cigarettes.

She just smiled her patient smile and said, "Harry, don't be so discouraged. I do have to make this call, and believe me, dear, it will be all right."

Don't you hate it when people reassure you and you haven't even admitted that you need to be reassured? So she coasted off to make her call and I coasted into the dining room.

Little Kerry Madura met me at the entrance, looking worried as hell. "Mr. Garnish," she said, "is everything all right? I mean, is Byron in trouble?"

Even if she did have gefilte fish for brains, she was a sweet kid. And I've always believed that, if you're talking to sweet people, lie if you have to.

"Everything's going fine." I smiled at her. "There may be a little flack one way or the other, but don't worry about Byron. He's got—what do you call it? Good karma."

She relaxed a little. I noticed she hadn't asked about Michelle.

Everybody in the dining room, of course, was relieved and anxious to see me, and to find out what had been going on with Frost. Hell, it could've been a college reunion. Except I never went.

I figured, you know, it was my turn to enjoy myself, so I asked Doc Logan if he'd go to Connors's office, poured myself a cup of coffee, and stared at the nearest wall, not talking at all.

Crazy Sam was the first to break the silence.

"Goddamn, Garment," he said, rising from his chair. "You know we're all as relaxed as a bunch of roosters with worms up their ass! What the hell is going on back there?"

"Well," I said, sipping my coffee, "as far as I can tell, Sheriff Frost is making some kind of headway in his investigation. And I think we'll probably all be out of here in just a little bit longer." The Schneidermans—or the people who wanted to be known as the Schneidermans—almost collapsed together in their mutual sigh. "Has anybody got a cigarette?" I concluded.

Nobody did, but Ross Connors, without a word, got up and stumped to the bar, fiddling with his keys. He came back with a virgin pack of Marlboros and a book of matches, both of which he'd got from the machine there, and tossed them in my lap.

He didn't answer me when I thanked him, but he did talk to the crowd. "Folks," he said, "there's really no way I can make up to you for the—the terrible things that have happened here. And if Mr. Garnish here is right, you'll all be free to leave in a little while. But if you want, you can stay the night. Anyhow, I'm closing down the resort for the season tomorrow. I'm sorry, but it just doesn't feel right to me to keep it open after what's happened. 'Course, those of you who've paid for more days will get your money back for the time you didn't spend here. And Kerry and Danny, I'm going to pay you right up to the end of the month, just like I said I would." He dropped his eyes. "And Michelle and Byron, too."

Everybody nodded and grunted support and sympathy. I lit my cigarette. Life's a bitch, all right, but you've got to stop along the way and smell the nicotine.

While we were all nodding and sympathizing Luther Frost came in, pipe in mouth and hand resting comfortably on his holster. Looking, I would say, like a cat who's had a three-canary lunch.

"Well, people," he said, "you're all free to go. Or for that matter, stay. Whatever you want to do. Our little problem appears to be just about all cleared up. Of course, now, we'll be needing your names and addresses, and I mean your *real* names and addresses"—I had to hand it to him, he didn't look at the Schneidermans when he said that —"but I'm sure you'll cooperate and give Officer Stewart all the information he needs before you pull out."

Everybody was sighing, when young Danny Bernstein spoke up. "Sheriff," he said, "if you don't mind my asking, is Michelle—is Miss Hill okay, or is she in some kind of trouble?"

Frost stared at him for a couple of seconds. "Sonny," he said, "I wouldn't worry my head, if I was you, about Miz Hill."

"But, sir," Danny went on.

"But nothing, lad," said Frost. "What's going to happen is going to happen, and there really ain't nothing you can do about it, now, is there?"

Poor Danny, he was about as gone on—do kids still say "gone on"? —Michelle as Byron was, except I didn't think he'd gotten as far, or maybe as low, as his co-worker. Anyhow, Frost wasn't going to have to clip Danny on the side of the head with his piece. Or at least I hoped not. Poor Danny hell, I thought. Poor Kerry. She was the one, as far as I could see, who was getting nothing out of the summer job except her salary.

But Danny, like a lot of kids his age, didn't know when he'd been told to shut up and piss off. "No, Sheriff," he said, "I just can't take that for an answer. I mean, I really want to know if Michelle is in any kind of trouble, and if she is, well you know, I want to know what her —her friends can do to help. Now I think you owe me—owe us that kind of information."

Frost was getting annoyed, I was getting another headache, or maybe it was the same one back from vacation, and everybody else, especially Ross Connors, was visibly wondering how much more crap there was going to be to be gone through before we all got to go home. And then Bridget galumphed into the room. She must have heard the last part of the conversation.

"My dear young man," she said to Danny Bernstein, "you can do your biggest favor for Miss Hill by possessing your soul in patience. Believe me, Sheriff Frost is expediting matters in the most efficient of ways, and the best course for all concerned is to stay out of his way. And I do understand your concern."

It pacified Danny, and Frost beamed and nodded at Bridget.

Damn, but they worked well together. I allowed myself the wish that maybe Bridget would decide to join the Wisconsin State Troopers and leave the agency in the hands it, by God, belonged in. I don't often win, but I never stop betting.

The dispersal didn't take long. The Schneidermans couldn't quit the premises soon enough, the Logans—Doc Logan came back in a few minutes—were off to their cabin to pack, Crazy Sam and Ross sauntered off to the bar, and Danny and Kerry disappeared. That left me and Bridget—oh yeah, and Winifred the cook, who was grumbling around the dining room picking up empty cups, and who didn't seem to know that anything unusual had gone on. World War III, I guessed, might have gotten a rise out of her. But only if she was real close to ground zero.

Bridget spoke first. "Harry," she said, "I know it's late, but don't you think we could drive back to Chicago tonight? I really don't feel like spending another night here, and there's nothing more we can do anyway."

Nothing more we could do? I didn't even know what the hell we'd done, except witness the afterbirth of two deaths and sit in on an interrogation that made the Constitution look about as serious as the playing rules for old maid. But here I was again, being asked for a free six-hour ride by a sixty-odd-year-old nun. I told you, didn't I?

"Okay, Bridget," I said. "Let me get my stuff together and we'll start out. But if it's not a state secret, could you tell me just what's going on with Michelle and Byron, and what was that phone call you made that was so damn important?"

"Thank you, dear," she said. "It won't take me any time at all to pack." And—you have my word for it—she turned to go.

"Bridget!" I shouted. "You're making me crazy. Did you hear what I asked you?"

She turned, benign. Nuns do a real good benign. "Oh," she said, "Miss Hill and Mr. Wilson are being bound over on suspicion of murder. Sheriff Frost suspects that Miss Hill killed Mrs. Howard because Mrs. Howard was threatening to reveal the blackmail operation, and then killed Mr. Schwartz because he might have been able to—what's the word? Oh yes, *finger* Miss Hill. By the way, Harry, do you have a cigarette?"

Just like that. I was too thunderstruck—not at the news, but at the offhand way she delivered it—to do anything but fish in my pocket and give her my pack.

She took it, looked at it, and handed it back to me. "Thank you," she said. "Perhaps I won't have one after all."

Swell. I wouldn't have given a fart in Florence if she'd asked me for two Cuban cigars to stick in her nose.

"And the phone call?" I persisted. "I mean, last time I looked, I was working for O'Toole Investigations, too."

"Oh, that," she said. "I just called Knobby to ask him to check some facts for me."

"Knobby? Facts?"

"Yes, dear, with Evanston Federal Savings and Loan."

"Bridget, are we done with this pile of—well, are we done with this business or not? I mean, face facts. All we have to do is give Thomas Howard his bill, tell him how sorry we are, and back off. You never listen to me, but I keep telling you that we're in *business,* and stuff like murder isn't what we get paid to screw around with."

She stared at me. "You were—you were really fond of her, weren't you?" she asked quietly. "I'm very sorry, Harry."

I lit a cigarette and watched Winifred pick up the last of the coffee cups.

"Well," Bridget went on brightly, "if we leave soon, we should have time for a short meal at the Bayou North. Wouldn't you like to say good-bye to Elliot? He was such a good student, and I so enjoyed the recordings he used to send me. And, Harry, in this sad affair, I wish you would remember Saint Thomas and the prostitute."

"Wha?"

"Remember, we're not being paid simply to transmit information, but to make sure, to the best of our abilities, that that information squares with the idea of justice."

"Wha?"

"There are facts, Harry, and there are truths. It may be a fact that a man gets drunk and murders his wife in a one-bedroom cold-water Chicago slum apartment. But the truth behind that fact may involve and imply the whole life history of two unfortunate people. Adam and Eve ate the apple: fact. But they ate it in search of, and finally in hostage to, the very knowledge of good and evil that was their exile and their salvation. Truth does not exonerate fact, it merely humanizes it."

Well, what can you do with a woman like that? It was the first time I'd heard that we were in the theology business, and I'll bet old Martin O'Toole would have cocked an eye at the news too. And I wished Saint Thomas had just told the merchant and the prostitute that he was on his way to a saints' convention in Verona or wherever, and couldn't talk to them. But anyway, the idea of a sandwich and a beer at the Bayou North was appealing, so I grunted and turned to go.

"And, Harry," Bridget said as I was almost out of the room, "you know, of course, that we can't let Michelle, bad girl though she is, suffer for murders she didn't commit. You have just helped me convince myself of her innocence, and for that I thank you, dear."

I just kept walking. What *can* you do with a woman like that?

# 17

THERE WERE NO affectionate good-byes to the people at the lodge. Everybody was a little shy, a little skittish, and a whole lot anxious to get the hell away. Luther Frost, with Michelle and Byron in tow, had headed back to town. Ross Connors bid us a gloomy farewell as we walked to my car. I'd thought about just leaving the ruined fishing pole and leprous tennis racket in my cabin. But then I remembered that they were Ben Gross's property, and figured that maybe, who knew? someday Ben might like to go fishing with two thirds of a pole for two thirds of a fish, or play tennis with a leper. So I took the stuff along, feeling even sillier carrying it out of the lodge than I had felt carrying it in. Ross smiled when he saw me.

"Harry," he said, "you're not a bad guy, but don't ever try to convince anybody you're an outdoorsman. Sorry, old boss, but it just don't take well on you."

I smiled back. "Okay, man," I said. "But next time you're in Chicago for the opera, I hope you give me a ring. Believe me, I'm great at trapping wild chateaubriand and Beefeater martinis. Hell, you dig Greek cooking? I even bagged me some saganaki in my time."

He laughed. "That I can believe about you. Yeah, next time we'll get together and have us a time."

"On my dime," I said.

"We'll fight over the bill after we eat." He laughed again.

We were both lying in our teeth. He knew he wasn't going to get in touch with me next time he was in town, and I knew it, and we both knew we'd probably never see one another again. But you know how it is. Sometimes you say good-bye—dig it, *good-bye*—to somebody you really like, and all those bullshit promises about writing, phoning, blah blah blah, are a kind of down payment on the guilt you know you're going to feel because you know you're not *gonna*. Listen, you think the phone companies don't know where you tie your goat?

So. Off to the Bayou North, where Elliot Andrews wouldn't hear of letting us pay for dinner, where I was dying to ask him what Bud

Powell was really like (he'd played with Bud during Bud's last, terrible years), and where all Elliot wanted to do was chew the fat—or the gumbo—with Bridget about the good old days in Louisiana grade school.

Swell. Eleanor kept feeding me Heinekens and asking me how my poor head felt, and the more Heinekens she fed me the better my head felt, till Bridget finally said, "Harry, this has been wonderful, especially after such a distressing time, but don't you think we'd better start?"

I assented—hoping the Wisconsin Highway Patrol had decided to take the evening off—when Elliot jumped to his feet, said, "No! Wait a minute," and ran into the back room.

"Honestly," said Eleanor, shaking her head. "That man. I don't think he knows what his next five minutes are going to be like. Lord, I don't think he cares."

Bridget was about to coo a response (ever see a very *big* pigeon?) when Elliot came charging back, grinning like twelve possums. He was carrying what looked like a cloth belt. He was carrying it the way the priest carries the chalice onto the altar. Reverently.

"Harry," he said. "One night at the Blackhawk, Bird was playing, and, dig, he was so far gone he forgot his horn after the gig. Well, anyhow, this was his neck strap. A cat gave it to me years ago, and I been keeping it since then. Why don't you take it along, man?"

Charlie Parker's neck strap? Hell, I stopped believing in relics before I got into high school. Saint Wulfstan's sandals, Saint Patagonia's fingernail, like that. In fact, in my old neighborhood there were probably enough relics of the True Cross on various living room walls to build a battleship if you brought them all together. And Bird had lost so many horns in his career that his collected missing neck straps could fill the hold of the good ship *True Cross.* But I remembered what Bridget had said about truth and fact, and I looked in Elliot's eyes and I went Bridget one better. This strap might not be fact, but because Elliot believed it, it sure as hell was some kind of truth.

"Jesus, Elliot," I said, "I can't. I mean, I can't. That's just too much."

"Hey, man." Elliot grinned. "I said take it *with*, not take it. It's a loan, you dig? Sometime I'll be down in Chicago, we'll lift a few, catch some sounds, and I'll take it back. But hell, you remembered me, you remember? Now, don't insult me by not letting me thank you."

"Oh, hell," I said, embarrassed.

"Sister—Miss O'Toole?" Elliot said, triumphant.

"Harry. Take it with you," Bridget said, softly.

"Elliot, you old fool," Eleanor said, lovingly.

The old fool and his wife escorted us to the parking lot, where I opened the trunk of my Duster and very carefully folded Bird's neck strap into my suitcase. Elliot smiled approvingly.

So. Off again, this time all the way back to Evanston, and would I ever love to get back. Cheryl Howard and Dick Schwartz were going back, too, but I figured we'd get there sooner.

Shock's a funny thing. I'd been in love with Cheryl Howard well before she got her head caved in. Okay, but since then I'd been walking around, talking to folks, and being my usual charming self. Ever get tagged on the jaw by a really big guy? You don't start to feel hurt and mean until the bastard has left the room and you've dragged yourself to the emergency ward for five stitches. Ever get busted for disorderly conduct, drunk driving, like that? They cuff you, they print you, they take mug shots and they put you for four hours in a holding cell that's filled with guys who look like runner-ups in an Attila the Hun look-alike contest and that smells like camel piss from Cleveland, and all the time you're so cool you can't *believe* anybody would take you for an offender. You even straighten your tie. And the next morning, bailed out (by Bridget) and waking up in your own bed, you're shaking so bad you have to pour the coffee into a bowl. Can't quite hit the cup, you dig?

Shock's a funny thing. My psychologist friend Marge talks about adrenaline and endorphins, which doesn't mean much to me except they're fancy ways of saying your body tries real hard not to fall apart on you until you have the leisure to fall apart. So now, driving back south, I found that my hands were trembling on the wheel and that my eyes kept watering and that I couldn't, without an effort, swallow.

Bridget was no help. She loves to talk, enough so that sometimes you calculate whether you can kill yourself jumping out of her second-story office window. But she loves to talk about things that don't mean anything. The first forty miles were devoted to what an interesting man Mr. Two Feathers seemed to be, and how exciting it must be to be involved in the video business. I grunted and tried to focus my eyes on the road. Wisconsin country roads after a late summer rain smell great, and you wouldn't, in your right mind, drive them on a dare.

The next sixty miles were devoted to Luther Frost, to what a fine officer he seemed to be. "Although," Bridget said, "I'm afraid he relies a bit too much on intuition—guesswork—for a professional investigator."

My hands had stopped shaking enough and my eyes were focused enough by now that I could do something more than grunt. I hollered.

"Intuition, Bridget?" I hollered. "Look, I don't want to drive the car into a ditch, or my point into the ground. But if you ask me, you're the one who relied on intuition, maybe even past the point of the law. What the hell is this stuff about Michelle being a blackmailer? You were right, okay, but don't tell me that's not guesswork."

She just stared straight ahead, her eyes a little raised—toward heaven or the sun-shield, don't ask me which.

"Harry, dear," she finally said. "Intuitive thought is a special variety of reasoning. I've never been capable of it myself, though that certainly doesn't mean I condemn it. But I've never—have *you*, dear?—had that inward flash that tells you you *know* why circumstances are the way they are, even if you don't quite know how they came to be that way. Great scientists, I'm told, rely very much more on that inward flash than they do on the experimental method. And investigators like Sheriff Frost. But all *I* did was form a few conclusions from a set of circumstances that could not be denied or altered. I'm afraid I'm not very good at the detective business," she concluded with a little girl's giggle and a fat woman's heaving of the shoulders.

If I can ever decide which one she really is, I will take over the agency.

"And," she went on (she always goes on), "I'm afraid Sheriff Frost relied much more on intuition, in that sense, than perhaps he should have. But it will probably all be all right in the end."

The miles were piling up, I was praying that my water pump would hold, and I was barely listening. Nevertheless, I heard that. And I didn't respond.

As you drive south from Wisconsin into northern Illinois, even in early fall and even after a bastard rain, you begin to notice differences. Not as many leaves on the road, I mean; more street signs at highway intersections. And those big houses way off the road get nearer to the road the farther south you drive, until finally they lose their mystery altogether and you pass a sign that says KENOSHA 5 MILES and you're back in civilization and the next stop is Chicago.

Now I was back on my turf, and I could respond.

"The *end?*" I said. "Bridget, we're well out of this now, so please—intuition or whatever—don't talk to me about the end of something I hope we never even started. For Christ's sake."

Kenosha rolled by. It doesn't take long. Bridget stared out the window. I wondered if Marianne would be available for a date tomorrow night, and then, thinking about Cheryl, I wondered if I would call Marianne tomorrow night or not. All I really wanted to do, I decided, was drop my boss off, get my ass home, and pour myself into bed and brandy. If the Duster didn't break down we'd be back in time for me to hit a liquor store.

"Harry," Bridget said, "would you mind dropping me at the agency instead of at home?" We were entering the outskirts of the city. "There are some things I should attend to tonight."

"Like what?" I said. "I know you're cooking something, and it sure as hell doesn't smell like goulash. You know I hate surprises. And, not that I give a healthy harooga, but if it's going to involve me or the business I'd really like to be let in on the gag. Damn it, Bridget! I'm tired, and I'd really like to be able to go to sleep tonight without worrying about what law I'll be violating tomorrow."

She continued to stare out the window. "Didn't you find that child —Kerry Madura—a sad young thing? So intelligent, and yet so distraught about being in love with a young black man. Goodness. I would have hoped parents by this late age would have stopped exposing their own children to that particular venom. Oh, well, she'll grow out of it. I hope."

"Bridget," I said with heroic self-restraint, "you're not answering my question."

"And," she went on, "the girl is studying oriental philosophy, too. You'd think that that alone would disabuse her of any silly prejudices, wouldn't you?"

"Bridget," I said with bulldog determination, "you're not answering my question."

"You know," she said, settling into the car seat and fitting her hands over her lap, "I haven't thought about Hinduism in years. Goodness, not since college. But that young lady jogged my memory. Have you heard of the *gunees,* Harry?"

I was in for it. No way out, no hope of escape. I've never been locked in a high school gym with a life insurance salesman, but it's a recurring nightmare of mine. And now, traveling forty miles per hour with Bridget in her lecture mood, I knew my dreams were coming true. "Gunees?" I said. "No. What are they? Some kind of bird, like a gull?"

"The gunees," she frowned at me, "are the fundamental constituents of the soul. There are three of them, *Tamas, Rajas,* and *Sattva.* They—"

"Bridget," I said, "you're not answering my question." If you transport a sixty-odd-year-old lecturer on Hinduism across state lines, I wondered, can't you invoke a reverse Mann Act and have *her* put away?

"They are not only descriptive of the soul, but in a way of the progress of most human affairs. Tamas includes all the vilest, most unruly of emotions. Fear, jealousy, lust—the seven deadlies, you know."

The seven *deadlies?* Leave it to her to be on nickname terms with the catechism.

"Rajas includes the noble, but still unruly passions. It may be cognate with our word *rage:* righteous anger, courage in battle, all the virtues of the noble warrior. But still not enough for the fully enlightened man. Sattva is that enlightenment, that wisdom that disciplines and organizes the lower impulses."

We were in front of the building that housed O'Toole Investigations. It was ten of ten, and the package stores would be closing soon. Life was a dog.

Oh, yeah. Knobby was waiting outside the building, red hair, bow tie, shit-eating grin, and a big wave to me as we pulled up to the curb. Life was *two* dogs.

"Bridget," I said as she opened the door, "a few days ago you were telling me about Saint Thomas and the whore. Now you tell me about the three gurneys, or gumballs, whatever the hell, and you think this makes sense of Cheryl's death?"

"*Yes!*" she said, smiling. Happily. "Oh, Harry, you do see, don't you? We know what Rajas did at the lodge, and for full Sattva we need only find out what special form of Tamas is at the root of it all. Now, you go home and get some sleep, dear. You must be simply exhausted." And with that she was gone, walking into the agency with Knobby chattering excitedly by her side.

I knew in my heart of weasels' hearts that things were going to get stickier than I wanted them to be. But the closest I'd ever come to higher Indian philosophy was shrimp curry and a quart of Golden Eagle at the Tandoori Restaurant on Michigan Avenue. And I was in the mood for a little Tamas. There were five minutes till the Bambi Bar package store closed. I could make it, and I'd wait till the first shot of brandy had hit my cerebral cortex before I decided whether to report for work tomorrow or quit and go into selling farm implements for K-Mart.

I gunned the motor.

# 18

I SPENT MOST of the night giving mouth-to-mouth resuscitation to a fifth of E & J brandy—lost the poor bastard, too. But my guardian gremlins must have been on the job, because I woke up next morning to Zoot Sims playing "Cherokee" on my cassette deck, and Zoot sounds so happy he can even make a hangover feel good.

Mrs. Chandler, in the apartment next to mine, hates music, and especially hates jazz. And adrenaline, I'm told, is especially good for muscle tone among those getting up in years. So, in a mood of Christian charity, I turned Zoot's volume all the way up, took off the clothes I'd slept in (yeah, the gremlins had screwed up there), and went to soak in the tub.

I was putting Tabasco on my poached eggs and talking to them— "Look guys, I'm in bad shape, so just be good eggs and get me through the morning, okay?"—when the phone rang.

"Sorry, Mrs. Chandler," I said into the receiver. "I'll turn it down right away."

"Mr. Garnish?" said a voice that was definitely not the voice of Mrs. Chandler. "Is this Mr. Garnish?"

I turned Zoot down. "Sorry," I said. "Yes, this is Harry Garnish."

"This is Thomas Howard, Mr. Garnish," said Thomas Howard, while Mr. Garnish thought *shit* to himself. "I . . . I just wanted to call and see if there was something—anything—you could tell me about what, uh, happened up there, or if—Oh, hell, Garnish, why did this happen? She's coming home today, you know. She's coming home in a plastic bag. Oh, Christ."

"Stop it!" I shouted over the phone. "Just fucking stop it, man. What are you, you going to get her back by pissing in your soup like this? You going to fix anything?"

If there's a book, *101 Things to Say to a Bereaved Husband,* what I said was probably number 102. But the hell with it. I was still hung over, my poached eggs were getting cold and staring at me like two abandoned school-girls, and Cheryl Howard *was* coming home in a body-bag.

"I'm sorry, Mr. Garnish," said Howard. "I just don't know who to turn to, who to call. I mean, I never wanted *this*, I wanted—"

"You want a drink, don't you?" I said.

There was a moment of silence over the line. "Why do you say that?" he asked.

"Because you told me the first time we talked that you're an alcoholic. Because your wife's dead and you and I both feel rotten about it. Because you had to call somebody just to hear another voice. Because *I* want a drink, damn it. Am I right?"

"You're right," he said, after a pause.

"Damn right I'm right," I said. "Now you hang up, and you find your AA sponsor—I figure you must be into that scam—or you go to the station and identify and pick up your wife's body, or, if you want, you drive over to O'Toole Investigations and you and I will go looking for a Scotch mine together. I don't care which, but I do care that we do something beside wail and moan on the goddamn phone, dig?"

Go ahead. Tell me I would make a rotten camp counselor. He hung up without another word; I scraped my disappointed eggs into the sink and went to brush my teeth for the fourth time that morning. Brandy does funny things to your mouth.

By the time I got to the agency it was ten in the morning; a nice, early autumn North Chicago morning, with just enough of the whiff of burning leaves and exhaust fumes in the air to tell you you're back in the city.

And there was Bridget.

"Harry!" she exclaimed as I walked into the office. Brenda stared at me quizzically, as if we might have met, those many years ago, on a terrace in Mozambique the night before the revolution. Or maybe it had just been a wild weekend in Springfield.

Fine. Nothing had changed.

Nothing ever does. Not in *my* life, anyhow, and I wish you better luck.

So. "Harry!" said Bridget as I walked in, "the most wonderful news, and all thanks to Knobby."

Now, you know how fond I am of Knobby, and how much I value wonderful news from him: my favorite item would be about his deportation back to the land of the toads. And my mouth felt like the way a dragon's mouth must feel, and my head felt like the dragon was trapped up there. So you won't be surprised at the next, very short, word I said to Bridget.

But she was. Alas.

"Harry," she said, blushing for Brenda (who I don't think had heard the word), "why don't you come into my office?"

I went in, nodding silently to Phil again. I was glad to see him doing so well. The trickle of water from his pot was only medium-size, and just one of his idiot-face leaves was getting brown around the edges.

"Sorry about the outburst, Bridget," I said as I settled into the chair across from her. "So what is this wonderful news Knobby has for you? I'd really like to hear it."

She sighed. Then she smiled. Then she put her hands together on the desk. I was about to ask her if she was going to do the last solo from *Swan Lake (is* there one?) when she decided to speak.

"Evanston Federal Savings and Loan," she said.

"Right," I said. "That's a bank, isn't it?" Since it was the middle of the month and I had a grand total of twenty-two dollars and seventy-one cents in my checkbook, I figured I was entitled to make fun of banks. Any banks.

"Harry, Mrs. Howard's account was at Evanston Federal. And Knobby knows a man there who—well, who owes him some favors."

Now, what that meant, even if Bridget didn't want to admit it, is why I like Chicago so much. Some poor bastard at Evanston Fed had let himself in to Knobby for a few shekels on the horses, or maybe something hairier, and Knobby was calling back his markers. I even felt a tiny twinge of respect for Knobby. It's how a big city works, and my city is a *big* city. It's called juice.

"And?" I said, master of dialogue that I am.

"And," she said, "Cheryl Howard *did* have a separate checking account there!"

Where was a plate of gumbo and a bottle of beer when you really needed them? "Wonderful, Bridget," I said. "We knew that."

"Yes," she said, "but we didn't know about *access.* Computer access. If you have an account with a bank under one name, and if you have another account with the same bank under a different name, you can access the blind account from the first account, if you know enough about the computer system and if you have just one important bit of information. It's all got to do with entry codes, and cross-filing of information, and what do they call it, interfaces—goodness, it's complicated. But there is one essential bit of information that, if you know the way the system works, allows you into it."

She looked at me like she expected me to ask the next question with baited breath. Unfortunately, all I know or care about computers is that for a quarter they'll play arcade games with you that you can't win and that are stupid in the first place. I mean, who *wants* to save the galaxy from the invading Jaxons or whatever? And besides, after the E & J, my breath was still strong enough it couldn't have been baited for anything less than a right whale.

"Yes?" I said.

"Yes," she said, a little disappointed. "Your *Social Security number.* Oh, it's all very complicated, and I don't believe poor Knobby even understands what his friend told him"—Poor Knobby, I reflected, couldn't understand the complexities of a flush toilet, probably, without printed instructions on the wall—"but the main point is, his friend from the bank could tell him that Cheryl's private account had been accessed—not just for the amounts of withdrawals, either, but also for a record of the fact that there were withdrawals to certain people."

I must have been tireder than I thought. Because none of this sounded real to me, and because I wished I was back in my apartment reading the *Tribune* comic page and watching reruns of *Mission: Impossible.*

"Bridget," I said, "that's really terrific, really interesting news. But I've got these three adulteries and four skipped checks to take care of right now. It's the business we're in, remember? And I'd like to go take care of them. So you and Knobby just go on meditating about Social Security numbers and computer access and stuff like that, and I'll go back to my tiny office and try to keep this agency afloat, okay? Oh, by the way, I think Phil could use a little water. He's not leaking bad enough."

She looked at me sadly. Phil, I swear to God, looked at me gratefully. Philodendrons are like turkeys, too damn dumb to know how much water is enough.

"Of course, dear," she said. "You should go and take care of those things. But I hope you will be able to take me to Mrs. Howard's wake. It's this afternoon, at Pernicone's Funeral Home on Howard Street. I'd like to get there by two o'clock. Do you mind?"

Did I mind? I don't even have to ask you to fill in the blanks, do I? But I don't have to tell you either that I said I'd pick her up at one thirty.

I went back to my office, opened a can of ale from the fridge, and dialed the three snoops I had doing piecework for us on the piecework other people were doing behind their spouses' backs. No answers. I dialed Marianne.

She was in. "Hello," she said.

"Hi," I said. "It's me. Back early. All kinds of good stuff to tell you about. What do you say to maybe some moussaka and fried squid at the Corinthian Columns tonight?"

"Oh," she said. She *didn't* say "Oh, Harry." "Listen, see, tonight's kind of bad for me." Period. I listened for a minute while everything she didn't say echoed over the wires.

"Well, yeah, okay. Tomorrow night?"

"Oh, I don't know. Listen, could you call me back over the weekend? I have to go out now."

"Right. Oh yeah—how's Fred Jr.?"

"Fine." That was it. *Fine.* Just "Fine." Like they say, reach out and lose someone. And as kiss-offs go, it was at least economical. We mumbled a few more inconsequentialities and hung up.

It's one of the nice things about my job that when there's nobody on the other end of the line or when the other end of the line doesn't want to be on the other end of the line, there's nothing you can do. So you can sit and sip ale and watch the sun take its boring arc across the sky.

Until one thirty, when it's time to pick up Bridget O'Toole and drive to the house of the dead.

# 19

PERNICONE'S FUNERAL HOME is on Howard. Howard is the street where Evanston ends and Chicago begins, where the street signs turn from green for Evanston to black for Chicago, and where the bars get raunchier and the winos get winier and the cops start wearing those dumb caps with checkers around the band, so you don't know if you're going to get busted or have to pay cab fare.

Things get noisier around Howard, too. Evanston is a quiet little old town, and Chicago is a city for shitkickers. The two ideas meet, look, and part at Howard. It's a kind of psychological DMZ, if you take my meaning.

And that's where Pernicone's Funeral Home is, and that's where Cheryl Howard was laid out. Damn! You know, I just noticed the echo in names?

Anyhow, I'd been there a few times. In my business, you get to know the local funeral homes. No, no, I'm not talking about killings and gangland slayings and Hollywood. I'm talking about the fact that funeral homes are where some of your friends end up, and more than that, where some of your best clients come from: the bereaved. Ask any lawyer.

And Vito Pernicone, who runs the place with his brother Carlo, is one of the truly nice guys I've met in the city. He's got a mop of gray hair and he's never been seen out of a three-piece gray suit, so he looks like a walking cigarette ash, except with a name like Vito Pernicone you'd think twice before rattling his cage, no?

And he's a pussycat. Takes his mother to mass three times a week, I mean, and couldn't hurt a moth unless the moth was armed and stoked on PCP. He also—and this is the one thing about him I don't like—plays chess like it was a blood sport. One afternoon I was playing black to his white—lots of wine and classic Sicilian defense. He laughed, looked at me, and said, "Harry, *ragazze*, don't you know you can't defend against a Sicilian?" He took my queen in ten moves.

Vito happened to be there when we arrived and had the warmest greetings for Bridget. *"Carissima,"* he effused as we walked in. "It's been so long since I've seen you. *Che fa?"*

Bridget didn't miss a stitch. *"Sta bene, Vito,"* she said. "You look healthier than ever. You know my associate, Harry, I think?"

Vito looked and nodded at me. "Yes, I know Mr. Garnish," he said. I owed him forty bucks from a chess game, and I'd owed it to him for about six months.

Bridget told him what we were there for and Vito, adopting his professional air, bowed us into the room marked HOWARD.

There weren't many people in the room, which surprised me because I would have thought Cheryl would have had a lot of friends. Well, maybe she did. A lot of flowers there were, just not many people. Bridget and I signed the register and went up to the casket. Cheryl was there, all right. The morticians had done a good job covering up the mess in her skull, but they hadn't caught that smile I'd seen in the picnic photo, that smile that made her look so excited and like so much fun. She just looked at peace. And bored.

After a while Bridget crossed herself, so I knew it was time to stop pretending like I was praying too. We got up from the kneelers and Bridget walked toward a tall thin anemic-looking man sitting along the wall.

"Excuse me, are you Mr. Howard?" she said. Tall thin and anemic jerked his head and stammered, "Yes—yes." Do I know you?"

"In a way. I am Bridget O'Toole, and this is Mr. Garnish."

It's funny meeting somebody you've only talked to on the phone. It's not so much that they look different than you'd imagined, but you're always surprised at how accurate the human voice is at shaping the human body. Howard was nervous and birdlike in his movements, and looked even too skinny for the thin black suit he was wearing. He had the long, nicotine-stained fingers of a piano player and the nose of a goshawk. All topped by a bush marine cut of dirty-blond hair.

I didn't like him.

"Can we go somewhere to talk?" asked Bridget. "I know this is an awful time for you, and, believe me, I share your grief, but there are a few questions I would really like to ask you."

I was along for the ride, I didn't know what the hell was going on, but any time I can get out of a funeral home I'll take any excuse. Thomas Howard seemed a little more doubtful but finally nodded, and we left, with Vito smiling and condoling his ass off till we got out the door.

In the coffee shop across the street from Pernicone's everything was bright, plastic, and noisy, just as everything back there had been velvet and silent. Howard's hands were shaking so badly that he had to bring the cup to his lips with both of them. I wondered if it was grief or if he'd fallen off the wagon. And then I thought what the hell, one way or the other life will always give you shaky hands.

After his first gulp of coffee, anyway, he seemed to settle down. "Miss O'Toole," he said. "Mr. Garnish. I'm sorry to be in such bad shape, but I'm sure you understand. Now, what can I do to help you?" He smiled.

"Well, Mr. Howard," said Bridget, "I wonder if you could simply enlighten me about your and Mrs. Howard's—Cheryl's—finances. I know that sounds like a terrible, crude thing to ask at this time, but I think it could be of great help in—in solving things."

Howard stared. "Finances? What do you mean, finances?"

"The two checking accounts, yours and hers," said Bridget.

"Two accounts?" said Howard. "We have—had—one account, at Evanston Federal. That's all I know about. If Cheryl has—had another one, I don't know anything about it. I'm very sorry, but I guess I can't be any help to you after all."

And then Bridget did something I've never seen her do as long as I've known her. She slurped her coffee. No, really, *slurped* it, with a long, lingering inhalation that was either lumbar pneumonia or deep meditation.

"You have helped," she said, dabbing at her lips with a paper napkin, "more than you know."

Conversation took, for a few minutes, the winding path it always takes when you're talking to someone who's just lost a loved one. You know—the weather, the traffic, congestion at O'Hare Airport, the basic sadness of life, and anything else except the central fact that somebody who was important to somebody else is dead. Howard eased up more, and I had to hand it to Bridget. She was making the guy feel half human again, even in spite of his loss.

"Miss O'Toole," said Howard after a while. "Mr. Garnish. I'm sorry I couldn't be more help to you, but you've both been a great help to me. You're both so kind to come by. I hope . . . well, I hope you'll join me after—after Cheryl's funeral."

I was moved, especially after the way I'd talked to him on the phone. I was about to say, "Oh, sure, man," but Bridget spoke first.

"I'm afraid not, Mr. Howard," she said. "I know how sad you are at this moment, but I also must admit that I have a constitutional aversion to dining with people I suspect of having committed murder."

Pregnant pause? You got it.

# 20

THOMAS HOWARD WAS the first to speak, though not very much to the point.

"What?" he said.

"What," said Bridget, "is the fact that I think you killed your wife, and that you are, sir, using me and Mr. Garnish as the most efficient alibis that you didn't kill her."

Enough is enough, as my old man always said after beer number twelve. "Bridget!" I said. "Christ, don't you see this guy's hurting?"

"Be still, Harry," she snapped—and I mean snapped. I was still. "Hurt? Of course poor Mr. Howard is hurt. He has lost his wife. I also think he caused that loss, and therefore his hurt must be even greater. Nevertheless, he is responsible for what now causes him so much pain."

The thing I noticed was that Thomas Howard hadn't yet gotten up to leave. That bothered me. And now he spoke, but he didn't rise.

"Miss O'Toole, I don't believe that you can be this cruel. My God! My wife. I—I loved my wife. And my wife is dead back there and you're insinuating that I—"

"I am insinuating nothing, Mr. Howard," she said." I am stating my conviction that you killed Cheryl, and that is neither an insinuation nor a legal charge. It is a statement of fact about what I believe to be the case. Would you like to hear why I believe what I believe?"

Howard didn't say anything and didn't move.

Bridget went on. "You just told me that you didn't know your wife had a second checking account at your bank. But I know—never mind how—that accounts can be accessed through a Social Security number, and that your wife's account *was* accessed two months ago. Now who, sir, who except you would know that Social Security number? And why would you want to access it?"

I stared at him, he stared at her, and she looked into her coffee cup.

*"Why,"* Bridget went on, "is easy. You knew that more money was being spent by your wife than you were willing to spend. And then

you found that the checks drawn on your wife's account were all, or most, to a college student named Michelle Hill, with some also to Mr. Richard Schwartz, attorney at law. Am I correct so far?"

We all kept staring in our various directions.

"You, probably with the aid of another detective agency, then discovered the relationship between Cheryl and Michelle Hill—and, Mr. Howard, you simply could not live with it."

Howard started to rise. Bridget held up a hand. Howard sat back down.

"You hired us as a blind," she said. "You knew that your wife and Dick Schwartz were not having an illicit affair, but you also knew from her canceled checks that she had reserved a cabin for this month at Lake Manitonaqua. And you were in pain at the thought of the wife who once saved you being intimate with another man—not Dick Schwartz, but Michelle's father."

"But that was before me!" shouted Howard, loud enough that at least five orders of scrambled eggs swished and sloshed to the floor out of the hands of stunned waitresses.

She didn't budge. "Before, after. Is there really a difference to the jealous mind? No. There is not. You were in pain at the thought of your Cheryl in another man's arms. Consumed with anger that they had made a daughter. So you killed the mother."

Howard laughed. I didn't like the laugh.

"You fool!" he said. "You think any of that bilge proves anything or could stand up in court? They've already found who killed my wife, and it was that little twit Michelle. They've got her cigarettes by Schwartz's body and everything."

Bridget sighed. "In court? No, I suppose it wouldn't hold up in court. But we both know I'm right, don't we? And, since you mention it, Harry, could I have a cigarette?"

Without thinking, I offered her one. She took the pack out of my hand and showed it, open end first, to Howard.

"I've noticed a curious thing about cigarettes," she said. "Well, about cigarette packages, actually. What do you call that little, ah, that little piece of tinfoil at the top of the pack? The thing you tear open to get the cigarettes out?"

"Flap," I said. I figured it was time I took an active part in the deductive process.

"Flap," said Bridget. "Well, that's a good enough name. You'll notice that Harry did to his pack what most men do: he tore it all the way off and threw the flap away. But women don't do that, you know. They tend to tear the flap open, and then, after taking out a cigarette, fold the flap back. I wonder if you know why."

I didn't know why, but in a funny way I knew where she was going.

"They do that," she went on, "because women carry their cigarettes in a purse, usually, where it's very easy for the tobacco to spill and make a mess, while men tend to carry them in their breast or jacket pockets, permanently upright."

"Now," she went on, "when we found Mr. Schwartz, nearby there was a pack of Michelle's brand of cigarettes—a little too conspicuously, not to say carefully, placed. I was bothered by the obviousness of the pack at the time, and I also noticed that the flap had been torn all the way off. Do you smoke, Mr. Howard?"

"No," he said. And since I was sitting next to him, and since I noticed the rectangular bulge in his jacket pocket, I decided to be even more brilliant help than I'd been so far. I snaked out my hand and had his pack of Pall Malls before he knew what hit him.

"Good for you," I said. "It's a filthy habit. But it's damn nice of you to carry a pack around with you, just in case a pal needs a hit. I haven't had a Pall Mall in years. You mind?" I tapped one out of the pack and lit it. The flap was torn all the way off.

"When Michelle offered Harry a cigarette," Bridget said, "I noticed that her pack had the flap folded in the—what shall I say?— ladylike fashion. The discrepancy bothered me. So did the fact that you yourself never came to our office in person. So did the fact that you were so difficult to reach by phone on the morning of your wife's . . . death."

Howard lit a Pall Mall. He inhaled deeply and blew the smoke directly at Bridget. His hands weren't shaking anymore.

"That's what you call evidence? Cigarette packs, bank statements, and, for Christ's sake, not being able to get me on the phone at five or six in the morning? You know, lady, I should sue you for slander, and for damages too. You take a husband away from his wife's casket and you say *this?* Just who the hell do you think you are?"

It wasn't the weeping wimp I had spoken with over the phone. It was an arrogant son of a bitch. And that's the moment when I knew Bridget was right. Howard was guilty as piss in the snow.

"Mr. Howard," said Bridget. "You know you're not going to sue me, because you know if this case ever came to court you would lose. Oh, to be sure, you wouldn't be tried for murder. The evidence is too flimsy for a jury. But we both know, don't we? You are bereaved, but you are also defiant, and that suggests to me once again that I'm right.

"Shall I tell you what happened? After setting up Mr. Garnish and me, you drove to Lake Manitonaqua, probably camped out in the forest, and on the fatal night you stole into your wife's cabin, killed her, dressed her in a swimsuit, and dropped her in the lake. You had killed Mr. Schwartz, or perhaps drugged him, at the same time you killed Cheryl, so you returned to the cabin, dragged him into the woods, slit his throat, and left a package of Michelle's brand of cigarettes nearby, where it couldn't help but be found. That way you had your revenge upon the wife who was no longer your private virgin, on the lawyer who knew, and on the stepdaughter whose existence on earth you loathed. Very efficient. Except, of course, you couldn't have known that there would be a torrential rain that night that would prevent you from driving back to Wilmette in time to receive the phone call telling you that Cheryl was dead."

"I don't have to hear any of this," said Howard, grinding out his cigarette and rising. "You'd better get a lawyer, because I am going to sue for libel. And Garnish here is my witness."

Like Bre'r Rabbit, I just lay low and say nothing.

Bridget shifted her weight. "Of course, that's your right," she said. "But allow me to remind you of two things. First, you insisted that Michelle is guilty because of the cigarettes found by Mr. Schwartz's body. Now, I don't know what Sheriff Frost told you on the phone, but I would be very surprised if he mentioned those cigarettes, especially since I asked him not to before I left Wisconsin. And," she went on, droning out Howard's gurgle, "since I do think that *you* left the pack by the body, that means you must have known what brand Michelle does smoke, and that means that you must have, in one way or another, met her face to face. Would you like to meet her now, with her knowing who you are? Don't you see that if her case were to come to trial she would have been bound to recognize you? You couldn't very well stay away from your wife's murder trial."

Howard was silent. So was I.

"No," Bridget said, "even in that eventuality there would not be enough hard evidence to send you to condemnation. I, for one, would not respect a jury who could find you guilty on the facts that I know make you guilty. But people would know, wouldn't they? The press is such a nasty thing."

Howard didn't speak when we left the coffee shop, just walked back toward the funeral home. I asked Bridget if she would like a ride home, to which she of course said yes. Then I drove her home, stopped off at the Bambi Bar on the way to my place for a half of bourbon (that's a half pint, if you're a novice), and drove home to find Bandit.

I haven't told you about Bandit, have I? He's a cat, a stray cat who hangs around my apartment. Fur like a cheap rug, eyes like a South Side junkie, stoned all the time, and a giant pain in the ass. I told you I hate cats. But one night I found him starving outside my door, so I gave him some leftover meat loaf. Nobody, not even a cat, should starve. But then the son of a bitch adopted me. He comes to my door every morning, whines, has fleas so I have to buy him a flea collar, catches cold so I have to take him to the vet, wanders away for a few days so I worry if he's been hit by a car—hell, I might as well be married.

"Hi, shithead," I said to him as I unlocked the door. "Missed me, didn't you, you little scumbag?"

Bandit wasn't talking. Just got his fresh tuna fish, gave me a classic junkie now-I-got-my-fix-you-can-fuck-off look, licked his ugly chops, and strolled off into the night.

Marianne wasn't talking either. No answer. No fun. I turned on TV, my favorite night-light, and went to sleep.

And I woke up to the ten P.M. news, just in time to hear that a local man, Mr. Thomas Howard of Wilmette, had apparently committed suicide by drinking a quart of Scotch in less than ten minutes. He had been distraught at the recent murder of his wife, Mrs. Cheryl Howard, and had left a strange note reading "Congratulations, O & G. May you rot."

I was on the phone as soon I could get the cobwebs out of my eyes. "Bridget," I said. "Something has happened."

"I know, Harry," she said. "I didn't think it would turn out this way, but, dear, I can't really say I'm sorry. Michelle, that naughty girl, will go through the discomfort she deserves but cannot possibly be punished for a crime she didn't commit. And Mr. Howard did bother to send us a certified check for our expenses before he chose his— unfortunate way out. It was decent of him."

I couldn't believe it. "Don't you care?" I shouted over the phone. "Damn, Bridget, don't you care this poor bastard is dead that way because of you?"

"Harry, dear," she said. "Believe me, I care. I hope that Mr. Howard did not die in full despair. But I had to confront him with his guilt, and with the fact that someone knew of that guilt. Remember Saint Thomas's harlot? She gave full satisfaction for wages proffered, and so did we—even to a killer."

"And remember what you said about enlightenment?" I said. "We may have found out who killed whom, but I'm damned if I think we found anything like enlightenment."

She sighed and hung up. I looked around and found the photo of Cheryl at the picnic, and wished I'd been there. Maybe—what the hell—to kiss her once. Just once.

I never had, you know.

# 21

THAT WAS AUGUST. Not one of the better months in my life, but then "better" is always a relative term, isn't it? A friend of mine once said that the great thing about sex is that it starts at great and works its way up; with me, as with most folks, life starts at okay and works its way down. I think they call it entropy.

The Cheryl Howard case was solved, right? Don't you just love it when they say on TV that the "case" is "solved" and Jack Lord can say "Book him, Dano—murder one" and you know the show is over and you can go to the john and get another Budweiser before the ten o'clock news?

I'll tell you something. Nothing is *ever* solved. Oh, sure, you can find out who axed who on the night of whatever, and with enough hard fact you can even send the son of a bitch over for it, fifteen to thirty, eligible for parole in ten. But then you ask yourself, why did he ax whomever? And as soon as you ask that you start making problems that can't be solved, unless you want to analyze the poor bastard's whole life, and you don't, so you just assume that the law's solution is the solution, and you know it's bullshit but you repress the knowledge because otherwise you'd spend your life trying to understand all the ways people can be unhappy, and that's madness.

Take Cheryl Howard.

It bothered me, and it bothered Bridget, and when Bridget and I are bothered about the same thing you know there's something wrong. Not that we talked about it. Much. But every once in a while Thomas Howard's suicide would sort of come up in conversation, and Bridget and I would do worse than talk about it. We wouldn't talk about it, each of us knowing that we were thinking about it. If you've ever had a bad marriage, you know what I'm talking about.

People kept bouncing checks and kept keeping Motel 6s open with people they weren't supposed to be in Motel 6s with, so the banks, the collection agencies, the Motel 6s, O'Toole Investigations, and I all stayed in business. Chicago did what Chicago always does in the fall

—turned just cold enough to get beautiful. Remember how burning autumn leaves used to smell when you were a kid? It made you want to buy a new sweater, a fresh notebook for school, and go to a football game. Well, in September the Chicago air looks and feels just like those leaves used to smell.

Bridget sailed, serene, through the office every day. Ben Gross caught a bad cold and had to lay off work for a whole week, so I lost a lot of good conversation and a lot of unwanted tea. I even drove to his little bungalow one night—he lives in Schaumburg, about fifteen miles from Skokie—with a pint of brandy. He met me at the door in a bathrobe that must, *must* have been born about the time of the Crimean War, cocked a hairy eyebrow at the brandy, then at me, and said, "Harry, it's a *mitzvah*, and I thank you. But why, my dear boy, do the goyim think that this stuff is some kind of universal cure? You never heard, I guess, of chicken soup—Jewish penicillin? Keep the brandy, I think maybe you like it more than I do. But come, have a little soup with me."

Ben got better. A few weeks later Kai Winding, that cheerful man who practically invented the bebop style of trombone playing, died. I stayed up all night, playing his records and toasting his memory with the brandy Ben had refused, and called in sick the next day. My life is so eventful, sometimes I could throw up.

And I almost forgot about Cheryl Howard.

Then, one afternoon in early November, I was puttering around the apartment—it was a Saturday—when my doorbell rang.

Now, if everybody used current as often as my doorbell rings, we wouldn't ever have an energy crisis. So, dig, I pulled on my shoes, frantically hollering, "Be right there," checked to see if my fly was zipped—it was—and opened the door.

It was Bandit. And Michelle.

"Hi," I said brilliantly.

"Can I come in for a minute?" she said. Bandit had already made his way to the couch and the afghan my aunt knitted me a few years ago. It's his fubby now; I can't use it anymore.

Her hands were shaking as she lit a cigarette. "I want to hire you," she said.

She hadn't gotten any uglier, and I guess I hadn't gotten any smarter. "Uh?" I uhhed.

"Look," she said. "I know this sounds weird, but I have to talk to somebody and you're the only—do you have an ashtray? Thanks. You're the only private eye I know." I liked that "private eye"; it made me feel like I was in a John Houston film. Black and white, of course. "They gave me a suspended sentence," she went on, "because . . . well, just because."

She meant for the blackmail charge. She hadn't been charged with the murders; the evidence was just too thin. And I could just see the judge looking at those melon breasts, thinking, hooters, and saying "first offense." If you're going to *get* busted, you can do worse than *having* a bust.

"And what do you want to hire me for?" I asked.

"To find out who really killed my mother," she said. Just like that. Now, I told you I'd forgotten, almost, about Cheryl Howard. But you knew it was a lie when I told you, didn't you? With the words "my mother," suddenly the picture in my mind revived again: that nice woman at the picnic. The one I never got to kiss.

My mouth tasted like tin. "Thomas Howard killed—your mother," I said. "And then he killed himself. I think, Michelle, you'd better go."

"No!" she said, rising out of her chair. "You and that fat lady you work with—"

"For," I put in.

"Okay, *for*. You and that fat lady you work for may have convinced yourselves and everybody else that Mr. Howard was responsible for my mother's death. But I know he wasn't."

"Know?" I said. "That's a pretty strong word in a business like this, Michelle."

"Know," she said. "Look. I don't have anything to hide anymore. I was way the hell mixed up back there in a lot of bad stuff. And I know what a bitch I was being to my mother. And I know what a bitch I was being, man! But you've got to believe me, I was working for somebody else."

My ears perked up and my palms started to sweat.

"I don't know who," she went on, calming my ears and drying my palms, "but I know that somebody was taking bread off the top of the operation. I only got paid in cash, see."

"But you must have been contacted at the beginning," I said. This was getting out of my depth. But then, almost everything does, sooner or later.

"Oh, sure," she said. "But I was contacted the way you get contacted for a chain letter. You know about those things? It was Kerry who contacted me. Yeah. Surprised, aren't you? Sweet little, nice little Kerry. She came up to me one day and told me that if I wanted to pick up some extra bucks, I could maybe check back on some of the ID's—license plates and stuff, you know—of, some of the guests, and if I could find anything funny, maybe pass it along."

"To her?"

"Oh, no, not to her. There was a place at the resort to drop the information, and to get instructions back about what to do about it."

"And you never tried to find out who was running the show? That doesn't seem too likely to me."

"Why should I?" she said. "I was getting paid, and I sure as hell didn't want to get any more mixed up in a blackmail operation." She caught herself and giggled—no, I swear, giggled, just like a little girl. "Know what I mean? That's why I didn't say anything about any of this to the judge. But I thought, well, like . . . I could tell you."

I looked to Bandit for advice, but he was twitching, dismembering mice or whatever in his sleep. Never count on a cat.

"Tell me?" I said. "Tell me what? That now that your mother is dead you've got a case of the regrets? That you're really a good girl after all, and all of a sudden you want to prove that to the world? Michelle, Michelle. Life isn't *The Rockford Files* and you don't always get a second chance before the last commercial. Didn't they teach you that in college?"

One of my best things, I've always said, is saying the wrong thing at the wrong time. She started to cry, the way you hate to see people cry —noiselessly, mouth pulled into a death's-head grin, tears but no sound coming out. I hate that.

I hate it because Newman or Eastwood or, God help us, Telly Savalas would go all tough-sensitive when that happened and would say the right thing to keep things moving and get the little girl (little! har har!) back on the track.

But I didn't even know what the right track was, let alone how to switch her onto it. So I did what I would always do in moments of maximum stress. I sat there and lit a cigarette.

I mean, Bridget O'Toole, to my sorrow, is usually *right*. And everything she'd deduced about Thomas Howard being the guy who eighty-sixed Cheryl made perfect sense, just like one of those Agatha

Christie mysteries where Miss Marple or whatever his name is, Hercule something, walks in after the crime and looks at everything in the room and picks out the killer because a teacup is out of place or some happy horseshit like that.

And then, while I waited for Michelle to stop crying, I realized that I'd always laughed at the few stories like that that I'd read. But Thomas Howard *had* killed himself. But Thomas Howard, as I'd known from my first phone conversation with him, was an Olympic-class flake capable of almost any silliness, up to and including that silliest of acts, suicide.

And wait a minute, I thought, what the hell had Bridget based her brilliant deduction on? Okay, she'd been right about Michelle being involved in blackmailing, and she'd been right about that just because she was smart enough to notice the typeface on the pasted letters—taped letters, I couldn't remember anymore—on the anonymous note. Good job, that, as my British friends would say (one of the advantages of being a Czech as opposed to an Irishman in Chicago is that you can *have* British friends). But Thomas Howard? Convicted of murder on the basis of a pack of cigarettes with the flap torn off the wrong way? God damn, that *was* the teacup placed in the wrong position.

But he had killed himself.

Bullshit. I wished I'd become a pharmacist. At least they got to deal with other people's headaches without contracting the headaches themselves.

Anyhow, while I went through that incredibly intricate logical process—ending, of course, with the conclusion that I didn't know what the hell I was doing—Michelle had stopped crying and seemed ready to talk again.

"Look," I said. "Do you have any hard evidence, any hard proof, that there was a—a big ring involved in all this? Because if you do, you should be talking to the cops, and if you don't, you shouldn't be talking to me."

"But I do know," she said, and I thought she was going to start crying again. "I just . . . know, you know?"

Well, there was no arguing with reasoning like that, now was there? I looked at her, and then at Bandit, asleep in his anemic bliss on the fubby that was supposed to have been my bedspread. Cats are generally a pain in the ass, but what the hell, they've got a right to cut it, too, and Bandit at least knew where to crash for his next dish of tuna or potpie or TV dinner. Michelle didn't look like as nice a person as my noncat, but I thought she might need a break too.

Besides, it would be my first independent case. Hooray.

"Okay." I sighed. I'll look into this mess for you. Now where do you want me to start?"

She looked relieved and puzzled at the same time—not an easy thing to do. "Start?" she said.

"Start," I said. "Look, sweetcakes, you're telling me that your momma was killed by somebody besides the guy that killed himself because everybody thought he killed your momma. You're telling me that somebody I knew was guilty as hell wasn't guilty as hell. That insults my intelligence, but my intelligence has been so insulted already that I don't care. Just don't care. You're telling me that there's a big, mysterious blackmail ring in north Wisconsin that's responsible for your momma getting offed. Like in a spy novel, yeah? So, okay. It's a crock, you know; any reasonably smart person in the business would tell you that right off. But I'll buy it, for the moment, because—well, because. I'll look into it, like they say. But I've got to have a place to start, dig? A name, an address, a suspicion—and *not* Kerry Madura, who's probably just as much a cog in the wheels as you are. Were."

Her eyes got wide and sexy, but by now I was used to that, at least from her. I wondered what Marianne was doing this afternoon; I hadn't talked to her for a while.

"Oh, gee," she said. "I don't know what I could tell you about who's really running things. But maybe Mr. Connors would know something about it. I mean, it's not like he was, you know, involved in anything, but he might, like, know, you know?"

Great. "Oh, gee," coming from a kid like that, was a sure sign that she was being bullshit—*disingenuous* I think is the college word for it. And mentioning Ross Connors was, then, a sure sign that Ross didn't have a damn thing to do with the blackmail ring, or a sure sign that he did. I was lost, halted without an effort to break through. But Cheryl was dead, and Dick Schwartz was dead, and Thomas Howard was dead, and if the whole damn thing had been for nothing . . .

My dad used to say about ugly situations, "It's just like shit. The more you stir it, the worse it stinks."

I picked up my stirrer.

"Right," I said. "I'll look around and see what I can find out."

"Oh, thank you," she gushed. Gushing I never liked. "And, uh, shouldn't I pay you a retainer, a fee? Something?"

"You back in college?" I asked.

"Uh, yeah," she said. College girls are so articulate.

"Okay," I said. "Save half your lunch money every month and three quarters of your dope money, and we'll dicker if this turns out to be anything."

She wide-eyed blinked again—I was getting kind of tired of it—and mumbled her way out of the apartment. I lurched toward the icebox where there were two Ballantine Ales left, fried myself a mess of mushrooms and garlic (when you live alone you don't have to chop the garlic too fine), and kicked back, turning on the public radio just in time to hear that Zoot Sims, that happiest and most listenable of tenor saxes, had died in a New York hospital. Fuck all, I thought, pulled my shoes back on, and sailed out the door to buy a quart of Scotch and conduct yet another private wake.

All my friends were dying on me: Cheryl Howard too. A pal of mine who teaches philosophy but still plays good poker once said to me after a long malt evening, "Harry, old man, this is not a world in which I choose much longer to exist." Well, yeah.

By the way, I never saw Michelle again.

# 22

I TOLD YOU that Chicago is great in the fall, didn't I? Another reason it's great is because it's great for hangovers; I mean, the sun rises so damn late. The morning after my one-man wake for Zoot—Sunday— I galumphed out of bed, dialed Bridget O'Toole, and told her that I was reinvestigating the Cheryl Howard murder case, and all without once gagging or missing a syllable.

Bridget wasn't as impressed as I was with my ability to operate my mouth.

"Really, Harry?" she said. "I thought we had come to an efficient conclusion of that business. What could possess you to pry into it again?" There was something cold in her voice, something that I hadn't heard before, in all the time we'd worked together. She didn't sound like Bridget.

Why not? I wondered, and then it came to me: damn it all, she'd been told she might be *wrong*.

Maybe there is a God.

"What could possess me, Bridget?" I said into the receiver as I flip-topped the last can of ale in the known universe. "Hell, I don't know. Maybe it's what you told me about, sat—Something."

"Sattva," she said. "Enlightenment. But, Harry, I fail to see—"

"Yeah, Sattva," I cut in. "That's it, and maybe you do fail to see. It's just that, you know, you reasoned this damn thing out so perfectly and we got that poor bastard Howard nailed, and like that, and there's still something wrong with the whole business. Don't you feel it?"

She didn't feel it. Or rather, I think she did, but she sure as hell wasn't going to admit that maybe an innocent if fucked up man canceled his own ticket because she had made a mistake. She told me I was on my own, and not to charge any of this to company time (company time! business being like it was, you could piss all our company time into a bottle of Michelob), and hung up.

Damn! I thought to myself. Here I am, with a chance to prove to

Bridget that she maybe isn't, after all, as smart as she claims not to be. Even a blind pig finds a truffle once in a while, hey? Michelle's story about the great Wisconsin blackmail ring sounded about as convincing as those conspiracies from Planet Zord I watched on the Saturday morning cartoons, and there wasn't even a cold trail to follow, and any cop will tell you that a murder not solved within forty-eight hours isn't likely to be solved at all (don't tell me about Manson and Josef Mengele—those guys practically advertised). And I knew I wasn't about to see a dollar of Michelle's money for this. But damn! if I could prove that Bridget had been wrong, that all that lovely logic had for once screwed up . . . Well, there's no real union of the nebbishes of the world, but I was beginning to feel like their representative. In other words, I was beginning to believe that what I was *supposed* to find out was what I *wanted* to find out and what with luck I *would* find out. That's not logic, but as Martin O'Toole used to tell me, if this business ran on logic, we'd all be wearing cheaper suits. (I didn't even own a suit, but for the moment I repressed the knowledge.)

Bandit interrupted my dreams of glory by scratching at my door to get out and staring at me with his big sick little-old-man eyes. The little bastard isn't healthy, but he's careful about my carpet. "Okay, asshole," I grunted, opening the door. "What is it, one or two?" And noticed my copy of the Sunday, *Chicago Tribune* on the stoop. While Bandit mroawed the cat version of "So long, sucker; see you for lunch" I carred the *Trib* back to the sofa, flicked the Zoot Sims tape back on, and started settling in to a Sunday morning suspended animation.

My eyes were already more than half glazed when, with a shock—I mean a *real* shock,—I realized that the *Tribune* is, or was on that day, what it claims to be: "the World's Greatest Newspaper." I jolted to the phone, losing half my head (the hangover was still in its ICBM mode), dialed the number from the page, read them my credit card number, cinched the deal, and then fished around in my desk until I found my address book and dialed the number in Wisconsin, hoping like hell I hadn't just blown eighty bucks I didn't have on a chance that wouldn't pay off. The great thing about hangover thinking is that it's so *fast*. The one drawback is that it's often so *dumb*.

I got a busy signal. They always sound like insults, don't they? So I did the grown-up thing: called the same number three times in the next five minutes, slammed down the phone in disgust, finished the finger or so of Scotch, took a shower, got dressed, wished I hadn't finished the Scotch, let Bandit back in—he likes to watch *Meet the Press*, since the guys on it are usually about as smart as he is—and dialed again. There was the reassuring long burp of a ring at the other end.

"Hello?"

"Hi. Ross Connors? Harry Garnish here."

The laugh at the other end was genuinely warm. "Harry!" Ross said. "God, boy, how've you been?"

"Oh, you know, hanging on by my fingernails as usual. Listen, Ross, why I called is, I just stumbled into a couple free tickets to the Chicago Lyric Opera. They're doing"—I had to check the paper—"uh, *The Magic. Flute*, and I wondered if maybe you'd like to come down and see it with me and make a night of it."

"You're kidding!" Ross said. *"The Magic Flute?* Who's Papageno?"

"Who's . . . ?" I began, wondering if he was talking about an Italian dinner before the opera. But he saved me.

"Oh, hell, what does it matter?" he went on. "That's damn nice of you, Harry. Especially after all—after all the trouble we've been through. Yeah, I'd love to. What's the date?"

I told him that it was a week from Tuesday, he told me that that would be terrific for him, insisted that he spring for dinner before and drinks after, and agreed to meet me at the Palmer House on the afternoon of the performance. Winter hadn't yet begun to fully strangle the city, so we could even walk from the Palmer House to the Lyric. If we were brave.

I hung up feeling very pleased with myself. Ross was a nice guy and I'd like to see him again. If I got him juiced enough—and you can get *anybody* juiced enough—I could find out something about this mysterious, grand, dark blackmail ring that was supposed to have offed Cheryl Howard. And I'd be seeing my first opera. Well, no plan is perfect.

At least I would be meeting him and dealing with this whole bundle of nonsense on my turf. I mean, the woods, the tiny lakes, the vacationers with their goddamn hiking shorts, all that was a little confusing to me. I like cities, with street signs and directions you don't need a compass to read and a cop at every major intersection.

It's real life, you know? Not natural foods and beautiful sunrises and John Denver.

Here I could work. Lake Michigan was always to the east, Lake Shore Drive took its S-curve a mile and a half from the Loop, there would never be lights in Wrigley Field even if the Cubs wanted them —whose baseball team was it, anyway?—and juice would always keep the wheels turning smoothly. And everybody could bitch from here to Tuesday about what was wrong with the city they loved to live in instead of mumbling *Boy's Life* crap like "Golly, Margaret, isn't the sunlight lovely through the pine trees?"

I mean, here you didn't have to worry about the muskrats or whatever creeping into your bed at night. They were all safe and well-fed where they belonged, in the Lincoln Park Zoo.

I was getting so good at making dates, I decided, that I ought to try my hand with Marianne again. A guy, yawning, answered her phone. Exit Sunday.

The next week was uneventful, except for one really nice messy tracking assignment—the other woman turned out to be the other man, or rather boy (he was working his way through college, for Christ's sake)—and except for the fact that the Bears were beginning to look like they actually might *do* it this year (by the time you read this, you know that they did, and take that, New England Patriots). Bridget was huffy around the office, though I didn't bring up the Howard business again, and I spent a lot of afternoons staring at the phone and convincing myself not to call Marianne again.

Came *Magic Flute* Tuesday, none too soon. I took the El to the Palmer House and got there about an hour before I was supposed to meet Ross. That was deliberate, because I knew I was going to be sitting through an opera and figured I could use fortification. Actually, I figured I could use a nice state of semiconsciousness.

Ross came into Don the Beachcomber's bar on the button, and on martini number three. Now, I'd like to tell you that the big cowboy looked uneasy and out of place in the big city surroundings; in fact, I'd been sort of counting on it, since if he was uneasy it would help my oh-so-clever design for weaseling some information out of him.

But by now, you know my luck.

He was wearing a three-piece blue pinstripe with a maroon silk tie that made my rumpled brown corduroy jacket (I *told* you Ben Gross is a bad dry cleaner) and yellow turtleneck look about as classy as a warm-up suit. Less; they tell me jogging is in. And the same *Arizona Highways* smile that in the woods made him look like Trapper Bob, here, in this outfit, made him look like an investment counselor you'd trust with your last dime.

"Harry!" he beamed, giving me a two-handed hand-shake. "Good to see you, pal!" And glancing at the debris in front of me on the bar, "Looks like you're a little ahead of me. Want to have another before dinner?"

I ordered another vodka mart, and Ross completed his transformation and my doubts about this whole thing by ordering a perfect Rob Roy, specifying Johnnie Walker Black Label Scotch, Martini & Rossi —not Tribuno—vermouth, and a lime twist.

I mean, if I was trying to impress the country mouse with my streetwise ways, I might as well have ordered a can of Sterno and a straw.

Dinner and the opera went the same way, with a lot of friendly talk about not much in particular. We might as well have been old army buddies trying to get together after years apart, and I've got to say that Ross carried more than his half of the cheerfulness.

Don't ask about the opera itself. Ross was nodding and smiling beside me all through it. I was trying to figure out when the magic flute would come on, and what the hell it had to do with anything, and why there was this one guy dressed like a bird, and how come he wound up with a girl dressed like a bird. And I love Mozart, but not when I have to listen to German or Italian as well as to him.

After it was over, just about when both my legs and my ass were stone asleep and I was beginning to worry about what you do when your lungs go numb too, Ross suggested a nightcap or two at his hotel, the Holiday Inn on Lake Shore Drive. I had already given up any hope of getting anything out of the evening and was kicking myself for spending the eighty bucks in the first place.

"Well, man," I said, as we strolled through the Lyric lobby, "it's kind of late, and you've got to get back tomorrow, so . . ."

He laughed and slapped—no, pounded me on the back. "Harry, for God's sake," he said. "Come on. We'll take a cab and you can get something out of the evening. I mean, old hoss, I can tell how much you enjoyed *Die Zauberflote,* and I surely do appreciate your being so quiet while I was loving it. Let me take you to Rick's at the Holiday Inn. We can catch Shearing's last set—he's playing there tonight, you know—and then you can tell me why the hell you bought those tickets that you told me were free, and what you really want to find out from me. Though"—and his face got serious—"I got a kind of feeling I know what this is all about."

# 23

LOOK, I *told* you I was not exactly a master of disguise. Like, I wouldn't go up against Lamont Cranston or any of those guys from *Mission: Impossible*. But this was a tad dicey, even for me.

I waited till we were seated at Rick's—Shearing was on break—before I sprung the big question.

"Ross," I said, "how'd you know?"

He laughed over the rim of his gin and tonic. "Harry, I like you. I really do. But hell, buddy, we just know each other from a few pretty unpleasant days in the woods. Now, would you really, with two tickets to the Lyric, think of calling me up just to celebrate old times? Damn, man, we don't *have* any old times! And I know you aren't exactly the toast of Chicago, but you've got to have a few friends down around here you'd treat to a free ticket."

"So," I said lamely (and I mean *lame*), "you didn't buy all this from the beginning?"

"Not really. But when you gave the doorman our tickets tonight, your credit card receipt fell out of the envelope. Harry, free tickets don't come with a Visa slip in your own name." He handed me the slip, grinning like he'd swallowed the Mr. T of canaries. "Anyhow, I did love the performance, and I do thank you for your trouble. Now. What can I do for you?"

What he could do for me, I was thinking, was help me get into a business I could really hack, like maybe janitoring in a whorehouse in Cleveland. But Shearing was being led back to the bandstand, and much as I love Shearing and much as I love Rick's, business is business, I thought, forgetting that nobody was *paying* me for this.

So, "Look," I said. "We can't talk while Shearing is playing. How about we just split and take a walk around the block? I know it's a shitty night, but—"

"No problem." He smiled and signaled the waitress over for the tab. I took a longing last look at my untouched martini—parting *is* such sweet sorrow—and decided that I'd better have as clear a head as I could for the rest of the night.

Rick's is on the access road off Lake Shore Drive, which means that during winter (don't tell me about Willard Scott—"winter" in Chicago begins in September and ends around Easter) it's a terrific place to walk if you like sleet in your face and the Hawk, the Lake Michigan wind, cutting through your three layers of clothes. The Hawk was out that night, but Ross pretended he didn't mind. Foreigners are always like that.

"Okay, Harry, what gives?" he said.

"What gives," I answered, wondering how long my lips would keep working in the cold, "is that I feel funny about the Cheryl Howard thing. But you knew that, didn't you?" Never look at a guy when you're asking him something important. Look at the ground and keep walking.

"I figured," I heard him say. "I figured it would be something like that. But, hell, Harry, you and Miss—what—Miss O'Toole practically wrapped the whole thing yourselves. I mean, Mr. Howard did . . . Well, you know."

I turned on him now, and looked him square in the eyes, just like good old John Wayne. "Me and Miss O'Toole?" I said. "Me and Miss O'Toole? Ross, man, me *and* Miss O'Toole didn't do jumping jack shit, as far as I can see. Miss—Bridget, for Christ's sake, she made a few passes with her cape and wand and came up with a poor confused bastard who looked guilty enough to off himself. Does that mean anything?"

For the first time, Ross looked bothered. "But he left a note, the papers said. Didn't he?"

As usual, I was getting madder than I had meant to be. "Yeah, Jack," I said. "He left a note. And you know what the note said? You remember what the note said? 'Congratulations, G and O, may you rot.' Some confession for a guy who's just killed his wife, right? It's been nagging at me since Howard eighty-sixed, and lately it's been a burr up my ass."

He stopped walking and looked at me strangely. "And what else?" he said. Like I told you, I can lie to anybody. I just hate meeting guys I don't *like* to lie to.

"Yeah," I said, trying to light a cigarette in the wind. The Hawk won. "What else is I had a talk with Michelle, and she—"

"Here," he said, and took my matches out of my hand, cupped his hands like the goddamn Marlboro Man, and lit my Lucky. "And Michelle said," he went on while I puffed, "that there's some kind of big blackmail ring in the resorts, with some mysterious fella at the top recruiting college kid workers to juice the clients, *no es verdad?*"

"*Es verdad* as all hell," I said, trying not to chew my cigarette, which at least was a filter tip. "Ross, if this is true, why didn't you tell me about it when— Well, you know? And if it's true and it did have something to do with Cheryl's death, why the *fuck* didn't you tell me, or Luther Frost, or somebody?"

Of course, I didn't think to ask the most important question.

He sighed, and said, "Harry, do you mind if we go back to my room to finish this? It's getting a little cold for me."

I told you, foreigners. Chicagoans know that it's always too cold, and aren't ashamed to bitch about it. We trudged back to the Holiday Inn in silence.

# 24

ROSS'S ROOM IN the Holiday Inn was huge and even had an icebox, which I didn't know they had in Holiday Inns but was grateful for when he pulled a bottle of Absolut vodka out of the freezer compartment. He'd even put some lemon twists and buffalo grass into the bottle before supercooling it, the way the Russians do.

"I guess I'm a real philosopher." He smiled, pouring us both a shot. "Always looking for the Absolut. A little pepper in yours?"—fishing a pepper shaker out of his overnight bag. Some backwoodsman, I thought. If Daniel Boone married James Bond . . .

"Thanks, no," I said. "Now if we could talk, I think I asked you a question. Is this *mishegoss* about a blackmail ring true or not?"

Ross gulped down his vodka—that's the way you do it—and sighed. "Harry, I don't know if it's true or not. But I know there've been rumors for—oh, hell. For a long time now. And I know that if it's true, I don't want to *know* it's true."

"You don't want to *know?* God damn it, man, that's your *business.* You—"

"Harry," he interrupted. "Look around you. What do you see?"

"Uh, a Holiday Inn room with an icebox?"

He smiled. "No. What you see is the top deck of a cruise ship. The executive lounge in an airport. The streets in Disneyland. You know how many people run the engines on a cruise ship, Harry? Or clean the latrines or punch tickets or haul luggage in an airport? Or sweep those streets all day every day and service the rides and cook the food in Disneyland? Do you?"

"Okay," I said. "A lot. But—"

"There ain't no *but,*" he said, shifting to his Dan'l Boone mode (he was very good at it). "This place is megabuck, multinational, so spread out that it can only compete against itself. Same with Ramada, Marriott, Hilton, you name it. And through all those systems, how many people you think come here to screw somebody not their spouse? Try the population of Louisville—per day. Harry," he smiled again, "that's *your* business. Am I wrong?"

"Okay," I grunted. "Maybe you're even a little conservative. But—"

"No *but*," he repeated. "Harry, if there was some big get-the-foolers-around blackmail ring in one of these companies, do you know what would happen? Nothing would happen. It would be found out, it would be dealt with, it might make a few front pages, and Holiday Inn and Ramada and the rest would go on just like before. Did the rumor about worm bits in Big Macs hurt McDonald's? Hell, no. Did the Tylenol scares hurt Johnson and Johnson? Come on. When you're big, you're *big*. Who has to worry about scandals? Not the cruise ships. They stay afloat because people keep going to them no matter what. But politicians do, because they've got nothing to sell but their personalities. And *I* do, and the other fellas who run the little resorts in north Wisconsin do, because *if* this ring is true, people will just stay away. And if they stay away, we all start thinking about going back to the farm. No, man. I don't *want* to know. It may be there and it may not, and that's fine with me. You *want* to know what your credit rating is, or you want to keep charging?"

He poured himself another shot of vodka, and I wondered, for the don't-know-how-manyth time, how decent people wound up, or got forced into, playing weasel games with their own heads.

"So," I said. "The bogeyman may be there or he may not, but you and your pals just don't want to hear about it. But Michelle came to me, man, because she's *sure* he's there, and that she's been working for him, and that he had something to do with her mother's getting offed. Now, can we cut the crap about business management and get down to whether the kid has a point or not? I don't like thinking I caused the death of a poor dumb innocent bastard, and I know Bridget O'Toole wouldn't like the news either. And I'd like some more Absolut, please."

He stared, not reaching for the bottle. "You're not as much of a wimp as you like to show, are you?" he said.

"Well, maybe not quite," I said, pouring my own. "It's pretty easy to jerk my chain, I admit. But after the third or fourth time even I get to paying attention. To things, I mean."

"Things?"

"Things. Like I know you like the opera. But you come down here, on a week's notice—and you say you knew I had something else in mind—and you treat me to drinks, dinner, and like that like I'm the Pope of Mars. And then, when we're walking around outside and I try to spring the Great Blackmail Plot on you, you tell me exactly what Michelle told me when she came to see me, and then get me up here for a lecture on capitalism with vodka on the side. Things like that, you know?"

He didn't quite smile, but he tried hard as hell to keep a straight face. "Well, the lecture's over," he said. "But at least you can have some more vodka."

"No thanks," I said as he extended the bottle. "Never try to drink a Czech under the table unless you've got insurance on your furniture. Wanna know what I think?" I leered at him, leaning across the coffee table and realizing I was a little drunker than I wanted to be. I was saying too much, and Martin O'Toole always used to say that the ideal investigator would be a nondeaf mute.

"What do you think, Harry?"

"I think I asked you the wrong question out there. I asked you why you didn't tell me about the big bad ring back—back when. I should've asked you why you told me *now*. But I don't gotta—don't hafta—fuck it. Don't have to ask you now. You told me because you knew I was gonna—going to ask you anyhow. Because you and Michelle set me up for this, didnya?" Christ, my head was splitting all of a sudden. I really wanted out of that hot room and back on the El to Evanston. Ross just sat and stared at me.

"What I want to know," I went on, fumbling for a cigarette that Ross lit for me, "is why you set me up? I mean, this whole thing was over with, right? Right. Hell, I may have thought Cheryl Howard was the most beautiful, precious girl I ever saw, but her death was solved, right? Right. Jesus, do you know how little time I spent with her? I never even kissed her, Ross."

Fuck, I thought, I'm on the edge of a crying jag. Something is not right.

"Ross? Ross? Wha'd you put in my drink here?" I wasn't quite sure which of the two Rosses across the table I was talking to. He stood up, and he was *huge*. Or rather, they were both *huge*.

"Nothing in your drink here, Harry," he said in a voice like a bad long-distance connection. "Maybe a little something back in the

Palmer House, but I can't pronounce its name. Wouldn't you like to lie down for a while?"

What a great idea. What a spectacular idea. I'd sleep for a while, and then Ross and I could finish our conversation about whatever it was so important to get settled. He really was a hell of a nice guy as he led me to the bed and helped me off with my clothes.

I told you I never saw Michelle after she came to my apartment. I lied. The next morning, when I woke up with the kind of hangover that makes your eyebrows hurt, I saw her again. She was nude, lewd, and looking screwed. She was in twelve Polaroid photos on the pillow beside my head. Or what was left of my head. In the photos she was in bed with two other girls and three other guys, only one of whom I recognized—me, drugged, fugged, and lewdly hugged by everybody else.

On the back of the last photo was a phone number and the scrawled message THERE ARE MORE CALL TODAY.

My clothes were neatly folded on the chair across from the bed. That, I thought through my headache, was a nice touch.

# 25

PHOTOGRAPHS, I THOUGHT. Voices over the phone. Torn cigarette packs. Cheryl's photos at the beginning of the whole thing, Thomas Howard's phone call, Bridget's insight about how men and women open packs of fags, and now I was in the picture too; me and Michelle. I didn't remember a goddamn thing after Ross put me to bed—I guess *in* bed is the better phrase—but I hoped I'd had a good time. I hadn't had a good time in a long time.

Vodka, I thought. The bottle of Absolut was still on the coffee table, and Ross had told me it, at least, wasn't drugged. And why not trust such a nice guy? And how else keep my hands from shaking and my eyes from dancing? I swigged from the bottle—if they used to call it a "belt," I had the whole damn harness—and waited for my mind to clear, or at least to unmurk a little.

Go ahead: tell me that mind altering substances are just a crutch. And then I'll tell you that if you've got one leg in your head, a crutch is damn well what you need.

My mind unmurked. A little. Photos and phone calls and cigarette packs and more photos, I kept thinking while I pulled on my pants, etc. (I was better at it than I thought I'd be—only fell down one time). This whole business was so—what's the word?—*abstract* that I wasn't sure I could really deal with it. And, oh yeah, there was Thomas Howard's suicide note which may or may not have been a suicide note and a confession to the murders back at Lake Manitonaqua.

I called the front desk and found out that the room was paid up till noon, which was just fine because it was nine thirty and I had exactly five dollars in my pocket and was overdrawn on both my credit cards. I called the number on the back of the photos of Michelle and me and got a recorded message from "Wisconsin Development Corporation" telling me that if I left my name and number they'd get back to me. I gave them the name Inspector Clarence Carp, and the number of the Skokie Homicide Division. Well, they don't actually call it "homicide," they call it Crimes Against People—CAP, as opposed to

Crimes Against Property—you got it, CAP again—but I figured, why not louse them up? I mean, they were going to blackmail *me*? Point one, I didn't have any reputation to ruin, and point two, I didn't have any money to save it even if there had been in the first place anything to save. It was like the old Jack Benny gag: "Your money or your life," says the robber to Benny. Two beats. "I'm thinking, I'm thinking," says Benny. Biggest laugh he ever got, he swore. With me, it was more like, "Your money or your life," to the punch line, "You can get fifty percent off on either," but you get the idea. Biggest headache I ever had.

But I *was* thinking, to my surprise. I was thinking photos, phone calls, and other abstractions. And this last business was so patently phony, misdirected, or whatever the hell you want to call it, that I began to see something. No, not a solution, but at least the glimmerings of the real problem.

And the real problem was not, who had killed Cheryl Howard? but, why did Cheryl Howard have to die? It was like in geometry class when you suddenly dug that the surface area of a sphere didn't have jackshit to do with the area of a circle because there was, you know, another dimension there, man.

You know that feeling when you get the shape of what's nagging your ass even though you don't know what's nagging your ass? It's a great feeling, because you don't really have to do a hell of a lot about it, just sit there and think to yourself how smart you're about to be.

I was still a little drunk or drugged or whatever, so I took another swig of vodka, and since I was thinking like Bridget O'Toole, I called Bridget O'Toole. It was already ten A.M., and I thought she might be worried, anyway.

She was. "Harry, where *are* you?" she demanded as soon as I got through Brenda to her. "Don't you know that we've got two new clients to see you this afternoon?"

In self-defense, I said, "Bridget, please don't talk so loud over the phone. I'm in a room at the Lake Shore Drive Holiday Inn, and I'm half snockered, and I'm about to get more snockered, and I *know* that you were wrong about Mr. Thomas Howard and that he didn't kill his wife, and I—For Christ's sake, Bridget, I need your help."

She could have said a lot of things, but she said the best. "You'd better come in," she said. "I'll send Knobby in the company car. He'll be waiting for you at the front entrance in forty-five minutes." And hung up.

I especially liked the bit about the "company car." The company car was a 1978 Camaro that Bridget had bought but refused to drive, and that nobody else wanted to drive. We needed it, she said regally, in case there was ever an important occasion for us to show our quality. Knobby and I would look at one another and think, Us? Important occasion? Quality?

Anyway, I got in when I found Knobby waiting for me outside the front entrance. And he was as much a sight for sore eyes as he ever is. Or sore ears.

"Hey, Boopsie!" he crowed as I crawled into the seat beside him. "You look like horseshit from hell! Wha'd you do, rip it off with one of the State Street Sadies? Balls, man. Hope you didn't forget your condominium."

Knobby—Mr. Conn, as I like to call him to his, I hope, everlasting annoyance—Knobby and I have a secure relationship. "Yeah, right," I said as I fastened my seat belt. "Except for that red fucking bow tie you got on, she looked a lot like your momma." Nobody laughed, but at least I didn't have to try and make conversation on the way back to Skokie.

Lake Shore Drive—I think I told you this—Lake Shore Drive from the Holiday Inn north to Skokie is one of the nice things you can do to yourself. Dig: half drugged, with two megaslugs of vodka, and confused as hell and being driven by a twerp with the instincts of Attila the Hun and the mind of a runt broccoli, in the November morning sunlight it's *still* beautiful. No, breathtaking, and I *mean* that. It took the glaciers eons or whatever to scratch out the lakes of northern Wisconsin. But it took human beings less than a hundred years, after the Big Fire, to build that dance of buildings. I've never seen London or Paris, and I don't have to. I know what a city looks like. It looks like my city.

# 26

BEN GROSS WAS back, healthy, and busy ruining the jackets and skirts of an unsuspecting public, and I waved to him on my way to the office.

Bridget was waiting for me in her hothouse cubicle, and Phil was looking about as wilted as I felt, but then Phil always looks that way. "Hi," I said brightly. "You watered Phil lately? You know, Bridget, sometimes I think you're trying to starve him just because he's the only vegetable here who really likes me."

Mother Superior was not amused. I swear to God, sometimes when she frowns you can almost see a ghostly wimple around her face. If *wimple* is the right word.

"Harry," she said. "What in the world have you gotten yourself— no, gotten us—into? I didn't like it, I confess, when you told me that you were looking at poor Mr. Howard's case again, and now I must say that it's becoming a positive annoyance. Please just tell me where you—we—stand in this matter."

I'd started the whole thing because I wanted, for once, to prove that Bridget had been terribly wrong, and that I was able to run down a case on my own. And now I was touched, really touched, by her including herself in my self-made problems: "we," not "you." Maybe, I thought generously, when I took over the agency I'd arrange a nice retirement party for her. It would be tax deductible, wouldn't it?

"Where I stand," I said, "is not exactly the right word. It's more like where I lay. Lie? Laid?" And I handed her the photos.

Her face didn't change: another minor disappointment for me. She examined each of the twelve Polaroids carefully, while Phil and I communed about the caprices of human destiny and such (I always talk better to plants).

"An interesting prelude, I must say," she did say when she'd finished her examination. "Now, would you like to give me the several thousand words I assume these pictures are worth?"

So I did. Starting with Michelle's visit to me, my calling Ross Connors, Mozart's *Magic Flute*, my less than magic fluke, the whole schmeer.

When I finished, Bridget did something weird. She started to cry. I don't mean weep or sniffle or get moist-eyed. I mean *cry*.

"Bridget," I said, "come on, it's not that bad."

If you ever want to stop somebody from breaking up before your very eyes, say something stupid enough to make them mad. I've been doing it all my life. Unintentionally.

"Not that *bad?*" she glared at me. "Not that *bad?*" Harry, don't you realize that this means I was wrong, terribly, unforgivably wrong about Mr. Howard. That poor man killed himself because of *me*, because of my damn—yes, *damn* arrogance, because I was so sure of myself, so sure that I could piece things together. Oh, Harry, I know you don't believe the way I do, but you have to see that I've sinned, and sinned in the worst way: through intellectual arrogance. I'll have to leave, of course. You can take over running the agency, can't you?"

I mean, God is a practical joker, right? I'd been waiting to hear those words from those balloon lips for years. And now I couldn't let her do it. She'd even said "damn," which in Bridget's vocabulary equals something you don't even want to guess at in mine. So I did the honorable thing. I lied.

"Bridget," I said. "You know I can't run the agency myself, and you know, or you ought to know that Howard offed—killed himself because he was incredibly screwed up from the start."

"But, Harry—" she began.

"But, my ass," I cut in. "Okay, so maybe you helped push him over the line." She winced. "Were you trying to get the bastard dead? You were not. Did you think you were right? You sure as hell did, and you convinced my genius-type brain that you were, too. And you were *wrong*, Bridget. You were *wrong*. You want to hear about how often I've been wrong? You free for the next twelve hours?"

"You don't understand," she said. Boy, this was fun. I was getting to give her advice for a change.

"Understand? I understand better than you think. I understand that you're going to take a bath up to your neck in self-pity and run away somewhere to lick your wounds. You Irish are all alike, you know? And whoever set this whole damn thing up is going to walk, and walk grinning to himself. Because you not only gave him, clever as you are, a scapegoat, but now that you know you've been had, you're going to fold and whimper. Christ, kid. On my side of the street we don't get weepy. We get even."

Remember those Foreign Legion films where one soldier slaps another who's breaking apart because the Bedouins, or whatever the hell they are, are about to attack an understaffed fort, and the guy who gets slapped jerks to attention and says, "Thanks. I needed that?"

"All right, Harry," Bridget said. "What do you think we should do?" One more time, sayonara Harold Garnish Detective Agency. I thought about wallowing in self-pity and finding a hole to lick my wounds in.

Instead, I lit a cigarette. "Bridget," I said, "I've been thinking about that long and hard. And I'll tell you. I don't know. Except call that damn number again, and see if Wisconsin Development Corporation is ready to do business yet. But even that doesn't make a lot of sense. Because who would want to blackmail *me?* I could call Ross Connors, but I get the impression he doesn't want to talk to me directly, and what could I charge him with if I called in the cops? I mean, it would be my word against his, and my credit card and phone record will show that I invited him down to Chicago. God, when I think about how I got suckered into all this by Michelle. . . ."

"Schrödinger's cat," she said.

"I was so damn dumb—what did you say?"

"Schrödinger's cat," she said again, with that faraway look I had learned to expect and dread. "Harry, you read novels, don't you?"

I was going to tell her that mainly, lately, I read centerfolds, but my eye caught the twelve Polaroids on her desk just in time to tell my brain to can it.

"Of course you do," she went on. "Well, then, what is the relation between a novel and a legal brief?"

"Uh, they're both written?" I guessed, expecting even Phil to give me a disapproving stare for that one.

"Yes!" she exploded, rising to her feet in excitement. Hell, all I'd wanted to do was give her a pep talk, not create a Frankensteinette. "Yes!" she said again. "Oh, Harry you do see."

"Oh, Bridget, I don't."

She sailed on, now starting to pace back and forth behind her desk. "Harry, something happens: a murder, an accident, a love affair, it doesn't really matter. It happens the way life happens, chaotically and unpredictably, and sometimes even crazily. And novels and legal briefs are both written records—fictions—imposed as an afterthought to reassure ourselves that life isn't as unruly as we fear."

"Yeah. Right," I said, meaning neither "yeah" nor "right." "But look, about Cheryl Howard—"

"Yes, about Cheryl Howard. The problem is that in telling the stories we tell about what happened, we *change* what happened, don't you see?"

"Bridget," I said. "If that's true, we're all out of business."

"No. We're just out of certainty. I was too certain about Mr. Howard being the sole culprit, the single solution, in that awful business with his wife. I don't think I'll ever forgive myself for that. The stupidity, the waste . . . Well, you're right, dear, the best we can do is try to help put things right. We have to reexplain things from the very beginning. And we shall."

"We shall," I said. "Uh, Bridget, I know I'm going to be sorry I asked this, but you said something about somebody's cat?"

She smiled. "Oh, *Schrödinger's* cat. Yes. It's a classic riddle illustrating quantum theory. A cat is in a box that may or may not release poison gas when you open it. You have to open it to find out whether the cat lives or dies. But your very act of opening it *determines*, you don't know how, whether there is poison gas or there isn't. See? Just like a novel or a legal brief."

Enough is enough. "No, I don't see," I said, lighting a cigarette. "In the first place, why not just leave the dumb cat"—I thought about Bandit, at home on his fubby—"alone in his box? And in the second place, what the hell does all this have to do with Cheryl Howard and with those damn pictures of me and Michelle?"

She opened her desk drawer and took out the ashtray she keeps there for our little visits, and I *hate* it when she does that. "To answer your first question, dear," she said, "we open the box because we have to. Maybe opening the box is what makes us human. And to answer your second question, what it all has to do with Mrs. Howard is what we are about to find out. I've had Brenda cancel your two appointments for this afternoon. Could you drive me to the Skokie Public Library?"

Well, I thought, of frigging course. Especially now that it was all so crystal clear. I *did* wish I'd gone into plumbing.

# 27

THE SKOKIE PUBLIC Library is right across from one of the great delicatessens in the world, I swear to God. So I dropped Bridget off at the front door of the library and cruised over to Irving's to save my life. I mean, this was turning into the kind of hangover where it's eat or die.

The Duchess, as usual, was seating people. The Duchess is older than you want to know, has skin like Godzilla, and a temper like Godzilla's mother, which she may be. And she's five four at best. I've been going to Irving's for fourteen years, minimum. She rustled up to me with a grease-spattered menu, looked at me like she'd never seen me before, and said, eloquently, "Yeah?"

Come on. Could you enjoy deli service with a smile?

Two cream sodas, one cole slaw, and one tongue and chopped liver sandwich later I looked up, wiping mustard from my lower lip, to see Bridget O'Toole hulking over me.

"Ohngh, hgyuh, Brghth. Cuppa cfee?" I said, swallowing the last of my tongue (no, dummy, not the one I *had*, the one I'd ordered).

She settled—and I mean settled—into the chair across from me. "Harry," she said, "did you know that there's no such place as you visited?"

Would you say "Huh"? *I* said "Huh."

"Lake Manitonaqua," she said, getting more excited by the minute. "I knew there was something bothersome about the name, and I couldn't get it right, couldn't quite bring it round. But now I can. The directory of Wisconsin Lakes lists no such place as Lake Manitonaqua! There *is* no 'Blood Lake.' For that precise location it lists a body of water whose name I won't even try to pronounce. Now, *was* there a Blood Lake or wasn't there?"

I tried not to swallow my tongue (not the one I'd ordered, the one I had) and told her that there sure as hell was a Lake Manitonaqua. I had seen a woman dead there.

She smiled and signaled for coffee. "No, Harry," she said. "There is no Lake Manitonaqua. Not on the Wisconsin plats, not in the record books. The place I sent you to doesn't really exist. Think about the name. The *name* is what began to bother me. 'Manitonaqua': is that an Indian name? It certainly sounds like one, until you remember that *aqua* is just the Latin for 'water' or 'waters,' and *manito* is a contraction of the word *manitou*, an Indian word for a presiding malevolent or beneficent spirit. So *Manitonaqua* signifies not 'Blood Lake' but 'Ghost Lake,' Harry, and that's just where you were. I think we should call Mr. Andrews."

"Bridget," I said. "There's a whole lot of crapola in the world. There's a whole lot of crapola I'll put up with from you. There's a whole lot of crapola all around. But *this* crapola I will not take. No. No. Call Mr. Andrews? I called Mr. Connors and damn near got my head taken off. I—"

I had heads turning toward me all around the deli. I settled down, lit a cigarette, and wondered what I was going to say to Elliot Andrews. Worse luck, I didn't have long to wait.

"Harry," she said. "We have to assume that Mrs. Howard died for reasons other than those I originally hypothesized. We also have to assume that Blood Lake itself is a fabrication, a mirage created for reasons we don't yet know. *Manitonaqua*, when you think about it, is a silly word. But what I need to know is when it became called Manitonaqua, and by whom it came to be called that."

"Bridget," I said, dabbing at the last bit of tongue on my plate with the last bit of my complimentary bagel, "Bridget. You're doing the same thing again, don't you see? You're sitting there like some god-damn spider, and every time you twitch a leg the strand turns and another fly falls into the everfucking web. But, kid, kid, don't you see that it's the same web? What was the name of that son of a bitch— Schrödinger? The one with the cat. Well, think about *him* for a change. You think he wants to see the cat die one time out of two? Don't ask me to call Elliot Andrews."

"But you have to, Harry," she said, sipping the coffee the waiter had brought her. "You have to open the box and see if the cat is dead or alive. Even if you determine it by opening the box."

"You're crazy, of course," I said. "You know that. I mean, I got naked pictures of myself with a campus cutie in bed, and we got two —no, three dead bodies, and we got a trail cold as three-week-old dog turds, and you talk to me about linguistics and you want me to call a dude who knows from nothing but *bebop*?"

I guess I was getting loud again. A large man came over and suggested that I might like to leave the place as quick as possible. Bridget seemed to agree. I left.

What would you do on a nice late spring, early winter afternoon in Skokie, when the air is almost breathable and the windchill factor is human? Would you drive to O'Toole Investigations and call Elliot Andrews? I did.

# 28

ELLIOT SOUNDED GLAD to hear from me. "Hey, man," he shouted over the phone. "I was wondering about you. You okay?"

"I'm okay," I said. "Just okay, but not much more. Listen, this is kind of a business call. You got a minute? I need to know when they started calling Lake Manitonaqua Lake Manitonaqua."

He laughed. "Say what? Hell, that's its *name.* They been calling it that as long as I can remember. You know the story behind the name, don't you? It's about—"

"Yeah," I said wearily. "It's about Indian maidens and death and Blood Lake and like that. You sure that's the whole story; it's just the name?"

"Well, it's on the maps, man. Who the hell changes names on maps?"

"Beats the hell out of me," I said. "Listen, have you heard anything about, well, about some kind of blackmail ring in the Wisconsin resorts?"

"Aw, *shee*-it." He laughed. "That bullshit's been going around for years. Harry, I am really surprised at you. You know how much hanky-panky goes on at those damn resorts, and you ought to know how often the hanky-pankiers get caught and stiffed. Now, wouldn't you think a rumor about some big fucking ring would get started in a situation like that? Come on, man. Where's the percentage? Hey—I read that Dexter Gordon's going to be at the Jazz Showcase next week. You want to make a night of it? I'm gonna drive down to hear him, and maybe party out with him later. We used to play together. How about it?"

Now, maybe you know or maybe you don't that Dexter Gordon, Long Tall Dexter, is *the* bop tenor saxophone player, and that he's thrived and survived for forty years, a lot of them lean, and that he sounds better now than he did when he was playing with Dizzy and Bird in those misty, magic years of the forties. But I knew, and the chance to hear him and party down with him made more sense than anything else I'd heard lately.

"Name the night and the time, man," I said. "First round's on me."

Elliot laughed again. "Man, you don't know Dex. You try to take the tab, he'll take your arm and give you back a bloody stump."

We set a date and I hung up and leaned back in my chair and sighed with the satisfaction that comes from knowing you've accomplished exactly nothing. Three people were dead and Lake Manitonaqua wasn't Lake Manitonaqua and I didn't have a clue to what was going on. No, cancel that. I had too many clues, and they were all the sort of bullshit clues that clutter up your basic boring English country-house murder, and you couldn't put your finger on any of them. So what had I done? I'd made a date to hear Dexter at the Jazz Showcase. Aargh.

I decided to do simply something useful. I dialed the number from the back of photo number twelve; by now I had it memorized.

To my surprise, someone answered. A voice I didn't know. "Yes?" she said. "Wisconsin Development Corporation."

"Yes," I said. "This is Harry Garnish. I believe someone there wants to talk to me."

"Mr.—Mr. Garnish? Could you hold a minute?" They never let you say okay before they punch you into telephone limbo.

What the hell was this? I thought. A blackmailer who's got, already, a secretary? After a while somebody pushed a button somewhere and I got clicked back into reality.

"Mr. Garnish?" said a man's voice, one again I didn't recognize. "I'm Donald Pearce, the district manager. You say that you have a call-back message from us?"

"Well, sort of," I said. "You've got some photographs, I think, and I'd like to talk to you about getting them back."

"I'm sorry, Mr. Garnish, but I think I don't know what you mean."

"What I mean?" I shouted. "What I mean, man, is that you better get your ass in gear and let me know what your fucking game is. I don't have the time or the money for jerking around like this."

"Mr. Garnish," said Mr. Pearce, "there's no need to be obscene over the phone. I assure you that I don't know what you mean. Perhaps you dialed the wrong number."

"I dialed the right number, God damn it! It's on the back of one of your goddamn Polaroids. What's your name—Pearce? You know a guy named Ross Connors?"

"Ross Connors? No, sir, I know nobody by that name. Look, Mr. Garnish, Wisconsin Development is involved with developing agribusiness in southern Wisconsin. I really think you must have gotten the wrong number. Please don't call us again." And he hung up.

And I hung up. And did what I should have done before making the phone call in the first place. I looked in the phone book, and there in the Ws, big and innocent as the day you were born, was Wisconsin Development Corporation, 2201 Wadsworth, Wilmette.

This was getting a little crazy. I was getting a little crazy. I buzzed Bridget's number. "Bridget?" I said when she picked up the phone. "Listen. I just called Wisconsin Development—"

"And spoke to Mr. Pearce, and discovered they're a legitimate, even a laudable enterprise," she finished for me. "I called them while you were on the phone to Mr. Andrews. They don't know anything about our problem, I think."

"Uh, yeah," I said. "So why?"

"Why what, dear?"

"Bridget, is Phil there? Cover his ears. Why is why the *fuck* did Ross Connors leave me a number that had nothing to do with him or his blackmail scheme, which wouldn't have worked in the first place? Any why is also why the bloody goddamn hell are we involved in this whole goddamn thing when we should be out chasing fornicators like any good self-respecting weasels? And I *hate* talking over the phone. I'm coming to your office." She was next door, for Christ's sake.

"Harry. Dear," she said. She'd deared me twice, which meant she was back in her complacent, high-cholesterol, habitual state of mind, and that she thought she knew what was going down. "Come by the office by all means. But please, the language you use is too much. I don't think it's healthy. I know a therapist, a wonderful man named Dominick Cain, who specializes in—"

I slammed down the receiver and paraded the whole ten feet to her door. I'd been drugged, blackmailed—if you could call it that— and I was in the middle of an investigation that wasn't even an investigation, and my boss was talking soulfully to me about my language. Fuck, I thought.

Bridget was studying the photographs. I mean studying them with,

I swear, a magnifying glass. It was embarrassing. I thought about asking her if I could just pop around the corner and buy her this month's *Hustler Magazine,* and then I thought about not asking her.

"Harry," she said, putting the glass down. "Do you remember anything about . . . about this?"—gesturing toward my publicity shots.

"Nothing. And for some things I have a good memory."

"Well, yes." She blushed. "But what disturbs me, dear, is that in none of these shots are you—uh, I mean you're not . . ."

"I know, Bridget, I noticed too. I'm not—uh, yeah."

Okay, *you* try and say "tumescent" to a nun—especially when you're talking about yourself.

She sailed on, sighing at getting past that little sticky patch. "Of course, you were drugged. But you see, in none of the—positions, I suppose, are you and Michelle ever likely of coitus."

*Likely* of *coitus?* Boy, I thought, Bridget could make *Debbie Does Dallas* sound like a stock folio.

"So?" I said. I say "so" a lot in Bridget's office.

"So," she said, "it seems to me odd that Michelle is not maneuvering you into more—*suggestive* postures."

"Bridget," I exclaimed, "how suggestive do you want it, for crying out loud?"

"No, Harry, don't you see? Michelle was being manipulated, too! She must have been as drugged as you were. Look at her face—in those few photos where you can see it."

I looked, and damn if she wasn't right. What I'd thought of as moaning, passionate looks on Michelle's face were, in another light, simply the expression of somebody stoned out of her skull. It was like that black and white drawing psychologists always rave about, what I think they call a "figure-ground problem." Look at it one way and it's two black faces looking at each other. Look at it another way and it's a white vase. Schrödinger's cat probably drew the damn thing.

"Hey, Bridget," I said. "If you're right then this means . . ."

"Yes," she said excitedly. "It means that nobody is trying to blackmail you—forgive me, dear, but you're not really a very lucrative target—but somebody is trying to blackmail Michelle."

"No," I said. "No. It doesn't make any sense. Look. Michelle came to see me, and she suggested I call Ross Connors. That means she and Ross set this whole scam up together, right? Right. So why would Ross then turn around and set Michelle up for a fall, especially when she's got no bread for him either? No. It doesn't make sense."

"Harry, dear, it makes perfect sense once you realize the real meaning of the question, cui bono?" And she sat back and sighed.

I sat forward and tried not to bite my tongue. "Bridget," I said, "I don't even know the *wrong* meaning of the question, cui bono? The only Bono I know used to sing with Cher. You want to explain to me, or should we just stay on separate planets?"

"Oh, Harry." She smiled, just the way Marlo Thomas used to say, "Oh, *Donald*" on *That Girl.* "It means, 'who profits?' To 'whose good is it?' But it doesn't necessarily refer to money. Now, think. Why would Ross Connors want to have Michelle contact you and then stage this elaborate charade? Why would he want to have the case of Mrs. Cheryl Howard reopened when it was already history? Why would he want to let himself in for a charge of assault at least and blackmail at most?"

"Uh, he was bored hanging around the house?" Honest, folks, it was the best I could come up with.

"Harry!" she said, shaking her head. "Think! Cui bono? Not yours, not Michelle's, certainly not his, so whose, then?"

"Okay, okay," I almost shouted, "for whoever's running the damn blackmail ring and needs Michelle out of the action because . . . because . . ."

"Because she's too dangerous to kill and too valuable not to be dealt with."

"Bullshit."

"On the contrary, dear. We have to assume that Michelle is two things at once, a little nasty and a little gullible. So she can be suborned into luring you into this little affair, for reasons probably venal and best left unexamined, and yet can also herself be pulled into the scenes we have a photographic record of, and which are doubtless being used against her right now for reasons we have yet to determine."

"Neat," I said. "And it still doesn't tell me who killed Cheryl Howard and Dick Schwartz, and it doesn't make any sense at all, and I'll tell you the truth, if I'd known it was going to get this crazy, I wouldn't have gotten involved in it in the first place."

Bridget laughed. No, not giggled, laughed; like in throwing your head back and going *Woo*-hah!

"I said something funny?" I said.

"Oh, Harry, I'm sorry," she said, still laughing. That's how you know they're not really sorry. "It's just that Schrödinger said the same thing about quantum theory."

"Schröd—the son of a bitch with the cat? Right. I'm out of here," I said, getting out of my chair. "A few hours ago you were ready to quit the business and now you're back to the same f—the same f—the same damn way you've always behaved. Bridget, this is the f—this is the *real world,* and people have died, and I don't know *why.* Doesn't that bother you?"

The laugh went and the smile went and if she'd been anybody but Bridget I would have gotten nervous about defending myself. "Care?" she began. "Don't I *care?*" But I was saved by the bell, or rather the knock on the door, followed by Knobby coming in without being asked to come in. He always does that; it's one of his less hateful traits.

"Here's that info you asked me to track down, Miss O'Toole," he said, handing her a sheet of paper. "Boopsie"—grinning at me.

"Hi, lover"—grinning at him. When Knobby and I go around and around one of these days, I'm going to fight dirty and I'm going to like it a lot. He left.

Bridget read the sheet, sighed, and stared at me. "You asked me some questions, dear," she said, "and I didn't answer them. Do I care who killed Mrs. Howard and Mr. Schwartz? Yes, I do. Do I care why you were entrapped? Yes, I do. Do I know what is going on? I fear so. But you're going to have to be patient. I wonder, could you get in touch with Mr. Elliot Andrews for me again? I'd like to talk to him."

"Hell, Bridget, I'm getting together with him next Thursday. I didn't tell you, I got him on the phone and he didn't know anything about the name of the lake, but he's going to be down in Chicago for a night. You want me to call him back?"

She stared. "No," she said, "that will be fine. Thursday, you say? Perhaps we could all meet for a drink before you two go off."

"Yeah," I said, getting a little uneasy. "Uh, Bridget? There are still those photos of me, and there's still Michelle around somewhere, and there's still—"

"Don't worry, dear," she said. "There's still some kind of order in the universe too. We know who killed Cheryl Howard and Dick

Schwartz. And we will find out, in a little while, why they both had to die."

My hangover was coming back, and it was coming back like the Apaches after their first attack on the wagon train. I went back to my office, canceled all the appointments for the afternoon, went home, and hoped the four o'clock rerun of *Star Trek* wouldn't be one I had seen too often. I was in luck. It was "The Trouble with Tribbles." Best part of my day.

# 29

I KNOW, I KNOW. Like any good private investigator, I should have been obsessed with the case of Cheryl Howard and spent the next week thinking of nothing else. That's the way it works in the movies, right?

Right. Now, you tell me. You've got chest pains because you smoke too much, or you've got an IRS audit coming up, or your kid's fifth grade teacher tells you he's got a serious attitude problem and may have to see a counselor. And that's all you can think about, isn't it?

It is not. Or if it is, there's something wrong with *you*, Jack. You think about it at three in the morning, maybe, when we all face God. But the rest of the day you go through the motions and jump through the hoops and shovel all the shit that we pile up between ourselves and whatever's out there waiting to bite us in the ass.

In other words, the week went by normally. An adultery here, an adultery there, and love makes the world go round, and if I worried about Cheryl Howard or Ross Connors it was only occasionally, when I was too sane or too drunk or too both to focus on the corners of my life. I didn't call Wisconsin Development Corporation again. If Bridget was right, they'd call me if they needed me. And once in a while I wondered, why leave me a number at all, if I wasn't the mark?

But, like I said, that was only a minor lapse. The rest of the time my life was as boring as ever. Till Thursday.

The Jazz Showcase isn't really a club, it's more like an idea. Joe Segal, a holy man, has been running it since God knows when and has been booking class—I mean class—acts into the Showcase from the year one, which is about 1947 on my calendar. Come on, who would sign Thelonious Monk, the most predictable pianist in the western world, with Clark Terry, the most lyrical and generous of players? Who? Joe Segal, that's who.

Thursday was Dexter. Bridget and I drove down to the Showcase and got there around six. Had drinks, since in this incarnation the Showcase was actually serving beer and wine. (It varies: Joe has moved the place so many times that you wouldn't be surprised to go hear Anthony Braxton in the basement of a Unitarian church.)

And at seven fifteen there was Elliot, big as life and good as gold, beard tilted into the air. He sat down enthusiastically (do you know anybody who can sit down enthusiastically?) and chattered away, to Bridget, mainly.

Dexter came in the back of the place around seven thirty, and all the heads—all the hip heads—turned in his direction.

"Gawd-*damn!*" said Elliot. "Dex is a *big* man, ain't he?"

"About as big as Sonny Rollins," said Bridget, shocking us both. "Now, Mr. Andrews, if you're through with pleasantries, maybe you'd like to help us with some details before the concert starts."

I was used to Bridget by now. Elliot wasn't. "Beg pardon?" he said lamely.

"There's no pardon to beg," she said. "At least, not from me. But there is some explaining to be done. For instance, why did you set Michelle up for the photos with Harry?"

"Oh, you *know* that?" He laughed. "Come on. How'd you guess?"

"Guessing had nothing to do with it," Bridget said, paraphrasing Mae West. "The records show that you, or Bayou North, own most of the land around Lake Manito—well, the lake you named when you bought the property in 1960."

Elliot stared at Bridget, while a crooked smile sneaked over his face. "Damn," he said. "You're good."

"Thank you," she said. "But I think Mr. Gordon is about to play."

And so he was, while I tried to keep my jaw from dropping all the way open.

Dexter *is* long and tall, and he has this habit of after every number holding his horn out to the audience during the applause. In his hands a tenor sax looks like a toy, and it's a big horn.

And I couldn't concentrate on the music. Bridget and Elliot were both the kind of people you want to be with at a performance; that is, they didn't talk while the musicians were playing. But for the first time in my life in a club, I wished they would talk.

During the break, Dexter came off the stand and shook hands with Elliot. I was impressed.

"First set's always the weakest." Elliot smiled at us as the Muzak—at least it was Gerry Mulligan—came on. "But I guess we're not going to hear the second set, are we?"

It was Bridget's turn to smile. "We can, Mr. Andrews," she said. "But I don't think you really want to prolong this, do you?"

"Aw, hell," he said. "Just let me say good-bye to Dexter," and strutted, cock of the walk, over to the great man's table while I whispered frantically to Bridget, "You're not going to tell me he did it?"

"Harry," she said. "Have a little faith in your instincts and in me."

Elliot had finished laughing with Dexter Gordon, and the three of us strolled out into the night. A cold Chicago night on Rush Street, it was; the air just sharp enough to feel like a jolt of bourbon, open your sinuses, and make you want to talk for hours for no reason at all.

Was I taking a stroll in the night air with a killer? I didn't think so.

"Why?" said Bridget. Apparently I was out of the conversation.

"Why not?" said Elliot, laughing. "You were right, Bridget—may I call you Bridget?—about Thomas Howard killing Cheryl Howard. But you were wrong about the reason. Look, you guys have been suckers all along. Sure, I own most of the land around Ross's place, and sure, I run—I help run—a little corporation that collects money from folks who come up to Wisconsin to do what they're not supposed to do."

"But why?" said Bridget, getting angry. "Why the elaborate farce with poor Harry here, and with Michelle?"

He stopped and turned to face the two of us. "Because," he said, "we—me and the people I work for—had to teach Michelle a lesson. Yeah, I own most of the land up there. But you know how I own it? I own it in trust. And you know who it's in trust to? Miss Michelle Hill, that's who. Sorry, Harry, but Cheryl Howard wasn't no damn saint. The land was hers before she married Thomas Howard, and she grandfathered—grand*mothered* it to me and my friends a long time ago. You think she was worried about her daughter? Christ, man, she got her daughter into the business. And she came up there—she *was* sleeping with Dick Schwartz, by the way—to try and keep Michelle in line, because Michelle was getting a little antsy about the whole business. Cheryl, she was one mean bitch."

I thought about the photo of her at the picnic, that fresh, sweet face. That surprised smile I'd fallen in love with. Andrews was grinning and the wind was getting colder.

"I don't mind telling you guys all this, because there ain't a god-damn thing you can do about it, you know?" He was really enjoying himself. "Yeah, her husband killed her because he found out she was having a little action on the side. And you, Bridget, you deduced that he was the bad guy. Oh, well, maybe you got some of the reasons wrong, but who's counting?"

I looked at Bridget, but she didn't look back.

"So," he went on, "after you two tidied things up so nicely for us, we still had a problem with Michelle. She's met this guy, an assistant professor or something. And she wants to marry him. I guess he wants to marry her too. Anyhow, she wanted out. She wanted to go public. The guy's respectable, see?

"Well, we couldn't have that. So we convinced her that if she contacted my main man, here"—slapping me on the back, the bastard—"one more time, we could set up a scam that would get her out with no bad publicity and no disrespect to her mother's memory. The rest was apple pie. Harry calls Ross, we get Ross and Michelle down here, get Michelle stoned out of her gourd, take the pictures, and she's in the hip pocket. The last thing in the world she wants is for that professor of hers to see pictures like that. Not bad, hey?"

"And why leave the fucking pictures with me?" I growled. And it's hard to growl into a twenty-five-mile-per-hour wind.

He laughed again. "Man, that was *my* idea. See, I like you, Harry, but I think you're a little naive. I think you've got an idea of this business that's kind of, well, simple. I just wanted you to know that there are guys out there, guys like me, that you'd best not take on. I knew you'd call me eventually, because I knew Miss O'Toole, at least, would think of it. And I got to hear Dexter, and Ross got to hear— what was it?"

"The Magic fucking Flute," I said.

"Yeah. And what did you guys get? Burned. You solved a murder and you didn't do a thing else. Michelle is going to go to college, and I'm going to hold on to all that nice land, and Ross is going to keep running his resort, and we're going to keep juicing our playboy visitors. And there ain't shit you can do about it. Satisfied?"

"Not quite," said Bridget. "You've proved to us sufficiently that we've ignored the salient points in this affair, Mr. Andrews. And you've certainly caused me a good deal of anguish over what I believed to be a mistaken deduction on my part."

"I'm truly sorry, ma'am," he said.

And then Bridget stopped. "Oh, no, Mr. Andrews, you're not

nearly sorry enough." By now we were across from the Wrigley Building, and I was thinking of walking back to the car and driving home with my exhaust pipe between my legs. Or whatever.

But Bridget wasn't thinking that way. "There's nothing, you're quite right, on which we can 'get' you. But you've just insulted me and my associate, and that means you've made a permanent enemy. Go back to Wisconsin, Mr. Andrews, and hope that we don't meet again."

He stared at her for a minute, and then he turned on his heel and walked away. I stared for longer than a minute. "What the hell do you think you're going to do?" I asked.

She stared back

"Do?" she said. "Harry, I'm going to let Mr. Andrews do it to himself. Arrogance is always suicidal, and Mr. Andrews is very arrogant. At this moment, Sheriff Luther Frost is waiting for Mr. Andrews to cross the Wisconsin state line; I called the sheriff this afternoon and explained about his peculiar real estate situation. Nothing, of course, will be done to Mr. Andrews. But he is going to find himself harassed and watched and bothered as he has never been before. And likewise his associate, Mr. Connors."

"Swell," I said. "And three people are still dead, and you were right for all the wrong reasons. So who won?"

"Nobody," she said. "Especially not me. But winning isn't everything, I think. Can you drive me home now? I'm very tired."

I drove her home, giving her on the way my thumbnail oral biography of Vince Lombardi.